Rossiter Johnson

Single famous poems

Rossiter Johnson

Single famous poems

ISBN/EAN: 9783337712112

Printed in Europe, USA, Canada, Australia, Japan

Cover: Foto ©Andreas Hilbeck / pixelio.de

More available books at **www.hansebooks.com**

SINGLE FAMOUS POEMS

EDITED

BY

ROSSITER JOHNSON

Does he paint? he fain would write a poem;
Does he write? he fain would paint a picture,—
Put to proof art alien to the artist's,
Once, and only once, and for One only.
          ROBERT BROWNING.

NEW YORK
HENRY HOLT AND COMPANY
1877

PREFACE.

There are wide differences in the fame of the poems here collected, as well as in their merits. Some are familiar to everybody who reads poetry at all; others find reputation and perpetuity only with particular classes. A few, like those of Bishop Berkeley and Michael Barry, have been saved from oblivion by a single happy line or quatrain; while the richness and perfection of many leave us in wonder that their authors produced no more. If critical judgment in such matters is worth anything when opposed to a popular verdict, some of these authors have written better poems for no reward at all, than those which have given them fame. However this may be, the present volume is intended to represent popular rather than critical taste, and to include all the poems in the language which fairly come under its title,—excepting only those numerous anonymous ballads belonging to the early centuries of our literature, which are preserved in Percy's and other collections. In cases of doubt, I have generally decided in favor of insertion. It is not expected that any one reader will prize all the poems here brought together; if each finds what he looks for, no one need be offended because the volume also includes some which he could have spared.

Thanks are due to living writers represented, for permission to use their poems. In but one instance was this refused,—though in two or three cases their address could not be obtained.

The poems are arranged nearly, if not exactly, in chronological order. Where any special history attaches to them, it will generally be found in the Notes at the end of the book.   R. J.

New York, August 1, 1877.

CONTENTS.

CONTENTS.

CONTENTS.

SINGLE FAMOUS POEMS.

My Mind to me a Kingdom is.

My mind to me a kingdom is,
  Such perfect joy therein I find
As far exceeds all earthly bliss
  That God or nature hath assigned;
Though much I want that most would have,
Yet still my mind forbids to crave.

Content I live, this is my stay:
  I seek no more than may suffice:
I press to bear no haughty sway:
  Look! what I lack, my mind supplies.
Lo! thus I triumph like a king,
Content with what my mind doth bring.

I see how plenty surfeits oft,
  And hasty climbers soonest fall;
I see that such as sit aloft
  Mishap doth threaten most of all:
These get with toil and keep with fear;
Such cares my mind could never bear.

Some have too much, yet still they crave;
　　I little have, yet seek no more;
They are but poor, though much they have,
　　And I am rich with little store.
They poor, I rich; they beg, I give;
They lack, I lend; they pine, I live.

I laugh not at another's loss,
　　I grudge not at another's gain:
No worldly wave my mind can toss,
　　I brook that is another's bane:
I fear no foe, nor fawn on friend;
I loathe not life, nor dread mine end.

I wish but what I have at will,
　　I wander not to seek for more,
I like the plain, I climb no hill,
　　In greatest storms I sit on shore,
And laugh at them that toil in vain,
To get what must be lost again.

My wealth is health and perfect ease,
　　My conscience clear my chief defense;
I never seek by bribes to please,
　　Nor by desert to give offense;
Thus do I live, thus will I die,
Would all did so as well as I.

　　　　　　　　　　WILLIAM BYRD.

The Lye.

Goe, soule, the bodie's guest,
　　Upon a thanklesse arrant;
Feare not to touche the best—
　　The truth shall be thy warrant!
　　Goe, since I needs must dye,
　　And give the world the lye.

Goe tell the court it glowes
  And shines like rotten wood;
Goe tell the church it showes
  What 's good, and doth no good;
    If church and court reply,
    Then give them both the lye.

Tell potentates they live
  Acting by others' actions—
Not loved unlesse they give,
  Not strong but by their factions;
    If potentates reply,
    Give potentates the lye.

Tell men of high condition,
  That rule affairs of state,
Their purpose is ambition,
  Their practice only hate;
    And if they once reply,
    Then give them all the lye.

Tell them that brave it most
  They beg for more by spending,
Who in their greatest cost
  Seek nothing but commending;
    And if they make reply,
    Spare not to give the lye.

Tell zeale it lacks devotion;
  Tell love it is but lust;
Tell time it is but motion;
  Tell flesh it is but dust;
    And wish them not reply,
    For thou must give the lye.

Tell age it daily wasteth;
  Tell honour how it alters;

Tell beauty how she blasteth;
　Tell favour how she falters:
　　And as they then reply,
　　Give each of them the lye.

Tell wit how much it wrangles
　In tickle points of nicenesse;
Tell wisdome she entangles
　Herselfe in over-wisenesse;
　　And if they do reply,
　　Straight give them both the lye.

Tell physicke of her boldnesse;
　Tell skill it is pretension;
Tell charity of coldnesse;
　Tell law it is contention;
　　And as they yield reply,
　　So give them still the lye.

Tell fortune of her blindnesse;
　Tell nature of decay;
Tell friendship of unkindnesse;
　Tell justice of delay;
　　And if they dare reply,
　　Then give them all the lye.

Tell arts they have no soundnesse,
　But vary by esteeming;
Tell schooles they want profoundnesse,
　And stand too much on seeming;
　　If arts and schooles reply,
　　Give arts and schooles the lye.

Tell faith it 's fled the citie;
　Tell how the country erreth;
Tell, manhood shakes off pitie;
　Tell, vertue least preferreth;

And if they do reply,
Spare not to give the lye.

So, when thou hast, as I
    Commanded thee, done blabbing—
Although to give the lye
    Deserves no less than stabbing—
        Yet stab at thee who will,
        No stab the soule can kill.
                        SIR WALTER RALEIGH.

Lament for Sir Philip Sidney.

You knew—who knew not Astrophel?
    That I should live to say I knew,
And have not in possession still!—
    Things known permit me to renew.
Of him you know his merit such
I cannot say—you hear—too much.

Within these woods of Arcady
    He chief delight and pleasure took;
And on the mountain Partheny,
    Upon the crystal liquid brook,
The muses met him every day,—
Taught him to sing, and write, and say.

When he descended down the mount
    His personage seemed most divine;
A thousand graces one might count
    Upon his lovely, cheerful eyne.
To hear him speak, and see him smile,
You were in Paradise the while.

A sweet, attractive kind of grace;
    A full assurance given by looks;

Continual comfort in a face;
  The lineaments of gospel books:
I trow that countenance cannot lie
Whose thoughts are legible in the eye.

Above all others this is he
  Who erst approvèd in his song
That love and honor might agree,
  And that pure love will do no wrong.
Sweet saints, it is no sin or blame
To love a man of virtuous name.

Did never love so sweetly breathe
  In any mortal breast before;
Did never muse inspire beneath
  A poet's brain with finer store.
He wrote of love with high conceit,
And beauty reared above her height.

MATHEW ROYDON

Man's Mortality.

LIKE as the damask rose you see,
Or like the blossoms on the tree,
Or like the dainty flower of May,
Or like the morning of the day,
Or like the sun, or like the shade,
Or like the gourd which Jonas had;
Even such is man, whose thread is spun,
Drawn out and cut, and so is done.
The rose withers, the blossom blasteth,
The flower fades, the morning hasteth,
The sun sets, the shadow flies,
The gourd consumes, and man—he dies!

Like to the grass that 's newly sprung,
Or like a tale that 's new begun,

Or like a bird that 's here to-day,
Or like the pearlèd dew of May,
Or like an hour, or like a span,
Or like the singing of a swan;
Even such is man, who lives by breath,
Is here, now there, in life and death.
The grass withers, the tale is ended,
The bird is flown, the dew 's ascended,
The hour is short, the span not long,
The swan near death,—man's life is done!

Like to a bubble in the brook,
Or in a glass much like a look,
Or like a shuttle in a weaver's hand,
Or like the writing on the sand,
Or like a thought, or like a dream,
Or like the gliding of a stream;
Even such is man, who lives by breath,
Is here, now there, in life and death.
The bubble 's out, the look 's forgot,
The shuttle 's flung, the writing 's blot,
The thought is past, the dream is gone,
The water glides,—man's life is done!

Like to a blaze of fond delight,
Or like a morning clear and bright,
Or like a frost, or like a shower,
Or like the pride of Babel's tower,
Or like the hour that guides the time,
Or like to Beauty in her prime;
Even such is man, whose glory lends
That life a blaze or two, and ends.
The morn 's o'ercast, joy turned to pain,
The frost is thawed, dried up the rain,
The tower falls, the hour is run,
The beauty lost,—man's life is done!

Like to an arrow from the bow,
Or like swift course of water-flow,
Or like that time 'twixt flood and ebb,
Or like the spider's tender web,
Or like a race, or like a goal,
Or like the dealing of a dole;
Even such is man, whose brittle state
Is always subject unto Fate.
The arrow 's shot, the flood soon spent,
The time 's no time, the web soon rent,
The race soon run, the goal soon won,
The dole soon dealt,—man's life is done!

Like to the lightning from the sky,
Or like a post that quick doth hie,
Or like a quaver in a short song,
Or like a journey three days long,
Or like the snow when summer's come,
Or like the pear, or like the plum;
Even such is man, who heaps up sorrow,
Lives but this day, and dies to-morrow.
The lightning 's past, the post must go,
The song is short, the journey 's so,
The pear doth rot, the plum doth fall,
The snow dissolves,—and so must all!

SIMON WASTEL.

Willy Drowned in Yarrow.

"WILLY 's rare, and Willy 's fair,
    And Willy 's wondrous bonny;
And Willy heght to marry me,
    Gin e'er he married ony.

"Yestreen I made my bed fu' braid,
    This night I 'll make it narrow;
For a' the livelang winter night
    I ly twined of my marrow.

VERSES.

"Oh came you by yon water-side?
    Pou'd you the rose or lily?
Or came you by yon meadow green?
    Or saw you my sweet Willy?"

She sought him east, she sought him west,
    She sought him braid and narrow;
Syne in the cleaving of a craig,
    She found him drowned in Yarrow.

ANONYMOUS.

Verses.

WRITTEN IN THE TOWER, THE NIGHT BEFORE HIS EXECUTION.

My prime of youth is but a frost of cares,
    My feast of joy is but a dish of pain,
My crop of corn is but a field of tares,
    And all my goodes is but vain hope of gain.
The day is fled, and yet I saw no sun;
And now I live, and now my life is done!

My spring is past, and yet it hath not sprung,
    The fruit is dead, and yet the leaves are green,
My youth is past, and yet I am but young,
    I saw the world, and yet I was not seen.
My thread is cut, and yet it is not spun;
And now I live, and now my life is done!

I sought for death and found it in the wombe,
    I lookt for life, and yet it was a shade,
I trade the ground, and knew it was my tombe,
    And now I die, and now I am but made.
The glass is full, and yet my glass is run;
And now I live, and now my life is done!

CHEDIOCK TICHEBORNE.

1*

The Ballad of Agincourt.

FAIR stood the wind for France,
When we our sails advance,
Nor now to prove our chance
    Longer will tarry;
But putting to the main,
At Kaux, the mouth of Seine,
With all his martial train,
    Landed King Harry.

And taking many a fort,
Furnished in warlike sort,
Marched toward Agincourt
    In happy hour—
Skirmishing day by day
With those that stopped his way,
Where the French general lay
    With all his power,

Which in his height of pride,
King Henry to deride,
His ransom to provide
    To the king sending;
Which he neglects the while,
As from a nation vile,
Yet, with an angry smile,
    Their fall portending.

And turning to his men,
Quoth our brave Henry then:
Though they be one to ten,
    Be not amazed;
Yet have we well begun—
Battles so bravely won
Have ever to the sun
    By fame been raised.

And for myself, quoth he,
This my full rest shall be ;
England ne'er mourn for me,
    Nor more esteem me.
Victor I will remain,
Or on this earth lie slain :
Never shall she sustain
    Loss to redeem me.

Poitiers and Cressy tell,
When most their pride did swell,
Under our swords they fell ;
    No less our skill is
Than when our grandsire great,
Claiming the regal seat,
By many a warlike feat
    Lopped the French lilies.

The Duke of York so dread
The eager vaward led ;
With the main Henry sped,
    Amongst his henchmen.
Excester had the rear—
A braver man not there :
O Lord! how hot they were
    On the false Frenchmen!

They now to fight are gone ;
Armor on armor shone ;
Drum now to drum did groan—
    To hear was wonder ;
That with the cries they make
The very earth did shake ;
Trumpet to trumpet spake,
    Thunder to thunder.

Well it thine age became,
O noble Erpingham!

Which did the signal aim
   To our hid forces;
When, from a meadow by,
Like a storm suddenly,
The English archery
   Struck the French horses,

With Spanish yew so strong,
Arrows a cloth-yard long,
That like to serpents stung,
   Piercing the wether;
None from his fellow starts,
But playing manly parts,
And like true English hearts,
   Stuck close together.

When down their bows they threw,
And forth their bilbows drew,
And on the French they flew,
   Not one was tardy:
Arms were from shoulders sent;
Scalps to the teeth were rent;
Down the French peasants went;
   Our men were hardy.

This while our noble king,
His broadsword brandishing,
Down the French host did ding,
   As to o'erwhelm it;
And many a deep wound lent,
His arms with blood besprent,
And many a cruel dent
   Bruised his helmet.

Glo'ster, that duke so good,
Next of the royal blood,
For famous England stood,
   With his brave brother—

Clarence, in steel so bright,
Though but a maiden knight,
Yet in that furious fight
    Scarce such another.

Warwick in blood did wade;
Oxford the foe invade,
And cruel slaughter made,
    Still as they ran up.
Suffolk his axe did ply,
Beaumont and Willoughby
Bare them right doughtily,
    Ferrers and Fanhope.

Upon St. Crispin's day
Fought was this noble fray,
Which fame did not delay
    To England to carry;
Oh, when shall Englishmen
With such acts fill a pen,
Or England breed again
    Such a King Harry?

                MICHAEL DRAYTON.

Take thy Old Cloake about thee.

THIS winter weather, it waxeth cold,
    And frost doth freese on every hill;
And Boreas blows his blastes so cold
    That all our cattell are like to spill.
Bell, my wife, who loves no strife,
    Shee sayd unto me quietlye,
"Rise up, and save cowe Crumbocke's life—
    Man, put thy old cloake about thee."

"O Bell, why dost thou flyte and scorne?
    Thou kenst my cloake is very thin;
2

It is so bare and overworne
   A cricke he thereon can not renn.
Then Ile no longer borrowe or lend—
   For once Ile new apparelled be;
To-morrow Ile to town, and spend,
   For Ile have a new cloake about me."

"Cow Crumbocke is a very good cow—
   She has been alwayes true to the payle;
She has helped us to butter and cheese, I trow,
   And other things she will not fayle;
I wold be loth to see her pine;—
   Good husbande, counsel take of me—
It is not for us to go so fine;
   Man, take thy old cloake about thee."

"My cloake, it was a very good cloake—
   It hath been alwayes true to the weare;
But now it is not worth a groat,
   I have had it four-and-forty year.
Sometime it was of cloth in graine;
   'T is now but a sigh clout as you may see;
It will neither hold nor winde nor raine—
   And Ile have a new cloake about me."

"It is four-and-forty yeares ago
   Since the one of us the other did ken;
And we have had betwixt us towe
   Of children either nine or ten.
We have brought them up to women and men—
   In the fere of God I trowe they be;
And why wilt thou thyself misken—
   Man, take thy old cloake about thee."

"O Bell, my wife, why dost thou floute?
   Now is now, and then was then;

Seeke now all the world throughout,
    Thou kenst not clownes from gentlemen;
They are clad in blacke, greene, yellowe, or gray,
    So far above their own degree—
Once in my life Ile do as they,
    For Ile have a new cloake about me."

"King Stephen was a worthy peere—
    His breeches cost him but a crowne;
He held them sixpence all too deere,
    Therefore he called the tailor lowne.
He was a wight of high renowne,
    And thou'se but of a low degree—
It 's pride that puts this countrye downe;
    Man, take thy old cloake about thee."

Bell, my wife, she loves not strife,
    Yet she will lead me if she can;
And oft to live a quiet life
    I 'm forced to yield though I be good-man.
It 's not for a man with a woman to threepe,
    Unless he first give o'er the plea;
As we began sae will we leave,
    And Ile take my old cloake about me.

ANONYMOUS.

A Contented Mind.

I WEIGH not fortune's frown or smile;
    I joy not much in earthly joys;
I seek not state, I seek not style;
    I am not fond of fancy's toys.
I rest so pleased with what I have,
I wish no more, no more I crave.

I quake not at the thunder's crack;
    I tremble not at noise of war;

I swound not at the news of wrack,
  I shrink not at a blazing star;
I fear not loss, I hope not gain;
I envy none, I none disdain.

I see ambition never pleased;
  I see some Tantals starved in store;
I see gold's dropsy seldom eased;
  I see even Midas gape for more;
I neither want, nor yet abound—
Enough 's a feast, content is crowned.

I feign not friendship where I hate;
  I fawn not on the great (in show);
I prize, I praise a mean estate,
  Neither too lofty nor too low:
This, this is all my choice, my cheer—
A mind content, a conscience clear.

JOSHUA SYLVESTER.

Love me Little, Love me Long.

Love me little, love me long!
Is the burden of my song:
Love that is too hot and strong
  Burneth soon to waste.
Still I would not have thee cold—
Not too backward, nor too bold;
Love that lasteth till 't is old
  Fadeth not in haste.
Love me little, love me long!
Is the burden of my song.

If thou lovest me too much,
'T will not prove as true a touch;
Love me little more than such,—
  For I fear the end.

I 'm with little well content,
And a little from thee sent
Is enough, with true intent
　To be steadfast, friend.

Say thou lovest me, while thou live
I to thee my love will give,
Never dreaming to deceive
　While that life endures;
Nay, and after death, in sooth,
I to thee will keep my truth,
As now when in my May of youth:
　This my love assures.

Constant love is moderate ever,
And it will through life persever;
Give me that with true endeavor,—
　I will it restore.
A suit of durance let it be,
For all weathers,—that for me,—
For the land or for the sea:
　Lasting evermore.

Winter's cold or summer's heat,
Autumn's tempests on it beat;
It can never know defeat,
　Never can rebel;
Such the love that I would gain,
Such the love, I tell thee plain,
Thou must give, or woo in vain:
　So to thee—farewell!

　　　　　　　　　　　ANONYMOUS.

Good Ale.

I can not eat but little meat—
  My stomach is not good;
But sure, I think that I can drink
  With him that wears a hood.
Though I go bare, take ye no care;
  I am nothing a-cold—
I stuff my skin so full within
  Of jolly good ale and old.
Back and side go bare, go bare;
  Both foot and hand go cold;
But, belly, God send thee good ale enough,
  Whether it be new or old!

I love no roast but a nut-brown toast,
  And a crab laid in the fire;
A little bread shall do me stead—
  Much bread I not desire.
No frost or snow, nor wind, I trow,
  Can hurt me if I wold—
I am so wrapt, and thorowly lapt
  Of jolly good ale and old.
Back and side go bare, go bare;
  Both foot and hand go cold;
But, belly, God send thee good ale enough,
  Whether it be new or old!

And Tyb, my wife, that as her life
  Loveth well good ale to seek,
Full oft drinks she, till you may see
  The tears run down her cheek;
Then doth she trowl to me the bowl,
  Even as a malt-worm should;
And saith, "Sweetheart, I took my part
  Of this jolly good ale and old."

Back and side go bare, go bare;
  Both foot and hand go cold;
But, belly, God send thee good ale enough,
  Whether it be new or old!

Now let them drink till they nod and wink,
  Even as good fellows should do;
They shall not miss to have the bliss
  Good ale doth bring men to;
And all poor souls that have scoured bowls,
  Or have them lustily trowled,
God save the lives of them and their wives,
  Whether they be young or old!
Back and side go bare, go bare;
  Both foot and hand go cold;
But, belly, God send thee good ale enough,
  Whether it be new or old!

JOHN STILL.

Exequy.

ACCEPT, thou shrine of my dead saint,
Instead of dirges, this complaint;
And for sweet flowers to crown thy hearse
Receive a strew of weeping verse
From thy grieved friend, whom thou might'st see
Quite melted into tears for thee.

Dear loss! since thy untimely fate,
My task hath been to meditate
On thee, on thee; thou art the book,
The library whereon I look,
Thou almost blind; for thee (loved clay)
I languish out, not live, the day,
Using no other exercise
But what I practice with mine eyes,

By which wet glasses I find out
How lazily Time creeps about
To one that mourns; this, only this,
My exercise and business is:
So I compute the weary hours
With sighs dissolvèd into showers.

Nor wonder if my time go thus
Backward and most preposterous;
Thou hast benighted me; thy set
This eve of blackness did beget,
Who wast my day (though overcast
Before thou hast thy noontide passed),
And I remember must in tears
Thou scarce hadst seen so many years
As day tells hours: by thy clear sun
My love and fortune first did run:

But thou wilt never more appear
Folded within my hemisphere,
Since both thy light and motion
Like a fled star is fallen and gone,
And 'twixt me and my soul's dear wish
The earth now interposèd is,
Which such a strange eclipse doth make
As ne'er was read in almanac.

I could allow thee for a time
To darken me and my sad clime:
Were it a month, or year, or ten,
I would thy exile live till then.
And all that space my mirth adjourn,
So thou wouldst promise to return,
And, putting off thy ashy shroud,
At length disperse this sable cloud!

But woe is me! the longest date
Too narrow is to calculate

These empty hopes: never shall I
Be so much blessed as to descry
A glimpse of thee, till that day come
Which shall the earth to cinders doom,
And a fierce fever must calcine
The body of this world like thine,
(My little world!) that fit of fire
Once off, our bodies shall aspire
To our souls' bliss: then we shall rise,
And view ourselves with clearer eyes
In that calm region where no night
Can hide us from each other's sight.

Meantime thou hast her, Earth: much good
May my harm do thee! Since it stood
With Heaven's will I might not call
Her longer mine, I give thee all
My short-lived right and interest
In her whom living I loved best;
With a most free and bounteous grief
I give thee what I could not keep.
Be kind to her, and, prithee, look
Thou write into thy doomsday book
Each parcel of this Rarity
Which in thy casket shrined doth lie.
See that thou make thy reckoning straight,
And yield her back again by weight:
For thou must audit on thy trust
Each grain and atom of this trust,
As thou wilt answer Him that lent,
Not gave thee, my dear monument.
So, close the ground, and 'bout her shade
Black curtains draw: my bride is laid.

Sleep on, my love, in thy cold bed
Never to be disquieted!
　2*

My last good-night! Thou wilt not wake
Till I thy fate shall overtake:
Till age or grief, or sickness must
Marry my body to that dust
It so much loves, and fill the room
My heart keeps empty in thy tomb.
Stay for me there: I will not fail
To meet thee in that hollow vale.
And think not much of my delay;
I am already on the way,
And follow thee with all the speed
Desire can make, or sorrows breed.
Each minute is a short degree,
And every hour a step toward thee.
At night when I betake to rest,
Next morn I rise nearer my west
Of life, almost by eight hours' sail,
Than when Sleep breathed his drowsy gale.
Thus from the sun my bottom steers,
And my day's compass downward bears;
Nor labor I to stem the tide
Through which to thee I swiftly glide.

'T is true, with shame and grief I yield;
Thou, like the van, first took'st the field,
And gotten hast the victory,
In thus adventuring to die
Before me, whose more years might crave
A just precedence in the grave.
But hark! my pulse, like a soft drum,
Beats my approach, tells thee I come;
And slow howe'er my marches be,
I shall at last sit down by thee.

The thought of this bids me go on,
And wait my dissolution
With hope and comfort. Dear (forgive
The crime) I am content to live,

Divided, with but half a heart,
Till we shall meet and never part.

HENRY KING.

The Angler's Wish.

I IN these flowery meads would be,
These crystal streams should solace me;
To whose harmonious bubbling noise
I, with my angle, would rejoice,
   Sit here, and see the turtle-dove
   Court his chaste mate to acts of love;

Or, on that bank, feel the west wind
Breathe health and plenty; please my mind,
To see sweet dew-drops kiss these flowers,
And then washed off by April showers;
   Here, hear my kenna sing a song:
   There, see a blackbird feed her young,

Or a laverock build her nest;
Here, give my weary spirits rest,
And raise my low-pitched thoughts above
Earth, or what poor mortals love.
   Thus, free from lawsuits, and the noise
   Of princes' courts, I would rejoice;

Or, with my Bryan and a book,
Loiter long days near Shawford brook;
There sit by him, and eat my meat;
There see the sun both rise and set;
There bid good-morning to next day;
There meditate my time away;
   And angle on; and beg to have
   A quiet passage to a welcome grave.

IZAAK WALTON.

Death's Final Conquest.

THE glories of our birth and state
    Are shadows, not substantial things;
'There is no armor against fate—
    Death lays his icy hands on kings; .
        Sceptre and crown
        Must tumble down
And in the dust be equal made
With the poor crooked scythe and spade.

Some men with swords may reap the field,
    And plant fresh laurels where they kill;
But their strong nerves at last must yield—
    They tame but one another still;
          Early or late
          They stoop to fate,
And must give up their murmuring breath,
When they, pale captives, creep to death.

The garlands wither on your brow—
    Then boast no more your mighty deeds;
Upon death's purple altar, now,
    See where the victor victim bleeds!
        All heads must come
        To the cold tomb—
Only the actions of the just
Smell sweet, and blossom in the dust.

                    JAMES SHIRLEY.

The Bride.

FROM A BALLAD UPON A WEDDING.

THE maid, and thereby hangs a tale,
For such a maid no Whitsun-ale
    Could ever yet produce:

No grape that 's kindly ripe could be
So round, so plump, so soft as she,
    Nor half so full of juice.

Her finger was so small, the ring
Would not stay on which they did bring—
    It was too wide a peck;
And, to say truth—for out it must—
It looked like the great collar—just—
    About our young colt's neck.

Her feet beneath her petticoat,
Like little mice, stole in and out,
    As if they feared the light;
But O, she dances such a way!
No sun upon an Easter-day
    Is half so fine a sight.

Her cheeks so rare a white was on,
No daisy makes comparison;
    Who sees them is undone;
For streaks of red were mingled there,
Such as are on a Cath'rine pear,
    The side that 's next the sun.

Her lips were red; and one was thin,
Compared to that was next her chin.
    Some bee had stung it newly;
But, Dick, her eyes so guard her face,
I durst no more upon them gaze,
    Than on the sun in July.

Her mouth so small, when she does speak,
Thou 'dst swear her teeth her words did break,
    That they might passage get;
But she so handled still the matter,
They came as good as ours, or better,
    And are not spent a whit.
                 SIR JOHN SUCKLING.

Ye Gentlemen of England.

Ye gentlemen of England
  That live at home at ease,
Ah! little do you think upon
  The dangers of the seas.
Give ear unto the mariners,
  And they will plainly show
All the cares and the fears
  When the stormy winds do blow.

If enemies oppose us
  When England is at war
With any foreign nation,
  We fear not wound or scar;
Our roaring guns shall teach 'em
  Our valor for to know,
Whilst they reel on the keel,
  And the stormy winds do blow.

Then courage, all brave mariners,
  And never be dismay'd;
While we have bold adventurers,
  We ne'er shall want a trade:
Our merchants will employ us
  To fetch them wealth, we know;
Then be bold—work for gold,
  When the stormy winds do blow.

                              MARTYN PARKER.

Song.

Love still has something of the sea,
  From whence his mother rose;
No time his slaves from doubt can free,
  Nor give their thoughts repose.

They are becalmed in clearest days,
  And in rough weather tossed;
They wither under cold delays,
  Or are in tempests lost.

One while they seem to touch the port,
  Then straight into the main
Some angry wind, in cruel sport,
  The vessel drives again.

At first disdain and pride they fear,
  Which if they chance to 'scape,
Rivals and falsehood soon appear,
  In a more cruel shape.

By such degrees to joy they come,
  And are so long withstood;
So slowly they receive the sun,
  It hardly does them good.

'T is cruel to prolong a pain;
  And to defer a joy,
Believe me, gentle Celemene,
  Offends the wingèd boy.

An hundred thousand oaths your fears,
  Perhaps, would not remove;
And if I gazed a thousand years,
  I could not deeper love.

                    SIR CHARLES SEDLEY.

My Dear and Only Love.

PART FIRST.

My dear and only love, I pray,
  This noble world of thee
Be governed by no other sway
  But purest monarchie.

For if confusion have a part,
　　Which virtuous souls abhore,
And hold a synod in thy heart,
　　I 'll never love thee more.

Like Alexander I will reign,
　　And I will reign alone,
My thoughts shall evermore disdain
　　A rival on my throne.
He either fears his fate too much,
　　Or his deserts are small,
That puts it not unto the touch,
　　To win or lose it all.

But I must rule and govern still
　　And always give the law,
And have each subject at my will,
　　And all to stand in awe.
But 'gainst my battery if I find
　　Thou shun'st the prize so sore
As that thou set'st me up a blind,
　　I 'll never love thee more.

If in the empire of thy heart,
　　Where I should solely be,
Another do pretend a part,
　　And dares to vie with me;
Or if committees thou erect,
　　And go on such a score,
I 'll sing and laugh at thy neglect,
　　And never love thee more.

But if thou wilt be constant then,
　　And faithful of thy word,
I 'll make thee glorious by my pen,
　　And famous by my sword.
I 'll serve thee in such noble ways
　　Was never heard before;

I 'll crown and deck thee all with bays,
  And love thee evermore.

PART SECOND.

My dear and only love, take heed,
  Lest thou thyself expose,
And let all longing lovers feed,
  Upon such looks as those.
A marble wall then build about,
  Beset without a door;
But if thou let thy heart fly out,
  I 'll never love thee more.

Let not their oaths, like volleys shot,
  Make any breach at all;
Nor smoothness of their language plot
  Which way to scale the wall;
Nor balls of wild-fire love consume
  The shrine which I adore;
For if such smoke about thee fume,
  I 'll never love thee more.

I think thy virtues be too strong
  To suffer by surprise;
Those victualed by my love so long,
  The siege at length must rise,
And leave thee ruled in that health
  And state thou wast before;
But if thou turn a commonwealth,
  I 'll never love thee more.

Or if by fraud, or by consent,
  Thy heart to ruine come,
I 'll sound no trumpet as I wont,
  Nor march by tuck of drum;
But hold my arms, like ensigns, up,
  Thy falsehood to deplore,

And bitterly will sigh and weep,
  And never love thee more.

I 'll do with thee as Nero did
  When Rome was set on fire,
Not only all relief forbid,
  But to a hill retire,
And scorn to shed a tear to see
  Thy spirit grown so poor;
But smiling sing, until I die,
  I 'll never love thee more.

Yet, for the love I bare thee once,
  Lest that thy name should die,
A monument of marble-stone
  The truth shall testifie;
That every pilgrim passing by
  May pity and deplore
My case, and read the reason why
  I can love thee no more.

The golden laws of love shall be
  Upon this pillar hung,—
A simple heart, a single eye,
  A true and constant tongue;
Let no man for more love pretend
  Than he has hearts in store;
True love begun shall never end;
  Love one and love no more.

Then shall thy heart be set by mine,
  But in far different case;
For mine was true, so was not thine,
  But lookt like Janus' face.
For as the waves with every wind,
  So sail'st thou every shore,
And leav'st my constant heart behind,—
  How can I love thee more?

My heart shall with the sun be fixed
   For constancy most strange,
And thine shall with the moon be mixed,
   Delighting ay in change.
Thy beauty shined at first more bright,
   And woe is me therefore,
That ever I found thy love so light
   I could love thee no more!

The misty mountains, smoking lakes,
   The rocks' resounding echo,
The whistling wind that murmur makes,
   Shall with me sing hey ho!
The tossing seas, the tumbling boats,
   Tears dropping from each shore,
Shall tune with me their turtle notes—
   I 'll never love thee more.

As doth the turtle, chaste and true,
   Her fellow's death regrete,
And daily mourns for his adieu,
   And ne'er renews her mate;
So, though thy faith was never fast,
   Which grieves me wondrous sore,
Yet I shall live in love so chaste,
   That I shall love no more.

And when all gallants ride about
   These monuments to view,
Whereon is written, in and out,
   Thou traitorous and untrue;
Then in a passion they shall pause,
   And thus say, sighing sore,
"Alas! he had too just a cause
   Never to love thee more."

And when that tracing goddess Fame
   From east to west shall flee,

She shall record it, to thy shame,
How thou hast lovèd me;
And how in odds our love was such
As few have been before;
Thou loved too many, and I too much,
So I can love no more.

JAMES GRAHAM, MARQUIS OF MONTROSE.

The Splendid Shilling.

". . . . . Sing, heavenly Muse!
Things unattempted yet, in prose or rhyme,"
A shilling, breeches, and chimeras dire.

HAPPY the man, who, void of cares and strife,
In silken or in leather purse retains
A Splendid Shilling: he nor hears with pain
New oysters cried, nor sighs for cheerful ale;
But with his friends, when nightly mists arise,
To Juniper's Magpie, or Town-hall repairs:
Where, mindful of the nymph, whose wanton eye
Transfix'd his soul, and kindled amorous flames,
Chloe, or Phillis, he each circling glass
Wisheth her health, and joy, and equal love.
Meanwhile, he smokes, and laughs at merry tale,
Or pun ambiguous, or conundrum quaint.
But I, whom griping penury surrounds,
And Hunger, sure attendant upon Want,
With scanty offals, and small acid tiff,
(Wretched repast!) my meagre corpse sustain:
Then solitary walk, or doze at home
In garret vile, and with a warming puff
Regale chill'd fingers: or from tube as black
As winter-chimney, or well-polish'd jet,
Exhale mundungus, ill-perfuming scent:
Not blacker tube, nor of a shorter size,
Smokes Cambro-Briton (vers'd in pedigree,

Sprung from Cadwallador and Arthur, kings
Full famous in romantic tale) when he,
O'er many a craggy hill and barren cliff,
Upon a cargo of fam'd Cestrian cheese,
High over-shadowing rides, with a design
To vend his wares, or at th' Avonian mart,
Or Maridunum, or the ancient town
Yclep'd Brechinia, or where Vaga's stream
Encircles Ariconium, fruitful soil!
Whence flow nectareous wines, that well may vie
With Massic, Setin, or renown'd Falern.

    Thus while my joyless minutes tedious flow,
With looks demure, and silent pace, a Dun,
Horrible monster! hated by gods and men,
To my aërial citadel ascends,
With vocal heel thrice thundering at my gate,
With hideous accent thrice he calls; I know
The voice ill-boding, and the solemn sound.
What should I do? or whither turn?　Amaz'd,
Confounded, to the dark recess I fly
Of wood-hole; straight my bristling hairs erect
Through sudden fear; a chilly sweat bedews
My shuddering limbs, and (wonderful to tell!)
My tongue forgets her faculty of speech;
So horrible he seems!　His faded brow,
Intrench'd with many a frown, and conic beard,
And spreading band, admir'd by modern saints,
Disastrous acts forbode; in his right hand
Long scrolls of paper solemnly he waves,
With characters and figures dire inscrib'd,
Grievous to mortal eyes; (ye gods, avert
Such plagues from righteous men!)　Behind him stalks
Another monster, not unlike himself,
Sullen of aspect, by the vulgar call'd
A catchpole, whose polluted hands the gods,
With force incredible, and magic charms,
First have endued: if he his ample palm
   3*

Should haply on ill-fated shoulder lay
Of debtor, straight his body, to the touch
Obsequious (as whilom knights were wont,)
To some enchanted castle is convey'd,
Where gates impregnable, and coercive chains,
In durance strict detain him, till, in form
Of money, Pallas sets the captive free.

Beware, ye debtors! when ye walk, beware,
Be circumspect; oft with insidious ken
The caitiff eyes your steps aloof, and oft
Lies perdu in a nook or gloomy cave,
Prompt to enchant some inadvertent wretch
With his unhallowed touch. So, (poets sing)
Grimalkin, to domestic vermin sworn
An everlasting foe, with watchful eye
Lies nightly brooding o'er a chinky gap,
Portending her fell claws, to thoughtless mice
Sure ruin. So her disembowell'd web
Arachne, in a hall or kitchen, spreads
Obvious to vagrant flies: she secret stands
Within her woven cell: the humming prey,
Regardless of their fate, rush on the toils
Inextricable, nor will aught avail
Their arts, or arms, or shapes of lovely hue;
The wasp insidious, and the buzzing drone,
And butterfly, proud of expanded wings
Distinct with gold, entangled in her snares,
Useless resistance make; with eager strides,
She towering flies to her expected spoils;
Then, with envenomed jaws, the vital blood
Drinks of reluctant foes, and to her cave
Their bulky carcasses triumphant drags.

So pass my days. But when nocturnal shades
This world envelop, and th' inclement air
Persuades men to repel benumbing frosts
With pleasant wines, and crackling blaze of wood;
Me, lonely sitting, nor the glimmering light

Of make-weight candle, nor the joyous talk
Of loving friend, delights: distress'd, forlorn,
Amidst the horrors of the tedious night,
Darkling I sigh, and feed with dismal thoughts
My anxious mind: or sometimes mournful verse
Indite, and sing of groves and myrtle shades,
Or desperate lady near a purling stream,
Or lover pendent on a willow tree.
Meanwhile I labor with eternal drought,
And restless wish, and rave; my parched throat
Finds no relief, nor heavy eyes repose:
But if a slumber haply does invade
My weary limbs, my fancy 's still awake,
Thoughtful of drink, and eager, in a dream,
Tipples imaginary pots of ale,
In vain; awake I find the settled thirst
Still gnawing, and the pleasant phantom curse.

　　Thus do I live, from pleasure quite debarred,
Nor taste the fruits that the sun's genial rays
Mature, john-apple, nor the downy peach,
Nor walnut in rough-furrow'd coat secure,
Nor medlar, fruit delicious in decay;
Afflictions great! yet greater still remain:
My galligaskins, that have long withstood
The winter's fury, and encroaching frosts,
By time subdued (what will not time subdue!)
An horrid chasm disclos'd with orifice
Wide, discontinuous; at which the winds
Eurus and Auster, and the dreadful force
Of Boreas, that congeals the Cronian waves,
Tumultuous enter with dire chilling blasts,
Portending agues. Thus a well-fraught ship,
Long sail'd secure, or through th' Ægean deep,
Or the Ionian, till cruising near
The Lilybean shore, with hideous crush
On Scylla, or Charybdis (dangerous rocks!)
She strikes rebounding; whence the shatter'd oak,

So fierce a shock unable to withstand,
Admits the sea: in at the gaping side
The crowding waves gush with impetuous rage
Resistless, overwhelming; horrors seize
The mariners; Death in their eyes appears,
They stare, they lave, they pump, they swear, they pray:
(Vain efforts!) still the battering waves rush in,
Implacable, till, delug'd by the foam,
The ship sinks foundering in the vast abyss.

JOHN PHILIPS.

Bonnie George Campbell.

HIE upon Hielands,
    And low upon Tay,
Bonnie George Campbell
    Rade out on a day.
Saddled and bridled
    And gallant rade he;
Hame cam his gude horse,
    But never cam he!

Out cam his auld mither,
    Greeting fu' sair;
And out cam his bonnie bride,
    Rivin' her hair.
Saddled and bridled
    And booted rade he;
Toom hame cam the saddle,
    But never cam he!

" My meadow lies green,
    And my corn is unshorn;
My barn is to big,
    And my baby's unborn."

Saddled and bridled
  And booted rade he;
Toom hame cam the saddle,
  But never cam he!

ANONYMOUS.

The Hermit.

FAR in a wild, unknown to public view,
From youth to age a reverend hermit grew;
The moss his bed, the cave his humble cell,
His food the fruits, his drink the crystal well:
Remote from men, with God he pass'd the days,
Prayer all his business, all his pleasure praise.

  A life so sacred, such serene repose,
Seem'd Heaven itself, till one suggestion rose;
That Vice should triumph, Virtue, Vice obey,
This sprung some doubt of Providence's sway:
His hopes no more a certain prospect boast,
And all the tenor of his soul is lost:
So when a smooth expanse receives imprest
Calm Nature's image on its watery breast,
Down bend the banks, the trees depending grow,
And skies beneath with answering colors glow:
But if a stone the gentle sea divide,
Swift ruffling circles curl on every side,
And glimmering fragments of a broken Sun,
Banks, trees, and skies, in thick disorder run.

  To clear this doubt, to know the world by sight,
To find if books, or swains, report it right,
(For yet by swains alone the world he knew,
Whose feet came wandering o'er the nightly dew)
He quits his cell; the pilgrim-staff he bore,
And fix'd the scallop in his hat before;
Then with the Sun a rising journey went,
Sedate to think, and watching each event.

  The morn was wasted in the pathless grass,

4

And long and lonesome was the wild to pass;
But when the southern Sun had warm'd the day,
A youth came posting o'er a crossing way;
His raiment decent, his complexion fair,
And soft in graceful ringlets wav'd his hair.
Then near approaching, " Father, hail! " he cried,
" And hail, my son," the reverend sire replied;
Words follow'd words, from question answer flow'd,
And talk of various kind deceiv'd the road;
Till each with other pleas'd, and loath to part,
While in their age they differ, join in heart.
Thus stands an aged elm in ivy bound,
Thus youthful ivy clasps an elm around.

   Now sunk the Sun: the closing hour of day
Came onward, mantled o'er with sober gray;
Nature in silence bid the world repose;
When near the road a stately palace rose:
There by the Moon through ranks of trees they pass,
Whose verdure crown'd their sloping sides of grass.
It chanced the noble master of the dome
Still made his house the wandering stranger's home:
Yet still the kindness, from a thirst of praise,
Prov'd the vain flourish of expensive ease.
The pair arrive: the liv'ried servants wait;
Their lord receives them at the pompous gate.
The table groans with costly piles of food,
And all is more than hospitably good.
Then led to rest, the day's long toil they drown,
Deep sunk in sleep, and silk, and heaps of down.

   At length 't is morn, and at the dawn of day,
Along the wide canals the zephyrs play:
Fresh o'er the gay parterres the breezes creep,
And shake the neighboring wood to banish sleep.
Up rise the guests, obedient to the call:
An early banquet deck'd the splendid hall;
Rich luscious wine a golden goblet grac'd,
Which the kind master forc'd the guests to taste.

Then, pleas'd and thankful, from the porch they go;
And, but the landlord, none had cause of woe:
His cup was vanish'd; for in secret guise
The younger guest purloin'd the glittering prize.

As one who spies a serpent in his way,
Glistening and basking in the summer ray,
Disorder'd stops to shun the danger near,
Then walks with faintness on, and looks with fear,
So seem'd the sire; when far upon the road,
The shining spoil his wily partner show'd.
He stop'd with silence, walk'd with trembling heart,
And much he wish'd, but durst not ask to part:
Murmuring he lifts his eyes, and thinks it hard,
That generous actions meet a base reward.

While thus they pass, the Sun his glory shrouds,
The changing skies hang out their sable clouds;
A sound in air presag'd approaching rain,
And beasts to covert scud across the plain.
Warn'd by the signs, the wandering pair retreat,
To seek for shelter at a neighboring seat.
'T was built with turrets on a rising ground,
And strong, and large, and unimprov'd around;
Its owner's temper, timorous and severe,
Unkind and griping, caus'd a desert there.

As near the miser's heavy doors they drew,
Fierce rising gusts with sudden fury blew;
The nimble lightning mix'd with showers began,
And o'er their heads loud rolling thunders ran.
Here long they knock, but knock or call in vain,
Driven by the wind, and batter'd by the rain.
At length some pity warm'd the master's breast,
('T was then his threshold first received a guest);
Slow creaking turns the door with jealous care,
And half he welcomes in the shivering pair;
One frugal fagot lights the naked walls,
And Nature's fervor through their limbs recalls:
Bread of the coarsest sort, with eager wine,

(Each hardly granted) serv'd them both to dine;
And when the tempest first appeared to cease,
A ready warning bid them part in peace.

    With still remark the pondering hermit view'd,
In one so rich, a life so poor and rude;
"And why should such," within himself he cried,
"Lock the lost wealth a thousand want beside?"
But what new marks of wonder soon take place,
In every settling feature of his face;
When from his vest the young companion bore
That cup, the generous landlord own'd before,
And paid profusely with the precious bowl
The stinted kindness of this churlish soul.

    But now the clouds in airy tumult fly!
The Sun emerging opes an azure sky;
A fresher green the smelling leaves display,
And, glittering as they tremble, cheer the day:
The weather courts them from the poor retreat,
And the glad master bolts the wary gate.

    While hence they walk, the pilgrim's bosom wrought
With all the travail of uncertain thought;
His partner's acts without their cause appear,
'T was there a vice, and seem'd a madness here:
Detesting that, and pitying this, he goes,
Lost and confounded with the various shows.

    Now Night's dim shades again involve the sky,
Again the wanderers want a place to lie,
Again they search, and find a lodging nigh,
The soil improv'd around, the mansion neat,
And neither poorly low, nor idly great:
It seem'd to speak its master's turn of mind,
Content, and not to praise, but virtue kind.

    Hither the walkers turn with weary feet,
Then bless the mansion, and the master greet:
Their greeting fair, bestow'd with modest guise,
The courteous master hears, and thus replies:

    "Without a vain, without a grudging heart,

To him who gives us all, I yield a part;
From him you come, for him accept it here,
A frank and sober, more than costly cheer."
He spoke, and bid the welcome table spread,
Then talk of virtue till the time of bed,
When the grave household round his hall repair,
Warn'd by a bell, and close the hours with prayer.

　At length the world, renew'd by calm repose,
Was strong for toil, the dappled Morn arose;
Before the pilgrims part, the younger crept
Near the clos'd cradle where an infant slept,
And writh'd his neck: the landlord's little pride,
O strange return! grew black, and gasp'd, and died.
Horror of horrors! what! his only son!
How look'd our hermit when the fact was done;
Not Hell, though Hell's black jaws in sunder part,
And breathe blue fire, could more assault his heart.

　Confus'd, and struck with silence at the deed,
He flies, but trembling, fails to fly with speed.
His steps the youth pursues; the country lay
Perplex'd with roads, a servant show'd the way:
A river cross'd the path; the passage o'er
Was nice to find; the servant trod before;
Long arms of oaks an open bridge supplied,
And deep the waves beneath them bending glide.
The youth, who seem'd to watch a time to sin,
Approach'd the careless guide, and thrust him in:
Plunging he falls, and rising lifts his head,
Then flashing turns, and sinks among the dead.

　Wild, sparkling rage inflames the father's eyes,
He bursts the bands of fear, and madly cries,
"Detested wretch!"—But scarce his speech began,
When the strange partner seem'd no longer man:
His youthful face grew more serenely sweet;
His robe turn'd white, and flow'd upon his feet;
Fair rounds of radiant points invest his hair;
Celestial odors breathe through purpled air;

And wings, whose colors glitter'd on the day,
Wide at his back their gradual plumes display.
The form ethereal burst upon his sight,
And moved in all the majesty of light.
   Though loud at first the pilgrim's passion grew,
Sudden he gaz'd, and wist not what to do;
Surprise in secret chains his words suspends,
And in a calm his settling temper ends.
But silence here the beauteous angel broke
(The voice of music ravish'd as he spoke).
   "Thy prayer, thy praise, thy life to vice unknown,
In sweet memorial rise before the throne:
These charms success in our bright region find
And force an angel down, to calm thy mind;
For this, commissioned, I forsook the sky,
Nay, cease to kneel—thy fellow-servant I.
   "Then know the truth of government divine,
And let these scruples be no longer thine.
   "The Maker justly claims that world he made,
In this the right of Providence is laid;
Its sacred majesty through all depends
On using second means to work his ends:
'T is thus, withdrawn in state from human eye,
The power exerts his attributes on high,
Your actions uses, nor controls your will,
And bids the doubting sons of men be still.
   "What strange events can strike with more surprise,
Than those which lately struck thy wondering eyes?
Yet, taught by these, confess th' Almighty just,
And where you can't unriddle, learn to trust!
   "The great, vain man, who far'd on costly food,
Whose life was too luxurious to be good;
Who made his ivory stands with goblets shine,
And forc'd his guests to morning draughts of wine,
Has, with the cup, the graceless custom lost,
And still he welcomes, but with less of cost.
   "The mean, suspicious wretch, whose bolted door

Ne'er mov'd in duty to the wandering poor;
With him I left the cup, to teach his mind
That Heaven can bless, if mortals will be kind.
Conscious of wanting worth, he views the bowl,
And feels compassion touch his grateful soul.
Thus artists melt the sullen ore of lead,
With heaping coals of fire upon his head;
In the kind warmth the metal learns to glow,
And loose from dross the silver runs below.

  "Long had our pious friend in virtue trod,
But now the child half-weaned his heart from God;
(Child of his age) for him he liv'd in pain,
And measured back his steps to Earth again.
To what excesses had his dotage run?
But God, to save the father, took the son.
To all but thee, in fits he seem'd to go,
(And 't was my ministry to deal the blow,)
The poor fond parent, humbled in the dust,
Now owns in tears the punishment was just.

  "But now had all his fortune felt a wrack,
Had that false servant sped in safety back;
This night his treasur'd heaps he meant to steal,
And what a fund of charity would fail!
Thus Heaven instructs thy mind: this trial o'er,
Depart in peace, resign, and sin no more."

  On sounding pinions here the youth withdrew,
The sage stood wondering as the seraph flew.
Thus look'd Elisha when, to mount on high,
His master took the chariot of the sky;
The fiery pomp ascending left to view;
The prophet gazed, and wish'd to follow too.

  The bending hermit here a prayer begun,
"*Lord! as in Heaven, on Earth thy will be done.*"
Then gladly turning sought his ancient place,
And passed a life of piety and peace.

THOMAS PARNELL.

On the Prospect of Planting Arts and Learning in America.

THE Muse, disgusted at an age and clime
  Barren of every glorious theme,
In distant lands now waits a better time,
  Producing subjects worthy fame;

In happy climes, where from the genial sun
  And virgin earth such scenes ensue,
The force of art by nature seems outdone,
  And fancied beauties by the true;

In happy climes the seat of innocence,
  Where nature guides and virtue rules,
Where men shall not impose, for truth and sense,
  The pedantry of courts and schools.

There shall be sung another golden age,
  The rise of empire and of arts,
The good and great uprising epic rage,
  The wisest heads and noblest hearts.

Not such as Europe breeds in her decay;
  Such as she bred when fresh and young,
When heavenly flame did animate her clay,
  By future poets shall be sung.

Westward the course of empire takes its way;
  The first four acts already past,
The fifth shall close the drama with the day;
  Time's noblest offspring is the last.

GEORGE BERKELEY.

Sally in our Alley.

OF all the girls that are so smart,
  There 's none like Pretty Sally;

She is the darling of my heart,
  And lives in our alley.
There 's ne'er a lady in the land
  That 's half so sweet as Sally;
She is the darling of my heart,
  And lives in our alley.

Her father he makes cabbage-nets,
  And through the streets does cry them;
Her mother she sells laces long
  To such as please to buy them:
But sure such folk can have no part
  In such a girl as Sally;
She is the darling of my heart,
  And lives in our alley.

When she is by, I leave my work,
  I love her so sincerely;
My master comes, like any Turk,
  And bangs me most severely:
But let him bang, long as he will,
  I 'll bear it all for Sally;
She is the darling of my heart,
  And lives in our alley.

Of all the days are in the week,
  I dearly love but one day,
And that 's the day that comes betwixt
  A Saturday and Monday;
For then I 'm dressed, all in my best,
  To walk abroad with Sally;
She is the darling of my heart,
  And lives in our alley.

My master carries me to church,
  And often am I blamed,
Because I leave him in the lurch,
  Soon as the text is named:

4*

I leave the church in sermon time,
　And slink away to Sally;
She is the darling of my heart,
　And lives in our alley.

When Christmas comes about again,
　O then I shall have money;
I 'll hoard it up and, box and all,
　I 'll give it to my honey;
Oh would it were ten thousand pounds,
　I 'd give it all to Sally;
For she 's the darling of my heart,
　And lives in our alley.

My master, and the neighbors all,
　Make game of me and Sally,
And but for her I 'd better be
　A slave, and row a galley:
But when my seven long years are out,
　O then I 'll marry Sally,
And then how happily we 'll live—
　But not in our alley.

HENRY CAREY.

Grongar Hill.

SILENT nymph, with curious eye,
Who the purple evening lie
On the mountain's lonely van,
Beyond the noise of busy man;
Painting fair the form of things,
While the yellow linnet sings;
Or the tuneful nightingale
Charms the forest with her tale;—
Come, with all thy various dues,
Come and aid thy sister Muse;
Now, while Phœbus riding high,
Gives lustre to the land and sky!

Grongar Hill invites my song,
Draw the landscape bright and strong;
Grongar, in whose mossy cells
Sweetly musing Quiet dwells;
Grongar, in whose silent shade,
For the modest Muses made,
So oft I have, the evening still,
At the fountain of a rill,
Sate upon a flowery bed,
With my hand beneath my head;
While stray'd my eyes o'er Towy's flood,
Over mead and over wood,
From house to house, from hill to hill,
Till Contemplation had her fill.

    About his chequer'd sides I wind,
And leave his brooks and meads behind,
And groves and grottoes where I lay,
And vistas shooting beams of day;
Wide and wider spreads the vale,
As circles on a smooth canal;
The mountains round, unhappy fate!
Sooner or later, of all height,
Withdraw their summits from the skies,
And lessen as the others rise:
Still the prospect wider spreads,
Adds a thousand woods and meads;
Still it widens, widens still,
And sinks the newly risen hill.

    Now, I gain the mountain's brow,
What a landscape lies below!
No clouds, no vapors intervene;
But the gay, the open scene
Does the face of Nature show,
In all the hues of Heaven's bow!
And, swelling to embrace the light,
Spreads around beneath the sight.

    Old castles on the cliffs arise,

Proudly towering in the skies!
Rushing from the woods, the spires
Seem from hence ascending fires!
Half his beams Apollo sheds
On the yellow mountain-heads!
Gilds the fleeces of the flocks,
And glitters on the broken rocks!
  Below me trees unnumber'd rise,
Beautiful in various dyes:
The gloomy pine, the poplar blue,
The yellow beach, the sable yew,
The slender fir that taper grows,
The sturdy oak with broad-spread boughs,
And beyond the purple grove,
Haunt of Phyllis, queen of love!
Gaudy as the opening dawn,
Lies a long and level lawn,
On which a dark hill, steep and high,
Holds and charms the wandering eye!
Deep are his feet in Towy's flood,
His sides are cloth'd with waving wood,
And ancient towers crown his brow,
That cast an awful look below;
Whose ragged walls the ivy creeps,
And with her arms from falling keeps;
So both a safety from the wind
In mutual dependence find.
'T is now the raven's bleak abode:
'T is now the apartment of the toad;
And there the fox securely feeds;
And there the poisonous adder breeds,
Conceal'd in ruins, moss, and weeds;
While, ever and anon, there falls
Huge heaps of hoary moulder'd walls.
Yet Time has seen, that lifts the low,
And level lays the lofty brow,
Has seen this broken pile complete,

Big with the vanity of state;
But transient is the smile of Fate!
A little rule, a little sway,
A sunbeam in a winter's day,
Is all the proud and mighty have
Between the cradle and the grave.

And see the rivers how they run,
Through woods and meads, in shade and sun,
Sometimes swift, sometimes slow,
Wave succeeding wave, they go
A various journey to the deep,
Like human life, to endless sleep!
Thus is Nature's vesture wrought,
To instruct our wandering thought;
Thus she dresses green and gay,
To disperse our cares away.

Ever charming, ever new,
When will the landscape tire the view!
The fountain's fall, the river's flow,
The woody valleys, warm and low;
The windy summit, wild and high,
Roughly rushing on the sky!
The pleasant seat, the ruin'd tower,
The naked rock, the shady bower;
The town and village, dome and farm,
Each gives each a double charm,
As pearls upon an Ethiop's arm.

See on the mountain's southern side
Where the prospect opens wide,
Where the evening gilds the tide;
How close and small the hedges lie!
What streaks of meadows cross the eye!
A step methinks may pass the stream,
So little distant dangers seem;
So we mistake the Future's face,
Ey'd through Hope's deluding glass;
As yon summit soft and fair,

Clad'in colors of the air,
Which to those who journey near,
Barren, brown, and rough appear,
Still we tread the same coarse way,
The present 's still a cloudy day.
  O may I with myself agree,
And never covet what I see;
Content me with an humble shade,
My passions tam'd, my wishes laid;
For, while our wishes wildly roll,
We banish quiet from the soul:
'T is thus the busy beat the air,
And misers gather wealth and care.
  Now, ev'n now, my joys run high,
As on the mountain-turf I lie;
While the wanton Zephyr sings,
And in the vale perfumes his wings;
While the waters murmur deep;
While the shepherd charms his sheep;
While the birds unbounded fly,
And with music fill the sky,
Now, ev'n now, my joys run high.
  Be full, ye courts; be great who will,
Search for Peace with all your skill:
Open wide the lofty door,
Seek her on the marble floor.
In vain you search, she is not there;
In vain you search the domes of Care!
Grass and flowers Quiet treads,
On the meads, and mountain-heads,
Along with Pleasure, close allied,
Ever by each other's side;
And often, by the murmuring rill,
Hears the thrush, while all is still,
Within the groves of Grongar Hill.

                          JOHN DYER.

A Soliloquy.

OCCASIONED BY THE CHIRPING OF A GRASSHOPPER.

HAPPY insect! ever blest
With a more than mortal rest,
Rosy dews the leaves among,
Humble joys, and gentle song!
Wretched poet! ever curst
With a life of lives the worst,
Sad despondence, restless fears,
Endless jealousies and tears.

In the burning summer thou
Warblest on the verdant bough,
Meditating cheerful play,
Mindless of the piercing ray;
Scorched in Cupid's fervors, I
Ever weep and ever die.

Proud to gratify thy will,
Ready Nature waits thee still;
Balmy wines to thee she pours,
Weeping through the dewy flowers
Rich as those by Hebe given
To the thirsty sons of heaven.

Yet alas, we both agree.
Miserable thou like me!
Each, alike, in youth rehearses
Gentle strains and tender verses;
Ever wandering far from home,
Mindless of the days to come
(Such as aged Winter brings
Trembling on his icy wings),
Both alike at last we die;
Thou art starved, and so am I!

WALTER HARTE.

The Braes of Yarrow.

"Busk ye, busk ye, my bonnie, bonnie bride!
    Busk ye, busk ye, my winsome marrow!
Busk ye, busk ye, my bonnie, bonnie bride,
    And think nae mair of the braes of Yarrow."

"Where got ye that bonnie, bonnie bride,
    Where got ye that winsome marrow?"
"I got her where I daurna weel be seen,
    Pu'ing the birks on the braes of Yarrow.

"Weep not, weep not, my bonnie, bonnie bride,
    Weep not, weep not, my winsome marrow!
Nor let thy heart lament to leave
    Pu'ing the birks on the braes of Yarrow."

"Why does she weep, thy bonnie, bonnie bride?
    Why does she weep, thy winsome marrow?
And why daur ye nae mair weel be seen
    Pu'ing the birks on the braes of Yarrow?"

"Lang maun she weep, lang maun she, maun she weep—
    Lang maun she weep wi' dule and sorrow;
And lang maun I nae mair weel be seen
    Pu'ing the birks on the braes of Yarrow.

"For she has tint her lover, lover dear—
    Her lover dear, the cause of sorrow;
And I hae slain the comeliest swain
    That e'er pu'd birks on the braes of Yarrow.

"Why runs thy stream, O Yarrow, Yarrow, red?
    Why on thy braes heard the voice of sorrow?
And why yon melancholious weeds
    Hung on the bonnie birks of Yarrow?

" What 's yonder floats on the rueful, rueful flood ?
    What 's yonder floats ?—Oh, dule and sorrow !
'T is he, the comely swain I slew
    Upon the dulefu' braes of Yarrow.

" Wash, oh, wash his wounds, his wounds in tears,
    His wounds in tears o' dule and sorrow ;
And wrap his limbs in mourning weeds,
    And lay him on the banks of Yarrow.

" Then build, then build, ye sisters, sisters sad,
    Ye sisters sad, his tomb wi' sorrow ;
And weep around, in waeful wise,
    His hapless fate on the braes of Yarrow !

" Curse ye, curse ye, his useless, useless shield,
    The arm that wrought the deed of sorrow,
The fatal spear that pierced his breast,
    His comely breast, on the braes of Yarrow !

" Did I not warn thee not to, not to love,
    And warn from fight ?   But, to my sorrow,
Too rashly bold, a stronger arm thou met'st,
    Thou met'st, and fell on the braes of Yarrow.

Sweet smells the birk; green grows, green grows the grass ;
    Yellow on Yarrow's braes the gowan ;
Fair hangs the apple frae the rock ;
    Sweet the wave of Yarrow flowing !

" Flows Yarrow sweet ?   As sweet, as sweet flows Tweed ;
    As green its grass ; its gowan as yellow ;
As sweet smells on its braes the birk ;
    The apple from its rocks as mellow !

" Fair was thy love ! fair, fair indeed thy love !
    In flowery bands thou didst him fetter ;

Though he was fair, and well-beloved again,
  Than I he never loved thee better.

"Busk ye, then, busk, my bonnie, bonnie bride!
  Busk ye, busk ye, my winsome marrow!
Busk ye, and lo'e me on the banks of Tweed
  And think nae mair on the braes of Yarrow."

"How can I busk a bonnie, bonnie bride?
  How can I busk a winsome marrow?
How can I lo'e him on the banks of Tweed,
  That slew my love on the braes of Yarrow?

"Oh Yarrow fields, may never, never rain,
  Nor dew, thy tender blossoms cover!
For there was basely slain my love,
  My love, as he had not been a lover.

"The boy put on his robes, his robes of green,
  His purple vest—'t was my ain sewing;
Ah, wretched me! I little, little kenned
  He was, in these, to meet his ruin.

"The boy took out his milk-white, milk-white steed,
  Unmindful of my dule and sorrow;
But ere the too fa' of the night,
  He lay a corpse on the banks of Yarrow!

"Much I rejoiced that waefu', waefu' day;
  I sang, my voice the woods returning;
But lang ere night the spear was flown
  That slew my love, and left me mourning.

"What can my barbarous, barbarous father do,
  But with his cruel rage pursue me?
My lover's blood is on thy spear—
  How canst thou, barbarous man, then woo me?

"My happy sisters may be, may be proud;
 With cruel and ungentle scoffing
May bid me seek, on Yarrow braes,
 My lover nailed in his coffin.

"My brother Douglas may upbraid,
 And strive, with threatening words, to move me;
My lover's blood is on thy spear—
 How canst thou ever bid me love thee?

"Yes, yes, prepare the bed, the bed of love!
 With bridal-sheets my body cover!
Unbar, ye bridal-maids, the door!
 Let in the expected husband-lover!

"But who the expected husband, husband is?
 His hands, methinks, are bathed in slaughter!
Ah me! what ghastly spectre 's yon
 Comes in his pale shroud, bleeding after?

"Pale as he is, here lay him, lay him down;
 Oh lay his cold head on my pillow!
Take off, take off these bridal weeds,
 And crown my careful head with willow.

"Pale though thou art, yet best, yet best beloved,
 Oh could my warmth to life restore thee!
Yet lie all night within my arms—
 No youth lay ever there before thee!

"Pale, pale indeed, O lovely, lovely youth!
 Forgive, forgive so foul a slaughter,
And lie all night within my arms,
 No youth shall ever lie there after!"

"Return, return, O mournful, mournful bride!
 Return, and dry thy useless sorrow!

Thy lover heeds nought of thy sighs;
  He lies a corpse on the braes of Yarrow."
WILLIAM HAMILTON.

The School-Mistress.

AH me! full sorely is my heart forlorn,
  To think how modest Worth neglected lies,
While partial Fame doth with her blast adorn
  Such deeds alone, as pride and pomp disguise;
  Deeds of ill sort, and mischievous emprise:
Lend me thy clarion, goddess! let me try
  To sound the praise of Merit, ere it dies,
  Such as I oft have chaunced to espy,
Lost in the dreary shades of dull Obscurity.

In every village mark'd with little spire,
  Embower'd in trees, and hardly known to Fame,
There dwells in lowly shed, and mean attire,
  A matron old, whom we School-mistress name,
  Who boasts unruly brats with birch to tame;
They grieven sore, in piteous durance pent,
  Aw'd by the power of this relentless dame
  And oft-times, on vagaries idly bent,
For unkempt hair, or task unconn'd, are sorely shent.

And all in sight doth rise a birchen tree
  Which Learning near her little dome did stowe
Whilom a twig of small regard to see,
  Though now so wide its waving branches flow
  And work the simple vassals mickle woe;
For not a wind might curl the leaves that blew,
  But their limbs shudder'd, and their pulse beat low;
  And as they look'd they found their horror grew,
And shap'd it into rods, and tingled at the view.

So have I seen (who has not, may conceive)
  A lifeless phantom near a garden plac'd;

So doth it wanton birds of peace bereave,
    Of sport, of song, of pleasure, of repast;
    They start, they stare, they wheel, they look aghast;
Sad servitude! such comfortless annoy
    May no bold Briton's riper age e'er taste!
    Ne superstition clog his dance of joy,
No vision empty, vain, his native bliss destroy.

Near to this dome is found a patch so green,
    On which the tribe their gambols do display,
    And at the door imprisoning-board is seen,
Lest weakly wights of smaller size should stray;
    Eager, perdie, to bask in sunny day!
    The noises intermix'd, which thence resound,
Do Learning's little tenement betray;
    Where sits the dame, disguis'd in look profound,
And eyes her fairy throng, and turns her wheel around.

Her cap, far whiter than the driven snow,
    Emblem right meet of decency does yield:
    Her apron dy'd in grain, as blue, I trow,
As is the hare-bell that adorns the field:
    And in her hand, for sceptre, she does wield
    Tway birchen sprays; with anxious fear entwin'd,
With dark distrust, and sad repentance fill'd:
    And stedfast hate, and sharp affliction join'd,
And fury uncontroll'd, and chastisement unkind.

Few but have kenn'd, in semblance meet portray'd,
    The childish faces of old Eol's train;
    Libs, Notus, Auster: these in frowns array'd,
How then would fare or Earth, or Sky, or Main,
    Were the stern god to give his slaves the rein?
    And were not she rebellious breasts to quell,
And were not she her statutes to maintain,
    The cot no more, I ween, were deem'd the cell,
Where comely peace of mind, and decent order dwell.

5

A russet stole was o'er her shoulders thrown;
A russet kirtle fenc'd the nipping air;
'T was simple russet, but it was her own;
'T was her own country bred the flock so fair!
'T was her own labor did the fleece prepare;
And, sooth to say, her pupils, rang'd around,
Through pious awe, did term it passing rare;
For they in gaping wonderment abound,
And think, no doubt, she been the greatest wight on ground.

Albeit ne flattery did corrupt her truth,
Ne pompous title did debauch her ear;
Goody, good-woman, gossip, n'aunt, forsooth,
Or dame, the sole additions she did hear;
Yet these she challeng'd, these she held right dear:
Ne would esteem him act as mought behove,
Who should not honor'd eld with these revere:
For never title yet so mean could prove,
But there was eke a mind which did that title love.

One ancient hen she took delight to feed,
The plodding pattern of the busy dame;
Which, ever and anon, impell'd by need,
Into her school, begirt with chickens, came!
Such favor did her past deportment claim:
And, if Neglect had lavish'd on the ground
Fragment of bread, she would collect the same,
For well she knew, and quaintly could expound
What sin it were to waste the smallest crumb she found.

Herbs too she knew, and well of each could speak
That in her garden sipp'd the silvery dew;
Where no vain flower disclos'd a gaudy streak;
But herbs for use, and physic, not a few,
Of gray renown, within those borders grew:
The tufted basil, pun-provoking thyme,
Fresh baum, and marigold of cheerful hue;

The lowly gill, that never dares to climb;
And more I fain would sing, disdaining here to rhyme.

Yet euphrasy may not be left unsung,
That gives dim eyes to wander leagues around;
And pungent radish, biting infant's tongue;
And plantain ribb'd, that heals the reaper's wound,
And marjoram sweet, in shepherd's posie found;
And lavender, whose spikes of azure bloom
Shall be, erewhile, in arid bundles bound,
To lurk amidst the labors of her loom,
And crown her kerchiefs clean, with mickle rare perfume.

And here trim rosemarine, that whilom crown'd
The daintiest garden of the proudest peer;
Ere, driven from its envied site, it found
A sacred shelter for its branches here;
Where edg'd with gold its glittering skirts appear.
Oh wassal days! Oh customs meet and well!
Ere this was banish'd from his lofty sphere:
Simplicity then sought this humble cell,
Nor ever would she more with thane and lordling dwell.

Here oft the dame, on Sabbath's decent eve,
Hymned such psalms as Sternhold forth did mete.
If winter 't were, she to her hearth did cleave,
But in her garden found a summer-seat;
Sweet melody! to hear her then repete
How Israel's sons, beneath a foreign king,
While taunting foemen did a song entreat,
All, for the nonce, untuning every string,
Uphung their useless lyres—small heart had they to sing.

For she was just, and friend to virtuous lore,
And pass'd much time in truly virtuous deed;
And in those elfins' ears would oft deplore
The times when Truth by Popish rage did bleed,

And tortious death was true Devotion's meed;
And simple Faith in iron chains did mourn,
That nould on wooden image place her creed;
And lawny saints in smouldering flames did burn:
Ah! dearest Lord, forefend, thilk days should e'er return.

In elbow-chair, like that of Scottish stem
By the sharp tooth of cankering eld defac'd,
In which, when he receives his diadem,
Our soverign prince and liefest liege is plac'd,
The matron sate; and some with rank she grac'd
(The source of children's and of courtiers' pride!)
Redress'd affronts, for vile affronts there pass'd;
And warn'd them not the fretful to deride,
But love each other dear, whatever them betide.

Right well she knew each temper to descry;
To thwart the proud, and the submiss to raise;
Some with vile copper-prize exalt on high,
And some entice with pittance small of praise,
And other some with baleful sprig she 'frays:
E'en absent, she the reins of power doth hold,
While with quaint arts the giddy crowd she sways:
Forewarn'd, if little bird their pranks behold,
'T will whisper in her ear, and all the scene unfold.

Lo now with state she utters the command!
Eftsoons the urchins to their tasks repair;
Their books of stature small they take in hand,
Which with pellucid horn secured are,
To save from finger wet the letters fair:
The work so gay that on their back is seen,
St. George's high achievements does declare;
On which thilk wight that has y-gazing been,
Kens the forthcoming rod, unpleasing sight, I ween!

Ah luckless he, and born beneath the beam
Of evil star! it irks me whilst I write:

As erst the bard * by Mulla's silver stream,
Oft, as he told of deadly dolorous plight,
Sigh'd as he sung, and did in tears indite.
For brandishing the rod, she doth begin
To loose the brogues, the stripling's late delight!
And down they drop; appears his dainty skin,
Fair as the furry-coat of whitest ermilin.

O ruthful scene! when from a nook obscure,
His little sister doth his peril see:
All playful as she sate, she grows demure;
She finds full soon her wonted spirits flee:
She meditates a prayer to set him free:
Nor gentle pardon could this dame deny
(If gentle pardon could with dames agree)
To her sad grief that swells in either eye,
And wrings her so that all for pity she could die.

No longer can she now her shrieks command;
And hardly she forbears, through awful fear,
To rushen forth, and, with presumptuous hand,
To stay harsh Justice in its mid career.
On thee she calls, on thee her parent dear!
(Ah! too remote to ward the shameful blow!)
She sees no kind domestic visage near,
And soon a flood of tears begins to flow;
And gives a loose at last to unavailing woe.

But ah! what pen his piteous plight may trace?
Or what device his loud laments explain?
The form uncouth of his disguised face?
The pallid hue that dyes his looks amain?
The plenteous shower that does his cheek distain?
When he, in abject wise, implores the dame,
Ne hopeth aught of sweet reprieve to gain;

* Spenser.

Or when from high she levels well her aim,
And, through the thatch, his cries each falling stroke pro-
     claim.

The other tribe, aghast, with sore dismay,
Attend, and con their tasks with mickle care:
By turns, astonied, every twig survey,
And, from their fellow's hateful wounds, beware,
Knowing, I wist, how each the same may share,
Till fear has taught them a performance meet,
And to the well-known chest the dame repair;
Whence oft with sugar'd cates she doth them greet,
And ginger-bread y-rare; now certes, doubly sweet.

See to their seats they hie with merry glee,
And in beseemly order sitten there;
All but the wight of bum y-galled, he
Abhorreth bench, and stool, and form, and chair;
(This hand in mouth y-fix'd, that rends his hair;)
And eke with snubs profound, and heaving breast,
Convulsions intermitting! does declare
His grievous wrong; his dame's unjust behest;
And scorns her offer'd love, and shuns to be caress'd.

His face besprent with liquid crystal shines,
His blooming face that seems a purple flower,
Which low to earth its drooping head declines,
All smear'd and sullied by a vernal shower.
O the hard bosoms of despotic power!
All, all, but she, the author of his shame,
All, all, but she, regret this mournful hour;
Yet hence the youth and hence the flower shall claim,
If so I deem aright, transcending worth and fame.

Behind some door, in melancholy thought,
Mindless of food, he, dreary caitiff! pines,
Ne for his fellows' joyaunce careth aught,
But to the wind all merriment resigns;

And deems it shame, if he to peace inclines:
And many a sullen look askance is sent,
Which for his dame's annoyance he designs;
And still the more to pleasure him she 's bent,
The more doth he, perverse, her havior past resent.

Ah me! how much I fear lest pride it be!
But if that pride it be, which thus inspires,
Beware, ye dames, with nice discernment see
Ye quench not too the sparks of nobler fires:
Ah! better far than all the Muses' lyres,
All coward arts, is Valor's generous heat;
The firm fixt breast which fit and right requires,
Like Vernon's patriot soul! more justly great
Than Craft that pimps for ill, or flowery false Deceit.

Yet nurs'd with skill, what dazzling fruits appear!
E'en now sagacious Foresight points to show
A little bench of heedless bishops here,
And there a chancellor in embryo,
Or bard sublime, if bard may e'er be so,
As Milton, Shakespeare, names that ne'er shall die!
Though now he crawl along the ground so low,
Nor weeting how the Muse should soar on high,
Wisheth, poor starveling elf! his paper kite may fly.

And this perhaps, who, censuring the design,
Low lays the house which that of cards doth build,
Shall Dennis be! if rigid Fate incline,
And many an epic to his rage shall yield;
And many a poet quit th' Aonian field;
And, sour'd by age, profound he shall appear,
As he who now with 'sdainful fury thrilled
Surveys mine work; and levels many a sneer,
And furls his wrinkly front, and cries, "What stuff is
    here?"

But now Dan Phœbus gains the middle skie,
And Liberty unbars her prison-door;
And like a rushing torrent out they fly,
And now the grassy cirque had covered o'er,
With boisterous revel-rout and wild uproar;
A thousand ways in wanton rings they run,
Heaven shield their short-liv'd pastime, I implore!
For well may Freedom erst so dearly won,
Appear to British elf more gladsome than the Sun.

Enjoy, poor imps! enjoy your sportive trade,
And chase gay flies, and cull the fairest flowers;
For when my bones in grass-green sods are laid,
O never may ye taste more careless hours
In knightly castles, or in ladies' bowers.
O vain to seek delight in earthly thing!
But most in courts where proud Ambition towers;
Deluded wight! who weens fair Peace can spring
Beneath the pompous dome of kesar or of king.

See in each sprite some various bent appear!
These rudely carol most incondite lay;
Those sauntering on the green, with jocund leer
Salute the stranger passing on his way;
Some builden fragile tenements of clay;
Some to the standing lake their courses bend,
With pebbles smooth at duck and drake to play;
Thilk to the huxter's savory cottage tend,
In pastry kings and queens th' allotted mite to spend.

Here, as each season yields a different store,
Each season's stores in order ranged been;
Apples with cabbage-net y-covered o'er,
Galling full sore th' unmoney'd wight, are seen;
And goose-b'rie clad in livery red or green;
And here of lovely dye, the Catharine pear,
Fine pear! as lovely for thy juice, I ween:

O may no wight e'er penniless come there,
Lest smit with ardent love he pine with hopeless care !

See ! cherries here, ere cherries yet abound,
 With thread so white in tempting posies tied,
Scattering like blooming maid their glances round,
 With pamper'd look draw little eyes aside;
And must be bought, though penury betide.
The plume all azure, and the nut all brown,
And here each season do those cakes abide,
 Whose honored names* th' inventive city own,
Rendering through Britain's isle Salopia's praises known;

 Admir'd Salopia ! that with venial pride
 Eyes her bright form in Severn's ambient wave,
 Famed for her loyal cares in perils tried,
 Her daughters lovely, and her striplings brave:
 Ah ! 'midst the rest, may flowers adorn his grave
 Whose heart did first these dulcet cates display !
 A motive fair to Learning's imps he gave,
 Who cheerless o'er her darkling region stray;
Till Reason's morn arise, and light them on their way.

WILLIAM SHENSTONE.

The Chameleon.

OFT has it been my lot to mark
A proud, conceited, talking spark,
With eyes, that hardly served at most
To guard their master 'gainst a post,
Yet round the world the blade has been
To see whatever could be seen,
Returning from his finished tour,
Grown ten times perter than before;
Whatever word you chance to drop,
The traveled fool your mouth will stop;

Shrewsbury cakes.

"Sir, if my judgment you 'll allow,
 I 've seen—and sure I ought to know,"
So begs you 'd pay a due submission,
And acquiesce in his decision.

Two travelers of such a cast,
As o'er Arabia's wilds they passed,
And on their way in friendly chat,
Now talked of this, and then of that,
Discoursed awhile, 'mongst other matter,
Of the chameleon's form and nature.
"A stranger animal," cries one,
"Sure never lived beneath the sun.
A lizard's body, lean and long,
A fish's head, a serpent's tongue,
Its foot with triple claw disjoined;
And what a length of tail behind!
How slow its pace; and then its hue—
Who ever saw so fine a blue?"

"Hold, there," the other quick replies,
"'T is *green*, I saw it with these eyes,
As late with open mouth it lay,
And warmed it in the sunny ray:
Stretched at its ease, the beast I viewed
And saw it eat the air for food."
"I 've seen it, sir, as well as you,
And must again affirm it blue;
At leisure I the beast surveyed,
Extended in the cooling shade."
"'T is green, 't is green, sir, I assure ye!"
"Green!" cries the other in a fury—
"Why, sir!—d' ye think I 've lost my eyes?"
"'T were no great loss," the friend replies,
"For, if they always serve you thus,
 You 'll find them of but little use."

So high at last the contest rose,
From words they almost came to blows;
When luckily came by a third—
To him the question they referred,
And begged he 'd tell 'em, if he knew,
Whether the thing was green or blue.
  "Sirs," cries the umpire, "cease your pother!
The creature 's neither one or t' other.
I caught the animal last night,
And viewed it o'er by candlelight:
I marked it well—'t was black as jet—
You stare—but, sirs, I 've got it yet,
And can produce it."   "Pray, sir, do:
I 'll lay my life the thing is blue."
"And I 'll be sworn, that when you 've seen
  The reptile, you 'll pronounce him green."

  "Well, then, at once to ease the doubt,"
Replies the man, " I 'll turn him out:
And when before your eyes I've set him,
If you don't find him black, I 'll eat him."
He said: then full before their sight
Produced the beast, and lo!—'t was white.

  Both stared, the man looked wondrous wise—
"My children," the chameleon cries,
  (Then first the creature found a tongue),
"You all are right, and all are wrong:
  When next you talk of what you view,
  Think others see as well as you:
  Nor wonder, if you find that none
  Prefers your eyesight to his own."

                              JAMES MERRICK.

Waly, Waly, but Love be Bonny.

O WALY, waly up the bank,
　　And waly, waly down the brae,
And waly, waly yon burn-side,
　　Where I and my love wont to gae.
I lean'd my back unto an aik,
　　And thought it was a trusty tree,
But first it bow'd, and syne it brak',
　　Sae my true love did lightly me.

O waly, waly but love be bonny,
　　A little time while it is new,
But when 't is auld it waxeth cauld
　　And fades away like morning dew.
Oh! wherefore should I busk my head?
　　Or wherefore should I kame my hair?
For my true love has me forsook,
　　And says he 'll never love me mair.

Now Arthur-Seat shall be my bed,
　　The sheets shall ne'er be fyled by me,
Saint Anton's well shall be my drink,
　　Since my true love 's forsaken me.
Martinmas wind, when wilt thou blaw,
　　And shake the green leaves off the tree?
Oh, gentle death! when wilt thou come?
　　For of my life I am weary.

'T is not the frost that freezes fell,
　　Nor blowing snaw's inclemency:
'T is not sic cauld that makes me cry,
　　But my love's heart grown cauld to me.
When we came in by Glasgow town,
　　We were a comely sight to see;
My love was clad in the black velvet,
　　And I mysel' in cramasie.

But had I wist before I kiss'd
    That love had been so ill to win,
I 'd lock'd my heart in a case of gold,
    And pinn'd it with a silver pin.
And oh! if my young babe were born,
    And set upon the nurse's knee,
And I mysel' were dead and gane,
    Wi' the green grass growing over me!

                        ANONYMOUS.

The Tears of Scotland.

MOURN, hapless Caledonia, mourn
Thy banish'd peace, thy laurels torn!
Thy sons, for valor long renown'd,
Lie slaughter'd on their native ground;
Thy hospitable roofs no more
Invite the stranger to the door;
In smoky ruins sunk they lie,
The monuments of cruelty.

The wretched owner sees afar
His all become the prey of war;
Bethinks him of his babes and wife,
Then smites his breast, and curses life.
Thy swains are famish'd on the rocks,
Where once they fed their wanton flocks:
Thy ravish'd virgins shriek in vain;
Thy infants perish on the plain.

What boots it then, in every clime,
Through the wide-spreading waste of time,
Thy martial glory, crown'd with praise,
Still shone with undiminish'd blaze?
Thy tow'ring spirit now is broke,
Thy neck is bended to the yoke.
What foreign arms could never quell,
By civil rage and rancor fell.

6*

The rural pipe and merry lay
No more shall cheer the happy day :
No social scenes of gay delight
Beguile the dreary winter night:
No strains but those of sorrow flow,
And nought be heard but sounds of woe,
While the pale phantoms of the slain
Glide nightly o'er the silent plain.

O baneful cause, O fatal morn,
Accurs'd to ages yet unborn !
The sons against their fathers stood,
The parent shed his children's blood.
Yet, when the rage of battle ceas'd,
The victor's soul was not appeas'd :
The naked and forlorn must feel
Devouring flames, and murd'ring steel !

The pious mother doom'd to death,
Forsaken wanders o'er the heath,
The bleak wind whistles round her head,
Her helpless orphans cry for bread ;
Bereft of shelter, food, and friend,
She views the shades of night descend,
And, stretch'd beneath th' inclement skies,
Weeps o'er her tender babes, and dies.

While the warm blood bedews my veins,
And unimpair'd remembrance reigns,
Resentment of my country's fate
Within my filial breast shall beat ;
And, spite of her insulting foe,
My sympathizing verse shall flow :
" Mourn, hapless Caledonia mourn
Thy banish'd peace, thy laurels torn ! "

TOBIAS SMOLLETT.

The Vicar of Bray.

In good King Charles's golden days,
  When loyalty no harm meant,
A zealous high-churchman was I,
  And so I got preferment.
To teach my flock I never missed:
· Kings were by God appointed,
And lost are those that dare resist
    Or touch the Lord's anointed.
      And this is law that I'll maintain
        Until my dying day, sir,
      That whatsoever King shall reign,
        Still I'll be Vicar of Bray, sir.

When royal James possessed the crown,
  And popery grew in fashion,
The penal laws I hooted down,
  And read the declaration;
The church of Rome I found would fit
  Full well my constitution;
And I had been a Jesuit
  But for the revolution.

When William was our king declared,
  To ease the nation's grievance;
With this new wind about I steered,
  And swore to him allegiance;
Old principles I did revoke,
  Set conscience at a distance;
Passive obedience was a joke,
  A jest was non-resistance.

When royal Anne became our queen,
  The church of England's glory,
Another face of things was seen,
  And I became a Tory;

Occasional conformists base,
   I blamed their moderation;
And thought the church in danger was,
   By such prevarication.

When George in pudding-time came o er,
   And moderate men looked big, sir,
My principles I changed once more,
   And so became a Whig, sir;
And thus preferment I procured
   From our new faith's defender;
And almost every day abjured
   The pope and the pretender.

The illustrious house of Hanover,
   And Protestant succession,
To these I do allegiance swear—
   While they can keep possession:
For in my faith and loyalty
   I nevermore will falter,
And George my lawful king shall be—
   Until the times do alter.
     And this is law that I'll maintain
      Until my dying day, sir,
     That whatsoever king shall reign,
      Still I'll be Vicar of Bray, sir.
               ANONYMOUS.

Cumnor Hall.

THE dews of summer night did fall;
   The moon, sweet regent of the sky,
Silvered the walls of Cumnor Hall,
   And many an oak that grew thereby.

Now naught was heard beneath the skies,
   The sounds of busy life were still,

Save an unhappy lady's sighs,
    That issued from that lonely pile.

"Leicester," she cried, "is this thy love
    That thou so oft hast sworn to me,
To leave me in this lonely grove,
    Immured in shameful privity?

"No more thou com'st with lover's speed,
    Thy once belovèd bride to see;
But be she alive, or be she dead,
    I fear, stern Earl, 's the same to thee.

"Not so the usage I received
    When happy in my father's hall;
No faithless husband then me grieved,
    No chilling fears did me appal.

"I rose up with the cheerful morn,
    No lark more blithe, no flower more gay;
And like the bird that haunts the thorn,
    So merrily sung the livelong day.

"If that my beauty is but small,
    Among court ladies all despised,
Why didst thou rend it from that hall,
    Where, scornful Earl, it well was prized?

"And when you first to me made suit,
    How fair I was, you oft would say!
And proud of conquest, plucked the fruit,
    Then left the blossom to decay.

"Yes! now neglected and despised,
    The rose is pale, the lily's dead;
But he that once their charms so prized,
    Is sure the cause those charms are fled.

7

"For know, when sick'ning grief doth prey,
    And tender love's repaid with scorn,
The sweetest beauty will decay,—
    What floweret can endure the storm?

"At court, I'm told, is beauty's throne,
    Where every lady's passing rare,
That Eastern flowers, that shame the sun,
    Are not so glowing, not so fair.

"Then, Earl, why didst thou leave the beds
    Where roses and where lilies vie,
To seek a primrose, whose pale shades
    Must sicken when those gauds are by?

"'Mong rural beauties I was one,
    Among the fields wild flowers are fair;
Some country swain might me have won,
    And thought my beauty passing rare.

"But, Leicester, (or I much am wrong,)
    Or 't is not beauty lures thy vows;
Rather ambition's gilded crown
    Makes thee forget thy humble spouse.

"Then, Leicester, why, again I plead,
    (The injured surely may repine,)—
Why didst thou wed a country maid,
    When some fair princess might be thine?

"Why didst thou praise my humble charms,
    And, oh! then leave them to decay?
Why didst thou win me to thy arms,
    Then leave to mourn the livelong day?

"The village maidens of the plain
    Salute me lowly as they go;

Envious they mark my silken train,
  Nor think a Countess can have woe.

" The simple nymphs! they little know
  How far more happy 's their estate ;
To smile for joy than sigh for woe—
  To be content—than to be great.

" How far less blest am I than them ?
  Daily to pine and waste with care !
Like the poor plant, that, from its stem
  Divided, feels the chilling air.

" Nor, cruel Earl! can I enjoy
  The humble charms of solitude ;
Your minions proud my peace destroy,
  By sullen frowns or pratings rude.

" Last night, as sad I chanced to stray,
  The village death-bell smote my ear;
They winked aside, and seemed to say,
  ' Countess, prepare, thy end is near.'

" And now, while happy peasants sleep,
  Here I sit lonely and forlorn ;
No one to soothe me as I weep,
  Save Philomel on yonder thorn.

" My spirits flag—my hopes decay—
  Still that dread death-bell smites my ear,
And many a boding seems to say,
  ' Countess, prepare, thy end is near!' "

Thus sore and sad that lady grieved,
  In Cumnor Hall so lone and drear,
And many a heartfelt sigh she heaved,
  And let fall many a bitter tear.

And ere the dawn of day appeared,
  In Cumnor Hall, so lone and drear,
Full many a piercing scream was heard,
  And many a cry of mortal fear.

The death-bell thrice was heard to ring,
  An aerial voice was heard to call,
And thrice the raven flapped its wing
  Around the towers of Cumnor Hall.

The mastiff howled at village door,
  The oaks were shattered on the green;
Woe was the hour, for nevermore
  That hapless Countess e'er was seen.

And in that manor now no more
  Is cheerful feast and sprightly ball;
For ever since that dreary hour
  Have spirits haunted Cumnor Hall.

The village maids, with fearful glance,
  Avoid the ancient moss-grown wall,
Nor ever lead the merry dance,
  Among the groves of Cumnor Hall.

Full many a traveler oft hath sighed,
  And pensive wept the Countess' fall,
As wandering onward they 've espied
  The haunted towers of Cumnor Hall.
                    WILLIAM JULIUS MICKLE.

The Sailor's Wife.

AND are ye sure the news is true?
  And are ye sure he 's weel?
Is this a time to think o' wark?
  Ye jades, lay by your wheel.

Is this the time to spin a thread,
   When Colin 's at the door ?
Reach down my cloak, I 'll to the quay,
   And see him come ashore.
For there 's nae luck about the house,
   There 's nae luck at a' ;
There 's little pleasure in the house
   When our gudeman 's awa'.

And gie to me my bigonet,
   My bishop's satin gown ;
For I maun tell the bailie's wife
   That Colin 's in the town.
My Turkey slippers maun gae on,
   My stockins pearly blue ;
It 's a' to pleasure our gudeman,
   For he 's baith leal and true.

Rise, lass, and mak a clean fireside,
   Put on the muckle pot ;
Gie little Kate her button gown,
   And Jock his Sunday coat ;
And mak their shoon as black as slaes,
   Their hose as white as snaw ;
It 's a' to please my ain gudeman,
   For he 's been lang awa'.

There 's twa fat hens upo' the coop,
   Been fed this month and mair ;
Mak haste and thraw their necks about,
   That Colin weel may fare ;
And spread the table neat and clean,
   Gar ilka thing look braw,
For wha can tell how Colin fared
   When he was far awa' ?

Sae true his heart, sae smooth his speech,
   His breath like caller air ;

His very foot has music in 't
  As he comes up the stair.
And will I see his face again?
  And will I hear him speak?
I'm downright dizzy wi' the thought—
  In troth I 'm like to greet!

If Colin 's weel, and weel content,
  I hae nae mair to crave;
And gin I live to keep him sae,
  I 'm blest aboon the lave.
And will I see his face again?
  And will I hear him speak?
I 'm downright dizzy wi' the thought—
  In troth I 'm like to greet.
For there 's nae luck about the house,
  There 's nae luck at a';
There's little pleasure in the house
  When our gudeman 's awa'.

JEAN ADAM.

The Toper's Apology.

I 'M often ask'd by plodding souls
  And men of crafty tongue,
What joy I take in draining bowls,
  And tippling all night long.
Now, though these cautious knaves I scorn,
  For once I 'll not disdain
To tell them why I sit till morn
  And fill my glass again.

'T is by the glow my bumper gives
  Life's picture 's mellow made;
The fading light then brightly lives,
  And softly sinks the shade;

Some happier tint still rises there
  With every drop I drain—
And that I think 's a reason fair
  To fill my glass again.

My Muse, too, when her wings are dry,
  No frolic flight will take;
But round a bowl she 'll dip and fly,
  Like swallows round a lake.
Then if the nymph will have her share
  Before she 'll bless her swain—
Why that I think 's a reason fair
  To fill my glass again.

In life I 've rung all changes too,—
  Run every pleasure down,—
Tried all extremes of fancy through,
  And lived with half the town;
For me there 's nothing new or rare,
  Till wine deceives my brain—
And that I think 's a reason fair
  To fill my glass again.

There 's many a lad I knew is dead,
  And many a lass grown old;
And as the lesson strikes my head,
  My weary heart grows cold.
But wine awhile drives off despair,
  Nay, bids a hope remain—
And that I think 's a reason fair
  To fill my glass again.

Then, hipp'd and vex'd at England's state
  In these convulsive days,
I can't endure the ruin'd fate
  My sober eye surveys;
But, 'midst the bottle's dazzling glare,
  I see the gloom less plain—

And that I think 's a reason fair
    To fill my glass again.

I find too when I stint my glass,
    And sit with sober air,
I 'm prosed by some dull reasoning ass,
    Who treads the path of care;
Or, harder tax'd, I 'm forced to bear
    Some coxcomb's fribbling strain—
And that I think 's a reason fair
    To fill my glass again.

Nay, do n't we see Love's fetters, too,
    With different holds entwine?
While nought but death can some undo,
    There 's some give way to wine.
With me the lighter head I wear
    The lighter hangs the chain—
And that I think 's a reason fair
    To fill my glass again.

And now I 'll tell, to end my song,
    At what I most repine;
This cursed war, or right or wrong,
    Is war against all wine;
Nay, Port, they say, will soon be rare
    As juice of France or Spain—
And that I think 's a reason fair
    To fill my glass again.

                   CHARLES MORRIS.

The Three Warnings.

THE tree of deepest root is found
Least willing still to quit the ground:
'T was therefore said by ancient sages,
    That love of life increased with years
So much, that in our later stages,

When pains grow sharp, and sickness rages,
  The greatest love of life appears.
This great affection to believe,
Which all confess, but few perceive,—
If old assertions can't prevail,—
Be pleased to hear a modern tale.
  When sports went round, and all were gay,
On neighbor Dodson's wedding-day,
Death called aside the jocund groom
With him into another room,
And looking grave—"You must," says he,
" Quit your sweet bride, and come with me."
" With you ! and quit my Susan's side !
With you ! " the hapless husband cried ;
" Young as I am 't is monstrous hard !
Besides, in truth, I 'm not prepared :
My thoughts on other matters go ;
This is my wedding-day you know."
    What more he urged, I have not heard,
      His reasons could not well be stronger ;
    So Death the poor delinquent spared,
      And left to live a little longer.
Yet calling up a serious look—
His hour-glass trembled while he spoke—
" Neighbor," he said, " Farewell !   No more
Shall Death disturb your mirthful hour ;
And farther, to avoid all blame
Of cruelty upon my name,
To give you time for preparation,
And fit you for your future station,
Three several warnings you shall have,
Before you 're summoned to the grave.
Willing for once I 'll quit my prey,
    And grant a kind reprieve,
In hopes you 'll have no more to say,
But, when I call again this way,
    Well pleased the world will leave."

7*

To these conditions both consented,
And parted perfectly contented.

What next the hero of our tale befell,
How long he lived, how wise, how well,
How roundly he pursued his course,
And smoked his pipe, and stroked his horse,
　The willing muse shall tell.
He chaffered then, he bought, he sold,
Nor once perceived his growing old,
　Nor thought of death as near;
His friends not false, his wife no shrew,
Many his gains, his children few,
　He passed his hours in peace.
But while he viewed his wealth increase,
While thus along life's dusty road
The beaten track content he trod,
Old Time, whose haste no mortal spares,
Uncalled, unheeded, unawares,
　Brought on his eightieth year.
And now, one night, in musing mood
　As all alone he sat,
Th' unwelcome messenger of fate
　Once more before him stood.
Half killed with anger and surprise,
"So soon returned!" old Dodson cries.
　"So soon, d' ye call it?" Death replies.
"Surely, my friend, you 're but in jest!
　Since I was here before
'T is six-and-thirty years at least,
　And you are now fourscore."
　"So much the worse," the clown rejoined;
"To spare the agèd would be kind:
However, see your search be legal;
And your authority—is 't regal?
Else you are come on a fool's errand,
With but a secretary's warrant.
Besides, you promised me Three Warnings,

Which I have looked for nights and mornings;
But for that loss of time and ease,
I can recover damages."

"I know," cries Death, that at the best
I seldom am a welcome guest;
But do n't be captious, friend, at least:
I little thought you 'd still be able
To stump about your farm and stable;
Your years have run to a great length;
I wish you joy, though, of your strength!"

"Hold," says the farmer, "not so fast!
I have been lame these four years past."

"And no great wonder," Death replies:
"However, you still keep your eyes;
And sure, to see one's loves and friends,
For legs and arms would make amends."

"Perhaps," says Dodson, "so it might,
But latterly I 've lost my sight."

"This is a shocking tale, 't is true,
But still there 's comfort left for you:
Each strives your sadness to amuse;
I warrant you hear all the news."

"There 's none," cries he; "and if there were,
I 'm grown so deaf I could not hear."
"Nay, then," the spectre stern rejoined,
"These are unwarrantable yearnings;
If you are lame, and deaf, and blind,
You 've had your three sufficient warnings.
So, come along, no more we.'ll part,"
He said, and touched him with his dart.
And now old Dodson, turning pale,
Yields to his fate—so ends my tale.

HESTER THRALE.

Life.

Life, I know not what thou art,
But know that thou and I must part;

And when, or how, or where we met,
I own to me 's a secret yet.

Life, we have been long together,
Through pleasant and through cloudy weather;
'T is hard to part when friends are dear,
Perhaps 't will cost a sigh, a tear;
Then steal away, give little warning,
    Choose thine own time,
Say not Good-Night, but in some brighter clime
    Bid me Good-Morning.
                          Anna Lætitia Barbauld.

When Shall we Three Meet Again?

When shall we three meet again?
When shall we three meet again?
Oft shall glowing hope expire,
Oft shall wearied love retire,
Oft shall death and sorrow reign,
Ere we three shall meet again.

Though in distant lands we sigh,
Parched beneath a burning sky;
Though the deep between us rolls,
Friendship shall unite our souls;
Oft in Fancy's rich domain;
Oft shall we three meet again.

When our burnished locks are gray,
Thinned by many a toil-spent day;
When around this youthful pine
Moss shall creep and ivy twine,—
Long may this loved bower remain—
Here may we three meet again.

When the dreams of life are fled;
When its wasted lamps are dead;

When in cold oblivion's shade
Beauty, wealth, and fame are laid,—
Where immortal spirits reign,
There may we three meet again.

ANONYMOUS.

Gaffer Gray.

"Ho! why dost thou shiver and shake,
    Gaffer Gray,
And why doth thy nose look so blue?"
   "'T is the weather that 's cold,
   'T is I 'm grown very old,
And my doublet is not very new,
    Well-a-day!"

"Then line that warm doublet with ale,
    Gaffer Gray,
And warm thy old heart with a glass."
   "Nay, but credit I 've none,
   And my money 's all gone;
Then say how may that come to pass?
    Well-a-day!"

"Hie away to the house on the brow,
    Gaffer Gray,
And knock at the jolly priest's door."
   "The priest often preaches
   Against worldly riches,
But ne'er gives a mite to the poor,
    Well-a-day!"

"The lawyer lives under the hill,
    Gaffer Gray,
Warmly fenced both in back and in front."
   "He will fasten his locks,
   And will threaten the stocks,

Should he evermore find me in want,
  Well-a day ! "

" The squire has fat beeves and brown ale,
    Gaffer Gray,
And the season will welcome you there."
    " His fat beeves and his beer,
      And his merry new year,
Are all for the flush and the fair,
      Well-a-day ! "

" My keg is but low, I confess,
      Gaffer Gray,
  What then ?   While it lasts, man, we 'll live."
    " The poor man alone,
      When he hears the poor moan,
Of his morsel a morsel will give,
      Well-a-day."

THOMAS HOLCROFT.

What Constitutes a State.

WHAT constitutes a state ?
Not high-raised battlement or labored mound,
    Thick wall or moated gate ;
Not cities proud with spires and turrets crowned ;
    Not bays and broad-armed ports,
Where, laughing at the storm, rich navies ride ;
    Not starred and spangled courts,
Where low-browed baseness wafts perfume to pride.
    No :—men, high-minded men,
With powers as far above dull brutes endued
    In forest, brake, or den,
As beasts excel cold rocks and brambles rude,—
    Men who their duties know,
But know their rights, and, knowing, dare maintain,
    Prevent the long-aimed blow,

And crush the tyrant while they rend the chain;
 These constitute a state;
And sovereign law, that state's collected will,
 O'er thrones and globes elate
Sits empress, crowning good, repressing ill.
 Smit by her sacred frown,
The fiend, Dissension, like a vapor sinks;
 And e'en the all-dazzling crown
Hides his faint rays, and at her bidding shrinks;
 Such was this heaven-loved isle,
Than Lesbos fairer and the Cretan shore!
 No more shall freedom smile?
Shall Britons languish, and be men no more?
 Since all must life resign,
Those sweet rewards which decorate the brave
 'Tis folly to decline,
And steal inglorious to the silent grave.
SIR WILLIAM JONES.

To the Cuckoo.

HAIL, beauteous stranger of the grove!
 Thou messenger of Spring!
Now heaven repairs thy rural seat,
 And woods thy welcome sing.

Soon as the daisy decks the green,
 Thy certain voice we hear.
Hast thou a star to guide thy path,
 Or mark the rolling year?

Delightful visitant! with thee
 I hail the time of flowers,
And hear the sound of music sweet
 From birds among the bowers.

The school-boy, wandering through the wood
 To pull the primrose gay,

Starts, thy most curious voice to hear,
   And imitates thy lay.

What time the pea puts on the bloom,
   Thou fliest thy vocal vale,
An annual guest in other lands,
   Another spring to hail.

Sweet bird! thy bower is ever green,
   Thy sky is ever clear;
Thou hast no sorrow in thy song,
   No winter in thy year!

Oh, could I fly, I 'd fly with thee!
   We 'd make, with joyful wing,
Our annual visit o'er the globe,
   Attendants on the Spring.

JOHN LOGAN.

Auld Robin Gray.

WHEN the sheep are in the fauld, and a' the kye at hame,
And a' the weary warld to sleep are gane,
The waes o' my heart fall in showers from my e'e,
While my gudeman sleeps sound by me.

Young Jamie lo'ed me weel, and sought me for his bride,
But saving a crown he had naithing else beside:
To mak' the crown a pound, my Jamie went to sea,
And the crown and the pound were baith for me.

He had nae been gane a year and a day,
When my faither brake his arm, and our cow was stole
      away;
My mither she fell sick, and Jamie at the sea,
And auld Robin Gray cam' a courting to me.

My faither could na wark, my mither could na spin,
I toil'd day and night, but their bread I could na win;
Auld Rob maintain'd 'em baith, and wi' tears in his ee,
Said, "Jennie, for their sakes, oh marry me."

My heart it said nay, for I look'd for Jamie back,
But the wind it blew hard, and the ship was a wrack—
The ship was a wrack, why did na Jamie dee?
Or why was I spared to cry, Wae's me!

My faither urged me sair, my mither did na speak,
But she look'd in my face till my heart was like to break:
They gi'ed him my hand, though my heart was at sea,—
So auld Robin Gray is gudeman to me!

I had na been a wife a week but only four,
When, sitting sae mournfully out at my door,
I saw my Jamie's wraith, for I could na think it he,
Till he said, "I'm come hame, love, to marry thee."

Sair, sair did we greet, and mickle did we say,—
We took but ae kiss, and tare oursels away:
I wish I were dead, but I am na lik' to dee,—
Oh, why was I born to say, Wae's me!

I gang like a ghaist, but I care not to spin;
I dare not think on Jamie, for that would be a sin;
So I will do my best a gude wife to be,
For auld Robin Gray is kind unto me.

LADY ANNE BARNARD.

Mary's Dream.

THE moon had climbed the highest hill
    Which rises o'er the source of Dee,
And from the eastern summit shed
    Her silver light on tower and tree,

When Mary laid her down to sleep,
　　Her thoughts on Sandy far at sea,
When, soft and slow, a voice was heard,
　　Saying, "Mary, weep no more for me!"

She from her pillow gently raised
　　Her head, to ask who there might be,
And saw young Sandy shivering stand,
　　With visage pale, and hollow e'e.
"O Mary dear, cold is my clay;
　　It lies beneath a stormy sea.
Far, far from thee I sleep in death;
　　So, Mary, weep no more for me!

"Three stormy nights and stormy days
　　We tossed upon the raging main;
And long we strove our bark to save,
　　But all our striving was in vain.
Even then, when horror chilled my blood,
　　My heart was filled with love for thee:
The storm is past, and I at rest;
　　So, Mary, weep no more for me!

"O maiden dear, thyself prepare;
　　We soon shall meet upon that shore,
Where love is free from doubt and care,
　　And thou and I shall part no more!"
Loud crowed the cock, the shadow fled,
　　No more of Sandy could she see;
But soft the passing spirit said,
　　"Sweet Mary, weep no more for me!"

　　　　　　　　　　　　　JOHN LOWE.

What is Time?

I ASKED an aged man, with hoary hairs,
Wrinkled and curved with worldly cares:

"Time is the warp of life," said he; "O, tell
  The young, the fair, the gay, to weave it well!"
  I asked the ancient, venerable dead,
  Sages who wrote, and warriors who bled:
  From the cold grave a hollow murmur flowed,
"Time sowed the seed we reap in this abode!"
  I asked a dying sinner, ere the tide
  Of life had left his veins: "Time!" he replied;
"I 've lost it! ah, the treasure!"—and he died.
  I asked the golden sun and silver spheres,
  Those bright chronometers of days and years:
  They answered, "Time is but a meteor glare,"
  And bade me for eternity prepare.
  I asked the Seasons, in their annual round,
  Which beautify or desolate the ground;
  And they replied (no oracle more wise),
"'T is Folly's blank, and Wisdom's highest prize!"
  I asked a spirit lost,—but O the shriek
  That pierced my soul! I shudder while I speak.
  It cried, "A particle! a speck! a mite
  Of endless years, duration infinite!"
  Of things inanimate, my dial I
  Consulted, and it made me this reply,—
"Time is the season fair of living well,
  The path of glory or the path of hell."
  I asked my Bible, and methinks it said,
"Time is the present hour, the past has fled;
  Live! live to-day! to-morrow never yet
  On any human being rose or set."
  I asked old Father Time himself at last;
  But in a moment he flew swiftly past,
  His chariot was a cloud, the viewless wind
  His noiseless steeds, which left no trace behind.
  I asked the mighty angel who shall stand
  One foot on sea and one on solid land:
"Mortal!" he cried, "the mystery now is o'er;
  Time was, Time is, but Time shall be no more!"

William Marsden.

The Groves of Blarney.

THE groves of Blarney, they look so charming,
  Down by the purlings of sweet silent brooks,
All decked with posies, that spontaneous grow there,
  Planted in order in the rocky nooks.
'T is there the daisy, and the sweet carnation,
  The blooming pink, and the rose so fair;
Likewise the lily, and the daffodilly—
  All flowers that scent the sweet, open air.

'T is Lady Jaffers owns this plantation,
  Like Alexander, or like Helen fair;
There 's no commander in all the nation
  For regulation can with her compare.
Such walls surround her, that no nine-pounder
  Could ever plunder her place of strength;
But Oliver Cromwell, he did her pommel,
  And made a breach in her battlement.

There 's gravel walks there for speculation,
  And conversation in sweet solitude;
'T is there the lover may hear the dove, or
  The gentle plover, in the afternoon.
And if a young lady should be so engaging
  As to walk alone in those shady bowers,
'T is there her courtier, he may transport her
  In some dark port, or under ground.

For 't is there 's the cave where no daylight enters,
  But bats and badgers are forever bred;
Being mossed by natur' which makes it sweeter
  Than a coach and six, or a feather bed.
'T is there 's the lake that is stored with perches,
  And comely eels in the verdant mud;
Besides the leeches, and the groves of beeches,
  All standing in order for to guard the flood.

'T is there 's the kitchen hangs many a flitch in,
  With the maids a-stitching upon the stair;
The bread and biske', the beer and whiskey,
  Would make you frisky if you were there.
'T is there you 'd see Peg Murphy's daughter
  A washing praties forenent the door,
With Roger Cleary, and Father Healy,
  All blood relations to my Lord Donoughmore.

There 's statues gracing this noble place in,
  All heathen goddesses so fair—
Bold Neptune, Plutarch, and Nicodemus,
  All standing naked in the open air.
So now to finish this brave narration,
  Which my poor geni' could not entwine;
But were I Homer, or Nebuchadnezzar,
  'T is in every feature I would make it shine.
                          RICHARD ALFRED MILLIKEN.

Helen of Kirkconnel.

I WISH I were where Helen lies,
For night and day on me she cries,
And, like an angel, to the skies
      Still seems to beckon me!
For me she lived, for me she sigh'd,
For me she wish'd to be a bride,
For me in life's sweet morn she died
      On fair Kirkconnel-Lee!

Where Kirtle waters gently wind,
As Helen on my arm reclined,
A rival with a ruthless mind
      Took deadly aim at me.
My love, to disappoint the foe,
Rush'd in between me and the blow;
And now her corse is lying low,
      On fair Kirkconnel-Lee!

8*

Though Heaven forbids my wrath to swell,
I curse the hand by which she fell,
The fiend who made my heaven a hell,
    And tore my love from me!
For if, when all the graces shine,
O, if on earth there 's aught divine,
My Helen, all these charms were thine,
    They centred all in thee!

Ah! what avails it that, amain,
I clove the assassin's head in twain?
No peace of mind, my Helen slain,
    No resting-place for me.
I see her spirit in the air—
I hear the shriek of wild despair,
When murder laid her bosom bare,
    On fair Kirkconnel-Lee!

O, when I 'm sleeping in my grave,
And o'er my head the rank weeds wave,
May He who life and spirit gave
    Unite my love and me!
Then from this world of doubts and sighs,
My soul on wings of peace shall rise,
And, joining Helen in the skies,
    Forget Kirkconnel-Lee.

                    JOHN MAYNE.

Connel and Flora.

DARK lowers the night o'er the wide stormy main,
Till mild rosy morning rise cheerful again;
Alas! morn returns to revisit the shore;
But Connel returns to his Flora no more.

For see, on yon mountain the dark cloud of death
O'er Connel's lone cottage, lies low on the heath;
While bloody and pale on a far distant shore
He lies, to return to his Flora no more.

Ye light fleeting spirits that glide o'er the steep,
O, would you but waft me across the wild deep,
There fearless I 'd mix in the battle's loud roar,
I 'd die with my Connel, and leave him no more.

ALEXANDER WILSON.

The Soldier.

WHAT dreaming drone was ever blest,
   By thinking of the morrow ?
To-day be mine—I leave the rest
   To all the fools of sorrow;
Give me the mind that mocks at care,
   The heart its own defender;
The spirits that are light as air,
   And never beat surrender.

On comes the foe—to arms—to arms—
   We meet—'t is death or glory;
'T is victory in all her charms,
   Or fame in Britain's story;
Dear native land! thy fortunes frown,
   And ruffians would enslave thee;
Thou land of honor and renown,
   Who would not die to save thee?

'T is you, 't is I, that meets the ball;
   And me it better pleases
In battle with the brave to fall,
   Than die of cold diseases;
Than drivel on in elbow-chair
   With saws and tales unheeded,
A tottering thing of aches and care,
   Nor longer loved nor needed.

But thou—dark is thy flowing hair,
   Thy eye with fire is streaming,
And o'er thy cheek, thy looks, thine air,
   Health sits in triumph beaming;

Then, brother soldier, fill the wine,
    Fill high the wine to beauty;
Love, friendship, honor, all are thine,
    Thy country and thy duty.

                 WILLIAM SMYTH.

The Beggar.

PITY the sorrows of a poor old man,
   Whose trembling limbs have borne him to your door,
Whose days are dwindled to the shortest span,
   O, give relief, and Heaven will bless your store.

These tattered clothes my poverty bespeak,
   These hoary locks proclaim my lengthened years;
And many a furrow in my grief-worn cheek
   Has been the channel of a stream of tears.

Yon house, erected on the rising ground,
   With tempting aspect drew me from my road,
For plenty there a residence has found,
   And grandeur a magnificent abode.

Hard is the fate of the infirm and poor!
   Here craving for a morsel of their bread,
A pampered menial forced me from the door,
   To seek a shelter in a humbler shed.

O, take me to your hospitable dome,
   Keen blows the wind, and piercing is the cold;
Short is my passage to the friendly tomb,
   For I am poor and miserably old.

Should I reveal the source of every grief,
   If soft humanity e'er touched your breast,
Your hands would not withhold the kind relief,
   And tears of pity could not be repressed.

Heaven sends misfortunes—why should we repine?
　'T is heaven has brought me to the state you see:
And your condition may be soon like mine,
　The child of sorrow and of misery.

A little farm was my paternal lot,
　Then like the lark I sprightly hailed the morn;
But ah! oppression forced me from my cot;
　My cattle died, and blighted was my corn.

My daughter, once the comfort of my age,
　Lured by a villain from her native home,
Is cast, abandoned, on the world's wild stage,
　And doomed in scanty poverty to roam.

My tender wife, sweet soother of my care,
　Struck with sad anguish at the stern decree,
Fell, lingering fell, a victim of despair,
　And left the world to wretchedness and me.

Then pity the sorrows of a poor old man,
　Whose trembling limbs have borne him to your door,
Whose days are dwindled to the shortest span,
　O, give relief, and Heaven will bless your store.
Thomas Moss.

The Orphan Boy.

Stay, lady, stay, for mercy's sake,
　And hear a helpless orphan's tale;
Ah, sure my looks must pity wake,—
　'T is want that makes my cheek so pale;
Yet I was once a mother's pride,
　And my brave father's hope and joy;
But in the Nile's proud fight he died,
　And I am now an orphan boy.

Poor, foolish child! how pleased was I,
　　When news of Nelson's victory came,
Along the crowded streets to fly,
　　To see the lighted windows flame!
To force me home my mother sought,—
　　She could not bear to hear my joy;
For with my father's life 't was bought,—
　　And made me a poor orphan boy.

The people's shouts were long and loud;
　　My mother, shuddering, closed her ears;
" Rejoice! rejoice! " still cried the crowd,—
　　My mother answered with her tears!
" O, why do tears steal down your cheek,"
　　Cried I, " while others shout for joy ? "
She kissed me, and in accents weak,
　　She called me her poor orphan boy.

" What is an orphan boy ? " I said;
　　When suddenly she gasped for breath,
And her eyes closed! I shrieked for aid,
　　But ah! her eyes were closed in death.
My hardships since I will not tell;
　　But now, no more a parent's joy,
Ah! lady, I have learned too well
　　What 't is to be an orphan boy.

O, were I by your bounty fed—
　　Nay, gentle lady, do not chide;
Trust me, I mean to earn my bread,—
　　The sailor's orphan boy has pride.
Lady, you weep; what is 't you say?
　　You 'll give me clothing, food, employ?
Look down, dear parents, look and see
　　Your happy, happy orphan boy!

　　　　　　　　　　　　AMELIA OPIE.

Night.

MYSTERIOUS Night, when our first parent knew
   Thee, from report divine, and heard thy name,
   Did he not tremble for this lovely frame,
This glorious canopy of light and blue?
Yet 'neath a curtain of translucent dew
   Bathed in the rays of the great setting flame,
   Hesperus with the host of heaven came,
And lo! Creation widened on Man's view.
Who could have thought such darkness lay concealed
   Within thy beams, O Sun! or who could find,
While flower, and leaf, and insect stood revealed,
   That to such countless orbs thou mad'st us blind!
Why do we then shun death with anxious strife?
If light can thus deceive, wherefore not life?
                  JOSEPH BLANCO WHITE.

The Tears I Shed.

THE tears I shed must ever fall:
   I mourn not for an absent swain;
For thoughts may past delights recall,
   And parted lovers meet again.
I weep not for the silent dead;
   Their toils are past, their sorrows o'er;
And those they loved their steps shall tread,
   And death shall join to part no more.

Though boundless oceans roll between,
   If certain that his heart is near,
A conscious transport glads each scene,
   Soft is the sigh, and sweet the tear.
E'en when by death's cold hand removed,
   We mourn the tenant of the tomb,
To think that e'en in death he loved,
   Can gild the horrors of the gloom.

But bitter, bitter are the tears
   Of her who slighted love bewails;
No hope her dreary prospect cheers,
   No pleasing melancholy hails.
Hers are the pangs of wounded pride,
   Of blasted hope, of wither'd joy;
The flatt'ring veil is rent aside,
   The flame of love burns to destroy.

In vain does memory renew
   The hours once tinged in transport's dye;
The sad reverse soon starts to view,
   And turns the past to agony.
E'en time itself despairs to cure
   Those pangs to ev'ry feeling due:
Ungenerous youth! thy boast how poor,
   To win a heart—and break it too!

[No cold approach, no alter'd mien,
   Just what would make suspicion start;
No pause the dire extremes between,
   He made me blest—and broke my heart.]
From hope, the wretched's anchor, torn;
   Neglected and neglecting all;
Friendless, forsaken, and forlorn;
   The tears I shed must ever fall.
                   HELEN CRANSTOUN STEWART.

To an Indian Gold Coin.

SLAVE of the dark and dirty mine,
   What vanity has brought thee here?
How can I love to see thee shine
   So bright, whom I have bought so dear?
   The tent-ropes flapping lone I hear
For twilight converse, arm in arm;
   The jackal's shriek bursts on mine ear
When mirth and music wont to charm.

By Cherical's dark wandering streams,
  Where cane-tufts shadow all the wild,
Sweet visions haunt my waking dreams
  Of Teviot loved while still a child,
  Of castled rocks stupendous piled
By Esk or Eden's classic wave,
  Where loves of youth and friendship smiled,
Uncursed by thee, vile yellow slave!

Fade, day-dreams sweet, from memory fade!
  The perished bliss of youth's first prime,
That once so bright on fancy played,
  Revives no more in after-time.
  Far from my sacred natal clime,
I haste to an untimely grave;
  The daring thoughts that soared sublime
Are sunk in ocean's southern wave.

Slave of the mine, thy yellow light
  Gleams baleful as the tomb-fire drear.
A gentle vision comes by night
  My lonely widowed heart to cheer:
  Her eyes are dim with many a tear,
That once were guiding stars to mine:
  Her fond heart throbs with many a fear!
I cannot bear to see thee shine.

For thee, for thee, vile yellow slave,
  I left a heart that loved me true!
I crossed the tedious ocean-wave,
  To roam in climes unkind and new.
  The cold wind of the stranger blew
Chill on my withered heart; the grave
  Dark and untimely met my view,—
And all for thee, vile yellow slave!

Ha! com'st thou now so late to mock
  A wanderer's banished heart forlorn,

Now that his frame the lightning shock
   Of sun-rays tipped with death has borne?
From love, from friendship, country, torn,
To memory's fond regrets the prey,
   Vile slave, thy yellow dross I scorn!
Go mix thee with thy kindred clay!

JOHN LEYDEN.

A Visit from St. Nicholas.

'T WAS the night before Christmas, when all through the
    house
Not a creature was stirring, not even a mouse;
The stockings were hung by the chimney with care,
In hopes that St. Nicholas soon would be there;
The children were nestled all snug in their beds,
While visions of sugar-plums danced in their heads;
And Mamma in her kerchief, and I in my cap,
Had just settled our brains for a long winter nap,—
When out on the lawn there arose such a clatter,
I sprang from my bed to see what was the matter.
Away to the window I flew like a flash,
Tore open the shutters and threw up the.sash.
The moon, on the breast of the new-fallen snow,
Gave a lustre of midday to objects below;
When, what to my wondering eyes should appear,
But a miniature sleigh and eight tiny reindeer,
With a little old driver, so lively and quick,
I knew in a moment it must be St. Nick.
More rapid than eagles his coursers they came,
And he whistled, and shouted, and called them by name:
'Now, Dasher! now, Dancer! now, Prancer and Vixen!
On! Comet, on! Cupid, on! Dunder and Blixen—
To the top of the porch, to the top of the wall!
Now, dash away, dash away, dash away all!"
As dry leaves that before the wild hurricane fly,
When they meet with an obstacle, mount to the sky,

So, up to the house-top the coursers they flew,
With the sleigh full of toys—and St. Nicholas too.
And then in a twinkling I heard on the roof
The prancing and pawing of each little hoof.
As I drew in my head, and was turning around,
Down the chimney St. Nicholas came with a bound.
He was dressed all in fur from his head to his foot,
And his clothes were all tarnished with ashes and soot;
A bundle of toys he had flung on his back,
And he looked like a peddler just opening his pack.
His eyes how they twinkle! his dimples how merry!
His cheeks were like roses, his nose like a cherry;
His droll little mouth was drawn up like a bow,
And the beard on his chin was as white as the snow.
The stump of a pipe he held tight in his teeth,
And the smoke, it encircled his head like a wreath.
He had a broad face and a little round belly
That shook, when he laughed, like a bowl full of jelly.
He was chubby and plump—a right jolly old elf;
And I laughed when I saw him, in spite of myself.
A wink of his eye, and a twist of his head,
Soon gave me to know I had nothing to dread.
He spoke not a word, but went straight to his work,
And filled all the stockings; then turned with a jerk,
And laying his finger aside of his nose,
And giving a nod, up the chimney he rose.
He sprang to his sleigh, to his team gave a whistle,
And away they all flew like the down of a thistle;
But I heard him exclaim, ere he drove out of sight,
"Happy Christmas to all, and to all a good-night!"

CLEMENT C. MOORE.

The Star-Spangled Banner.

O, say, can you see, by the dawn's early light,
   What so proudly we hailed at the twilight's last gleam-
      ing?

Whose broad stripes and bright stars through the perilous
  fight,
  O'er the ramparts we watched were so gallantly stream-
    ing;
And the rocket's red glare, the bombs bursting in air,
Gave proof through the night that our flag was still there.
  O, say, does that star-spangled banner yet wave
  O'er the land of the free and the home of the brave?

On the shore, dimly seen through the mists of the deep,
  Where the foe's haughty host in dread silence reposes,
What is that which the breeze, o'er the towering steep,
  As it fitfully blows, half conceals, half discloses?
Now it catches the gleam of the morning's first beam,
In full glory reflected now shines on the stream.
  'T is the star-spangled banner!   O, long may it wave
  O'er the land of the free and the home of the brave!

And where is that band who so vauntingly swore
  That the havoc of war and the battle's confusion
A home and a country should leave us no more?
  Their blood has washed out their foul footsteps' pollution.
No refuge could save the hireling and slave,
From the terror of death and the gloom of the grave.
  And the star-spangled banner in triumph shall wave
  O'er the land of the free and the home of the brave!

O, thus be it ever, when freemen shall stand
  Between their loved homes and the war's desolation;
Blest with victory and peace, may the heaven-rescued land
  Praise the power that has made and preserved us a na-
    tion.
Then conquer we must, for our cause it is just,
And this be our motto, "In God is our trust."
  And the star-spangled banner in triumph shall wave
  O'er the land of the free and the home of the brave!

                                    FRANCIS SCOTT KEY.

Lucy's Flittin'.

'T was when the wan leaf frae the birk tree was fa'in',
   And Martinmas dowie had wound up the year,
That Lucy row'd up her wee kist wi' her a' in 't
   And left her auld maister and neebours sae dear.
For Lucy had served in "The Glen" a' the simmer;
   She cam' there afore the flower bloom'd on the pea;
An orphan was she, and they had been gude till her,
   Sure that was the thing brocht the tear to her ee.

She gaed by the stable where Jamie was stannin',
   Richt sair was his kind heart the flittin' to see:
Fare-ye-weel, Lucy! quo Jamie, and ran in;
   The gatherin' tears trickled fast frae his ee.
As down the burn-side she gaed slow wi' the flittin',
   Fare-ye-weel, Lucy! was ilka bird's sang;
She heard the craw sayin' 't, high on the tree sittin',
   And robin was chirpin' 't the brown leaves amang.

Oh, what is 't that pits my puir heart in a flutter?
   And what gars the tears come sae fast to my ee?
If I wasna ettled to be ony better,
   Then what gars me wish ony better to be?
I 'm just like a lammie that loses its mither;
   Nae mither or friend the puir lammie can see;
I fear I ha'e tint my puir heart a'thegither,
   Nae wonder the tear fa's sae fast frae my ee.

Wi' the rest o' my claes I hae row'd up the ribbon,
   The bonnie blue ribbon that Jamie ga'e me;
Yestreen, when he ga'e me 't, and saw I was sabbin',
   I 'll never forget the wae blink o' his ee.
Though now he said naething but Fare-ye-weel, Lucy!
   It made me I neither could speak, hear, nor see;
He cudna say mair but just, Fare-ye-weel, Lucy!
   Yet that I will mind till the day that I dee.
  9*

The lamb likes the gowan wi' dew when its droukit;
    The hare likes the brake, and the braird on the lea;
But Lucy likes Jamie;—she turned and she lookit,
    She thocht the dear place she wad never mair see.
Ah, weel may young Jamie gang dowie and cheerless,
    And weel may he greet on the bank o' the burn;
For bonnie sweet Lucy, sae gentle and peerless,
    Lies cauld in her grave, and will never return.

WILLIAM LAIDLAW.

A Litany for Doneraile.

Alas! how dismal is my tale!—
I lost my watch in Doneraile;
My Dublin watch, my chain and seal,
Pilfered at once in Doneraile.

May fire and brimstone never fail
To fall in showers on Doneraile;
May all the leading fiends assail
The thieving town of Doneraile.

As lightnings flash across the vale,
So down to hell with Doneraile;
The fate of Pompey at Pharsale,
Be that the curse of Doneraile.

May beef or mutton, lamb or veal,
Be never found in Doneraile;
But garlic soup, and scurvy kail,
Be still the food for Doneraile.

And forward as the creeping snail
Th' industry be of Doneraile;
May Heaven a chosen curse entail
On rigid, rotten Doneraile.

May sun and moon forever fail
To beam their lights in Doneraile;

May every pestilential gale
Blast that cursed spot called Doneraile.

May no sweet cuckoo, thrush, or quail,
Be ever heard in Doneraile;
May patriots, kings, and commonweal,
Despise and harass Doneraile.

May every Post, Gazette, and Mail
Sad tidings bring of Doneraile;
May loudest thunders ring a peal,
To blind and deafen Doneraile.

May vengence fall at head and tail,
From north to south, at Doneraile;
May profit light, and tardy sale,
Still damp the trade of Doneraile.

May Fame resound a dismal tale,
Whene'er she lights on Doneraile;
May Egypt's plagues at once prevail,
To thin the knaves of Doneraile.

May frost and snow, and sleet and hail,
Benumb each joint in Doneraile;
May wolves and bloodhounds trace and trail
The cursed crew of Doneraile.

May Oscar, with his fiery flail,
To atoms thresh all Doneraile;
May every mischief, fresh and stale,
Abide, henceforth, in Doneraile.

May all, from Belfast to Kinsale,
Scoff, curse, and damn you, Doneraile;
May neither flour nor oatenmeal
Be found or known in Doneraile.

May want and wo each joy curtail
That e'er was known in Doneraile;
May no one coffin want a nail,
That wraps a rogue in Doneraile.

May all the thieves that rob and steal,
The gallows meet in Doneraile;
May all the sons of Granaweal
Blush at the thieves of Doneraile.

May mischief big as Norway whale
O'erwhelm the knaves of Doneraile;
May curses, wholesale and retail,
Pour with full force on Doneraile.

May every transport wont to sail,
A convict bring from Doneraile;
May every churn and milking-pail
Fall dry to staves in Doneraile.

May cold and hunger still congeal
The stagnant blood of Doneraile;
May every hour new woes reveal,
That hell reserves for Doneraile.

May every chosen ill prevail
O'er all the imps of Doneraile;
May no one wish or prayer avail
To soothe the woes of Doneraile.

May th' Inquisition straight impale
The rapparees of Doneraile;
May Charon's boat triumphant sail,
Completely manned from Doneraile.

Oh! may my couplets never fail
To find a curse for Doneraile;
And may grim Pluto's inner jail
For ever groan with Doneraile.

Patrick O'Kelly.

A Riddle.

'T was in heaven pronounced, and 't was muttered in hell,
And echo caught faintly the sound as it fell;
On the confines of earth 't was permitted to rest,
And the depths of the ocean its presence confessed.
'T will be found in the sphere when 't is riven asunder,
Be seen in the lightning and heard in the thunder.
'T was allotted to man with his earliest breath,
Attends him at birth, and awaits him in death,
Presides o'er his happiness, honor, and health,
Is the prop of his house, and the end of his wealth.
In the heaps of the miser 't is hoarded with care,
But is sure to be lost on his prodigal heir.
It begins every hope, every wish it must bound,
With the husbandman toils, and with monarchs is crowned.
Without it the soldier, the seaman, may roam;
But woe to the wretch who expels it from home!
In the whispers of conscience its voice will be found,
Nor e'en in the whirlwind of passion be drowned.
'T will not soften the heart; but, though deaf be the ear,
It will make it acutely and instantly hear.
Yet in shade let it rest, like a delicate flower,
Ah! breathe on it softly—it dies in an hour.

CATHERINE FANSHAWE.

The Philosopher's Scales.

A MONK, when his rites sacerdotal were o'er,
In the depths of his cell with its stone-covered floor,
Resigning to thought his chimerical brain,
Once formed the contrivance we now shall explain;
But whether by magic's or alchemy's powers
We know not; indeed, 't is no business of ours.

Perhaps it was only by patience and care,
At last, that he brought his invention to bear.

10

In youth 't was projected, but years stole away,
And ere 't was complete he was wrinkled and gray;
But success is secure, unless energy fails;
And at length he produced the Philosopher's Scales.

"What were they?" you ask.   You shall presently see;
These scales were not made to weigh sugar and tea.
O no; for such properties wondrous had they,
That qualities, feelings, and thoughts they could weigh,
Together with articles small or immense,
From mountains or planets to atoms of sense.

Naught was there so bulky but there it would lay,
And naught so ethereal but there it would stay,
And naught so reluctant but in it must go:
All which some examples more clearly will show.

The first thing he weighed was the head of Voltaire,
Which retained all the wit that had ever been there.
As a weight, he threw in a torn scrap of a leaf,
Containing the prayer of the penitent thief;
When the skull rose aloft with so sudden a spell
That it bounced like a ball on the roof of the cell.

One time he put in Alexander the Great,
With a garment that Dorcas had made for a weight;
And though clad in armor from sandals to crown,
The hero rose up, and the garment went down.

A long row of alms-houses, amply endowed
By a well-esteemed Pharisee, busy and proud,
Next loaded one scale; while the other was pressed
By those mites the poor widow dropped into the chest;
Up flew the endowment, not weighing an ounce,
And down, down the farthing-worth came with a bounce.

By further experiments (no matter how)
He found that ten chariots weighed less than one plough;

A sword with gilt trapping rose up in the scale,
Though balanced by only a ten-penny nail;
A shield and a helmet, a buckler and spear,
Weighed less than a widow's uncrystallized tear.

A lord and a lady went up at full sail,
When a bee chanced to light on the opposite scale;
Ten doctors, ten lawyers, two courtiers, one earl,
Ten counselors' wigs, full of powder and curl,
All heaped in one balance and swinging from thence,
Weighed less than a few grains of candor and sense;
A first-water diamond, with brilliants begirt,
Than one good potato just washed from the dirt;
Yet not mountains of silver and gold could suffice
One pearl to outweigh,—'t was the Pearl of Great Price.

Last of all, the whole world was bowled in at the grate,
With the soul of a beggar to serve for a weight,
When the former sprang up with so strong a rebuff
That it made a vast rent and escaped at the roof!
When balanced in air, it ascended on high,
And sailed up aloft, a balloon in the sky;
While the scale with the soul in 't so mightily fell
That it jerked the philosopher out of his cell.

JANE TAYLOR.

A Modest Wit.

A SUPERCILIOUS nabob of the East—
    Haughty, being great—purse-proud, being rich—
A governor, or general, at the least,
    I have forgotten which—
Had in his family a humble youth,
    Who went from England in his patron's suite,
An unassuming boy, in truth
    A lad of decent parts, and good repute.

This youth had sense and spirit;
    But yet with all his sense,
    Excessive diffidence
Obscured his merit.

One day, at table, flushed with pride and wine,
    His honor, proudly free, severely merry,
Conceived it would be vastly fine
    To crack a joke upon his secretary.

"Young man," he said, "by what art, craft, or trade,
    Did your good father gain a livelihood?"—
"He was a saddler, sir," Modestus said,
    "And in his time was reckon'd good."

"A saddler, eh! and taught you Greek,
    Instead of teaching you to sew!
Pray, why did not your father make
    A saddler, sir, of you?"

Each parasite, then, as in duty bound,
The joke applauded, and the laugh went round.
    At length Modestus, bowing low,
Said (craving pardon, if too free he made),
  "Sir, by your leave, I fain would know
Your father's trade!"

"My father's trade! by heaven, that's too bad!
My father's trade?   Why, blockhead, are you mad?
My father, sir, did never stoop so low—
He was a gentleman, I'd have you know."

"Excuse the liberty I take,"
    Modestus said, with archness on his brow,
"Pray, why did not your father make
    A gentleman of you?"

SELLECK OSBORNE.

Saint Patrick.

St. Patrick was a gentleman,
  Who came of decent people;
He built a church in Dublin town,
  And on it put a steeple.
His father was a Gallagher;
  His mother was a Brady;
His aunt was an O'Shaughnessy,
  His uncle an O'Grady.
So, success attend St. Patrick's fist,
  For he 's a saint so clever;
Oh! he gave the snakes and toads a twist,
  And bothered them forever!

The Wicklow hills are very high,
  And so 's the hill of Howth, sir;
But there 's a hill, much bigger still,
  Much higher nor them both, sir:
'T was on the top of this high hill
  St. Patrick preached his sarmint
That drove the frogs into the bogs,
  And banished all the varmint.

There 's not a mile in Ireland's isle
  Where dirty varmin musters,
But where he put his dear fore-foot,
  And murdered them in clusters.
The toads went pop, the frogs went hop,
  Slap-dash into the water;
And the snakes committed suicide
  To save themselves from slaughter.

Nine hundred thousand reptiles blue
  He charmed with sweet discourses,
And dined on them at Killaloe
  In soups and second courses.

Where blind-worms crawling in the grass
　　Disgusted all the nation,
He gave them a rise, which opened their eyes
　　To a sense of their situation.

No wonder that those Irish lads
　　Should be so gay and frisky,
For sure St. Pat he taught them that,
　　As well as making whiskey;
No wonder that the saint himself
　　Should understand distilling,
Since his mother kept a shebeen-shop
　　In the town of Enniskillen.

O, was I but so fortunate
　　As to be back in Munster,
'T is I 'd be bound that from that ground
　　I never more would once stir.
For there St. Patrick planted turf,
　　And plenty of the praties,
With pigs galore, ma gra, ma 'store,
　　And cabbages—and ladies.
So, success attend St. Patrick's fist,
　　For he 's a saint so clever;
O, he gave the snakes and toads a twist
　　And bothered them forever!

HENRY BENNETT.

The Cloud.

A CLOUD lay cradled near the setting sun,
　　A gleam of crimson tinged its braided snow;
Long had I watched the glory moving on,
　　O'er the still radiance of the lake below:
Tranquil its spirit seemed, and floated slow,
　　E'en in its very motion there was rest,
While every breath of eve that chanced to blow,

Wafted the traveler to the beauteous west.
Emblem, methought, of the departed soul,
   To whose white robe the gleam of bliss is given,
And by the breath of mercy made to roll
   Right onward to the golden gates of heaven,
While to the eye of faith it peaceful lies,
And tells to man his glorious destinies.
JOHN WILSON.

The Bucket.

How dear to this heart are the scenes of my childhood,
When fond recollection presents them to view!—
The orchard, the meadow, the deep-tangled wildwood,
And every loved spot which my infancy knew!
The wide-spreading pond, and the mill that stood by it;
The bridge, and the rock where the cataract fell;
The cot of my father, the dairy-house nigh it;
And e'en the rude bucket that hung in the well—
The old oaken bucket, the iron-bound bucket,
The moss-covered bucket which hung in the well.

That moss-covered vessel I hailed as a treasure;
For often at noon, when returned from the field,
I found it the source of an exquisite pleasure—
The purest and sweetest that nature can yield.
How ardent I seized it, with hands that were glowing,
And quick to the white-pebbled bottom it fell!
Then soon, with the emblem of truth overflowing,
And dripping with coolness, it rose from the well—
The old oaken bucket, the iron-bound bucket,
The moss-covered bucket arose from the well.

How sweet from the green, mossy brim to receive it,
As, poised on the curb, it inclined to my lips!
Not a full, blushing goblet could tempt me to leave it,
The brightest that beauty or revelry sips.

And now, far removed from the loved habitation,
The tear of regret will intrusively swell,
As fancy reverts to my father's plantation,
And sighs for the bucket that hangs in the well—
The old oaken bucket, the iron-bound bucket,
The moss-covered bucket that hangs in the well!

SAMUEL WOODWORTH.

The Soul's Defiance.

I said to sorrow's awful storm,
   That beat against my breast,
Rage on!—thou may'st destroy this form,
   And lay it low at rest;
But still the spirit that now brooks
   Thy tempest, raging high,
Undaunted on its fury looks,
   With steadfast eye.

I said to penury's meagre train,
   Come on! your threats I brave;
My last poor life-drop you may drain,
   And crush me to the grave;
Yet still the spirit that endures
   Shall mock your force the while,
And meet each cold, cold grasp of yours
   With bitter smile.

I said to cold neglect and scorn,
   Pass on! I heed you not;
Ye may pursue me till my form
   And being are forgot;
Yet still the spirit which you see
   Undaunted by your wiles,
Draws from its own nobility
   Its high-born smiles.

I said to friendship's menaced blow,
  Strike deep! my heart shall bear;
Thou canst but add one bitter woe
  To those already there;
Yet still the spirit that sustains
  This last severe distress,
Shall smile upon its keenest pains,
  And scorn redress.

I said to death's uplifted dart,
  Aim sure! oh, why delay?
Thou wilt not find a fearful heart—
  A weak, reluctant prey;
For still the spirit, firm and free,
  Unruffled by this last dismay,
Wrapt in its own eternity,
  Shall pass away.

LAVINIA STODDARD.

The Mitherless Bairn.

WHEN a' ither bairnies are hushed to their hame
By aunty, or cousin, or frecky grand-dame,
Wha stands last and lanely, an' naebody carin'?
'T is the puir doited loonie,—the mitherless bairn.

The mitherless bairn gangs to his lane bed;
Nane covers his cauld back, or haps his bare head;
His wee hackit heelies are hard as the airn,
And litheless the lair o' the mitherless bairn.

Aneath his cauld brow siccan dreams hover there,
O' hands that wont kindly to kame his dark hair;
But mornin' brings clutches, a' reckless an' stern,
That lo'e nae the locks o' the mitherless bairn.

Yon sister that seng o'er his saftly rocked bed
Now rests in the mools where her mammie is laid;
10*

The father toils sair their wee bannock to earn,
An' kens na the wrangs o' his mitherless bairn.

Her spirit, that passed in yon hour o' his birth,
Still watches his wearisome wanderings on earth;
Recording in heaven the blessings they earn
Wha couthilie deal wi' the mitherless bairn.

O, speak him na harshly,—he trembles the while,
He bends to your bidding, and blesses your smile;
In their dark hour o' anguish the heartless shall learn,
That God deals the blow for the mitherless bairn.

WILLIAM THOM.

Stanzas.

My life is like the summer rose
    That opens to the morning sky,
But, ere the shades of evening close,
    Is scattered on the ground—to die!
Yet on the rose's humble bed
The sweetest dews of night are shed,
As if she wept the waste to see,—
But none shall weep a tear for me!

My life is like the autumn leaf
    That trembles in the moon's pale ray;
Its hold is frail—its date is brief,
    Restless—and soon to pass away!
Yet, ere that leaf shall fall and fade,
The parent tree will mourn its shade,
The winds bewail the leafless tree,—
But none shall breathe a sigh for me!

My life is like the prints which feet
    Have left on Tampa's desert strand;
Soon as the rising tide shall beat,
    All trace will vanish from the sand;

Yet, as if grieving to efface
All vestige of the human race,
On that lone shore loud moans the sea,—
But none, alas! shall mourn for me!
                    RICHARD HENRY WILDE.

Afar in the Desert.

AFAR in the desert I love to ride,
With the silent Bush-boy alone by my side,
When the sorrows of life the soul o'ercast,
And, sick of the present, I cling to the past;
When the eye is suffused with regretful tears,
From the fond recollections of former years;
And shadows of things that have long since fled
Flit over the brain, like the ghosts of the dead:
Bright visions of glory that vanished too soon;
Day-dreams, that departed ere manhood's noon;
Attachments by fate or falsehood reft;
Companions of early days lost or left—
And my native land—whose magical name
Thrills to the heart like electric flame;
The home of my childhood; the haunts of my prime;
All the passions and scenes of that rapturous time
When the feelings were young, and the world was new,
Like the fresh bowers of Eden unfolding to view;
All—all now forsaken—forgotten—foregone!
And I—a lone exile remembered of none—
My high aims abandoned,—my good acts undone—
Aweary of all that is under the sun—
With that sadness of heart which no stranger may scan,
I fly to the desert afar from man.

Afar in the desert I love to ride,
With the silent Bush-boy alone by my side.
When the wild turmoil of this wearisome life,
With its scenes of oppression, corruption, and strife—

The proud man's frown, and the base man's fear,
The scorner's laugh, and the sufferer's tear,
And malice, and meanness, and falsehood, and folly,
Dispose me to musing and dark melancholy;
When my bosom is full, and my thoughts are high,
And my soul is sick with the bondman's sigh,—
O, then there is freedom, and joy, and pride,
Afar in the desert alone to ride!
There is rapture to vault on the champing steed,
And to bound away with the eagle's speed,
With the death-fraught firelock in my hand,—
The only law of the Desert Land!

Afar in the desert I love to ride,
With the silent Bush-boy alone by my side,
Away, away from the dwellings of men,
By the wild deer's haunt, by the buffalo's glen;
By valleys remote where the oribi plays,
Where the gnu, the gazelle, and the hartebeest graze,
And the kudu and eland unhunted recline
By the skirts of gray forest o'erhung with wild vine;
Where the elephant browses at peace in his wood,
And the river-horse gambols unscared in the flood,
And the mighty rhinoceros wallows at will
In the fen where the wild ass is drinking his fill.

Afar in the desert I love to ride,
With the silent Bush-boy alone by my side,
O'er the brown karroo, where the bleating cry
Of the springbok's fawn sounds plaintively;
And the timorous quagga's shrill whistling neigh
Is heard by the fountain at twilight gray;
Where the zebra wantonly tosses his mane,
With wild hoof scouring the desolate plain;
And the fleet-footed ostrich over the waste
Speeds like a horseman who travels in haste,
Hieing away to the home of her rest,
Where she and her mate have scooped their nest,

Far hid from the pitiless plunderer's view
In the pathless depths of the parched karroo.

Afar in the desert I love to ride,
With the silent Bush-boy alone by my side,
Away, away, in the wilderness vast
Where the white man's foot hath never passed,
And the quivered Coranna or Bechuan
Hath rarely crossed with his roving clan,—
A region of emptiness, howling and drear,
Which man hath abandoned from famine and fear;
Which the snake and the lizard inhabit alone,
With the twilight bat from the yawning stone;
Where grass, nor herb, nor shrub takes root,
Save poisonous thorns that pierce the foot;
And the bitter-melon, for food and drink,
Is the pilgrim's fare by the salt lake's brink;
A region of drought, where no river glides,
Nor rippling brook with osiered sides;
Where sedgy pool, nor bubbling fount,
Nor tree, nor cloud, nor misty mount,
Appears, to refresh the aching eye;
But the barren earth and the burning sky,
And the blank horizon, round and round,
Spread,—void of living sight or sound.
And here, while the night-winds round me sigh,
And the stars burn bright in the midnight sky,
As I sit apart by the desert stone,
Like Elijah at Horeb's cave, alone,
" A still small voice " comes through the wild
(Like a father consoling his fretful child),
Which banishes bitterness, wrath, and fear,
Saying,—Man is distant, but God is near!

THOMAS PRINGLE.

11

The Beacon.

THE scene was more beautiful far to the eye,
    Than if day in its pride had arrayed it:
The land-breeze blew mild, and the azure-arched sky
    Looked pure as the spirit that made it:
The murmur rose soft, as I silently gazed
    On the shadowy waves' playful motion,
From the dim distant hill, till the light-house fire blazed
    Like a star in the midst of the ocean.

No longer the joy of the sailor-boy's breast
    Was heard in his wildly-breathed numbers;
The sea-bird had flown to her wave-girdled nest,
    The fisherman sunk to his slumbers:
One moment I looked from the hill's gentle slope,
    All hushed was the billows' commotion,
And o'er them the light-house looked lovely as hope,—
    That star of life's tremulous ocean.

The time is long past, and the scene is afar,
    Yet when my head rests on its pillow,
Will memory sometimes rekindle the star
    That blazed on the breast of the billow:
In life's closing hour, when the trembling soul flies,
    And death stills the heart's last emotion;
O, then may the seraph of mercy arise,
    Like a star on eternity's ocean!

                       P. M. JAMES.

Mortality.

O WHY should the spirit of mortal be proud?
Like a fast-flitting meteor, a fast-flying cloud,
A flash of the lightning, a break of the wave,
He passes from life to his rest in the grave.

The leaves of the oak and the willow shall fade,
Be scattered around and together be laid;
And the young and the old, and the low and the high,
Shall moulder to dust and together shall lie.

The child that a mother attended and loved,
The mother that infant's affection that proved,
The husband that mother and infant that blessed,
Each, all, are away to their dwelling of rest.

The maid on whose cheek, on whose brow, in whose eye,
Shone beauty and pleasure,—her triumphs are by;
And the memory of those that beloved her and praised
Are alike from the minds of the living erased.

The hand of the king that the sceptre hath borne,
The brow of the priest that the mitre hath worn,
The eye of the sage, and the heart of the brave,
Are hidden and lost in the depths of the grave.

The peasant whose lot was to sow and to reap,
The herdsman who climbed with his goats to the steep,
The beggar that wandered in search of his bread,
Have faded away like the grass that we tread.

The saint that enjoyed the communion of heaven,
The sinner that dared to remain unforgiven,
The wise and the foolish, the guilty and just,
Have quietly mingled their bones in the dust.

So the multitude goes, like the flower and the weed
That wither away to let others succeed;
So the multitude comes, even those we behold,
To repeat every tale that hath often been told.

For we are the same that our fathers have been;
We see the same sights that our fathers have seen,—
We drink the same stream, and we feel the same sun,
And we run the same course that our fathers have run.

The thoughts we are thinking, our fathers would think;
From the death we are shrinking from, they too would
        shrink;
To the life we are clinging to, they too would cling;
But it speeds from the earth like a bird on the wing.

They loved, but their story we cannot unfold;
They scorned, but the heart of the haughty is cold;
They grieved, but no wail from their slumbers may come;
They joyed, but the voice of their gladness is dumb.

They died, ay! they died! and we things that are now,
Who walk on the turf that lies over their brow,
Who make in their dwellings a transient abode,
Meet the changes they met on their pilgrimage road.

Yea! hope and despondence, and pleasure and pain,
Are mingled together like sunshine and rain;
And the smile and the tear, and the song and the dirge,
Still follow each other, like surge upon surge.

'T is the wink of an eye, 't is the draught of a breath,
From the blossom of health to the paleness of death,
From the gilded saloon to the bier and the shroud,—
O why should the spirit of mortal be proud?

WILLIAM KNOX.

The Whistler.

"You have heard," said a youth to his sweetheart, who
        stood
    While he sat on a corn-sheaf, at daylight's decline,—
"You have heard of the Danish boy's whistle of wood:
    I wish that the Danish boy's whistle were mine."

"And what would you do with it?   Tell me," she said,
    While an arch smile played over her beautiful face.

"I would blow it," he answered, "and then my fair maid
   Would fly to my side and would there take her place."

"Is that all you wish for? Why, that may be yours
   Without any magic!" the fair maiden cried:
"A favor so slight one's good-nature secures;"
   And she playfully seated herself by his side.

"I would blow it again," said the youth; "and the charm
   Would work so that not even modesty's check
Would be able to keep from my neck your white arm."
   She smiled and she laid her white arm round his neck.

"Yet once more I would blow; and the music divine
   Would bring me a third time an exquisite bliss,—
You would lay your fair cheek to this brown one of mine;
   And your lips stealing past it would give me a kiss."

The maiden laughed out in her innocent glee,—
   "What a fool of yourself with the whistle you'd make!
For only consider how silly 't would be
   To sit there and whistle for what you might take."
                  ROBERT STORY.

We'll Go to Sea no More.

O, BLITHELY shines the bonny sun
   Upon the Isle of May,
And blithely comes the morning tide
   Into St. Andrew's Bay.
Then up, gudeman, the breeze is fair,
   And up, my braw bairns three;
There 's goud in yonder bonny boat
   That sails sae weel the sea!
      When haddocks leave the Firth o' Forth,
      An' mussels leave the shore,

When oysters climb up Berwick Law,
  We 'll go to sea no more,—
    No more,
  We 'll go to sea no more.

I 've seen the waves as blue as air,
  I 've seen them green as grass;
But I never feared their heaving yet,
  From Grangemouth to the Bass.
I 've seen the sea as black as pitch,
  I 've seen it white as snow;
But I never feared its foaming yet,
  Though the winds blew high or low.
    When squalls capsize our wooden walls,
      When the French ride at the Nore,
    When Leith meets Aberdour half way,
      We 'll go to sea no more,—
        No more,
      We 'll go to sea no more.

I never liked the landsman's life,
  The earth is aye the same;
Gie me the ocean for my dower,
  My vessel for my hame.
Gie me the fields that no man plows,
  The farm that pays no fee;
Gie me the bonny fish that glance
  So gladly through the sea.
    When sails hang flapping on the masts
      While through the waves we snore,
    When in a calm we 're tempest-tossed,
      We 'll go to sea no more,—
        No more,
      We 'll go to sea no more.

The sun is up, and round Inchkeith
  The breezes softly blaw;

The gudeman has the lines on board,—
    Awa, my bairns, awa!
An' ye be back by gloamin' gray,
    An' bright the fire will low,
An' in your tales and sangs we 'll tell
    How weel the boat ye row.
      When life's last sun gaes feebly down,
       An' death comes to our door,
     When a' the world 's a dream to us,
       We 'll go to sea no more,—
        No more,
       We 'll go to sea no more.

           Miss Corbett.

Geehale.

The blackbird is singing on Michigan's shore,
As sweetly and gayly as ever before;
For he knows to his mate he at pleasure can hie,
And the dear little brood she is teaching to fly.
The sun looks as ruddy, and rises as bright,
And reflects o'er the mountains as beamy a light
As it ever reflected, or ever expressed,
When my skies were the bluest, my dreams were the best.
The fox and the panther, both beasts of the night,
Retire to their dens on the gleaming of light,
And they spring with a free and a sorrowless track,
For they know that their mates are expecting them back.
Each bird and each beast, it is blessed in degree;
All nature is cheerful, all happy, but me.

I will go to my tent, and lie down in despair;
I will paint me with black, and will sever my hair;
I will sit on the shore where the hurricane blows,
And reveal to the god of the tempest my woes;
I will weep for a season, on bitterness fed,
For my kindred are gone to the hills of the dead;

But they died not by hunger, or lingering decay—
The steel of the white man hath swept them away.

This snake-skin, that once I so sacredly wore,
I will toss with disdain to the storm-beaten shore;
Its charms I no longer obey or invoke,
Its spirit hath left me, its spell is now broke.
I will raise up my voice to the source of the light;
I will dream on the wings of the blue-bird at night;
I will speak to the spirits that whisper in leaves,
And that minister balm to the bosom that grieves;
And will take a new Manito, such as shall seem
To be kind and propitious in every dream.

O, then I shall banish these cankering sighs,
And tears shall no longer gush salt from my eyes;
I shall wash from my face every cloud-colored stain;
Red, red shall alone on my visage remain!
I will dig up my hatchet, and bend my oak bow;
By night and by day I will follow the foe;
Nor lakes shall impede me, nor mountains, nor snows;
His blood can alone give my spirit repose.

They came to my cabin when heaven was black;
I heard not their coming, I knew not their track;
But I saw, by the light of their blazing fusees,
They were people engendered beyond the big seas.
My wife and my children—O, spare me the tale!
For who is there left that is kin to Geehale?

HENRY ROWE SCHOOLCRAFT.

I Would not Live Alway.

I WOULD not live alway: I ask not to stay
Where storm after storm rises dark o'er the way;
Where, seeking for rest, I but hover around
Like the patriarch's bird, and no resting is found;

Where Hope, when she paints her gay bow in the air,
Leaves her brilliance to fade in the night of despair,
And Joy's fleeting angel ne'er sheds a glad ray,
Save the gleam of the plumage that bears him away.

I would not live alway, thus fettered by sin,
Temptation without, and corruption within;
In a moment of strength if I sever the chain,
Scarce the victory 's mine ere I 'm captive again.
E'en the rapture of pardon is mingled with fears,
And the cup of thanksgiving with penitent tears.
The festival trump calls for jubilant songs,
But my spirit her own *miserere* prolongs.

I would not live alway: no, welcome the tomb;
Immortality's lamp burns there bright 'mid the gloom.
There too is the pillow where Christ bowed his head—
O, soft be my slumbers on that holy bed!
And then the glad morn soon to follow that night,
When the sunrise of glory shall burst on my sight,
And the full matin-song, as the sleepers arise
To shout in the morning, shall peal through the skies.

Who, who would live alway, away from his God,
Away from yon heaven, that blissful abode,
Where rivers of pleasure flow o'er the bright plains,
And the noontide of glory eternally reigns;
Where the saints of all ages in harmony meet,
Their Saviour and brethren transported to greet,
While the anthems of rapture unceasingly roll,
And the smile of the Lord is the feast of the soul?

That heavenly music! what is it I hear?
The notes of the harpers ring sweet on my ear.
And see soft unfolding those portals of gold,
The King all arrayed in his beauty behold!
  11*

O give me, O give me the wings of a dove!
Let me hasten my flight to those mansions above.
Ay, 't is now that my soul on swift pinions would soar,
And in ecstasy bid earth adieu evermore.

WILLIAM AUGUSTUS MUHLENBERG.

Lines Written in a Church-yard.

"It is good for us to be here. If thou wilt, let us make here three tabernacles; one for thee, one for Moses, and one for Elias."

METHINKS it is good to be here;
If thou wilt, let us build—but for whom?
    Nor Elias nor Moses appear;
But the shadows of eve that encompass with gloom
The abode of the dead and the place of the tomb.

Shall we build to Ambition? Ah no!
Affrighted he shrinketh away;
    For see, they would pen him below
In a small narrow cave and begirt with cold clay,
To the meanest of reptiles a peer and a prey.

To Beauty? Ah no! she forgets
The charms which she wielded before;
    Nor knows the foul worm that he frets
The skin which but yesterday fools could adore,
For the smoothness it held, or the tint which it wore.

Shall we build to the purple of pride?
To the trappings which dizen the proud?
    Alas! they are all laid aside,
And here 's neither dress nor adornment allowed,
But the long winding-sheet, and the fringe of the shroud

To Riches? Alas, 't is in vain!
Who hid, in their turns have been hid:
    The treasures are squandered again;

And here in the grave are all metals forbid,
But the tinsel that shines on the dark coffin-lid.

To the pleasures which Mirth can afford,
The revel, the laugh, and the jeer?
Ah! here is a plentiful board!
But the guests are all mute as their pitiful cheer,
And none but the worm is a reveler here.

Shall we build to Affection and Love?
Ah no! they have withered and died,
Or fled with the spirit above.
Friends, brothers, and sisters are laid side by side,
Yet none have saluted, and none have replied.

Unto Sorrow?—the dead cannot grieve;
Not a sob, not a sigh meets mine ear,
Which compassion itself could relieve.
Ah, sweetly they slumber, nor love, hope, or fear;
Peace, peace is the watchword, the only one here.

Unto Death, to whom monarchs must bow?
Ah no! for his empire is known,
And here there are trophies enow!
Beneath, the cold dead, and around, the dark stone,
Are the signs of a sceptre that none may disown.

The first tabernacle to Hope we will build,
And look for the sleepers around us to rise;
The second to Faith, that insures it fulfilled;
And the third to the Lamb of the great sacrifice,
Who bequeathed us them both when he rose to the skies.

HERBERT KNOWLES.

The Mariner's Dream.

In slumbers of midnight the sailor-boy lay;
His hammock swung loose at the sport of the wind;

But watch-worn and weary, his cares flew away,
　　And visions of happiness danced o'er his mind.

He dreamt of his home, of his dear native bowers,
　　And pleasures that waited on life's merry morn;
While memory stood sideways half covered with flowers,
　　And restored every rose, but secreted its thorn.

Then Fancy her magical pinions spread wide,
　　And bade the young dreamer in ecstasy rise;
Now far, far behind him the green waters glide,
　　And the cot of his forefathers blesses his eyes.

The jessamine clambers in flower o'er the thatch,
　　And the swallow chirps sweet from her nest in the wall;
All trembling with transport he raises the latch,
　　And the voices of loved ones reply to his call.

A father bends o'er him with looks of delight;
　　His cheek is impearled with a mother's warm tear;
And the lips of the boy in a love-kiss unite
　　With the lips of the maid whom his bosom holds dear.

The heart of the sleeper beats high in his breast;
　　Joy quickens his pulses,—his hardships seem o'er;
And a murmur of happiness steals through his rest,—
　　"O God! thou hast blest me,—I ask for no more."

Ah! whence is that flame which now bursts on his eye?
　　Ah! what is that sound which now 'larms on his ear?
'T is the lightning's red gleam, painting hell on the sky!
　　'T is the crashing of thunders, the groan of the sphere!

He springs from his hammock, he flies to the deck;
　　Amazement confronts him with images dire;
Wild winds and mad waves drive the vessel a-wreck;
　　The masts fly in splinters; the shrouds are on fire.

Like mountains the billows tremendously swell;
   In vain the lost wretch calls on mercy to save;
Unseen hands of spirits are ringing his knell,
   And the death-angel flaps his broad wings o'er the wave!

O sailor-boy, woe to thy dream of delight!
   In darkness dissolves the gay frost-work of bliss.
Where now is the picture that fancy touched bright,—
   Thy parents' fond pressure, and love's honeyed kiss?

O sailor-boy! sailor-boy! never again
   Shall home, love, or kindred thy wishes repay;
Unblessed and unhonored, down deep in the main,
   Full many a fathom, thy frame shall decay.

No tomb shall e'er plead to remembrance for thee,
   Or redeem form or fame from the merciless surge,
But the white foam of waves shall thy winding-sheet be,
   And winds in the midnight of winter thy dirge!

On a bed of green sea-flowers thy limbs shall be laid,—
   Around thy white bones the red coral shall grow;
Of thy fair yellow locks threads of amber be made,
   And every part suit to thy mansion below.

Days, months, years, and ages shall circle away,
   And still the vast waters above thee shall roll;
Earth loses thy pattern forever and aye,—
   O sailor-boy! sailor-boy! peace to thy soul!

WILLIAM DIMOND.

Old Grimes.

    OLD GRIMES is dead; that good old man
      We never shall see more;
    He used to wear a long, black coat,
      All buttoned down before.

His heart was open as the day,
　His feelings all were true;
His hair was some inclined to gray,
　He wore it in a queue.

Whene'er he heard the voice of pain,
　His breast with pity burned;
The large, round head upon his cane
　From ivory was turned.

Kind words he ever had for all,
　He knew no base design;
His eyes were dark and rather small,
　His nose was aquiline.

He lived at peace with all mankind,
　In friendship he was true;
His coat had pocket-holes behind,
　His pantaloons were blue.

Unharmed, the sin which earth pollutes
　He passed securely o'er,
And never wore a pair of boots
　For thirty years or more.

But good old Grimes is now at rest,
　Nor fears misfortune's frown;
He wore a double-breasted vest—
　The stripes ran up and down.

He modest merit sought to find,
　And pay it its desert;
He had no malice in his mind,
　No ruffles on his shirt.

His neighbors he did not abuse,
　Was sociable and gay;
He wore large buckles on his shoes,
　And changed them every day.

His knowledge, hid from public gaze,
  He did not bring to view,
Nor make a noise town-meeting days,
  As many people do.

His worldly goods he never threw
  In trust to fortune's chances,
But lived (as all his brothers do)
  In easy circumstances.

Thus undisturbed by anxious cares
  His peaceful moments ran;
And everybody said he was
  A fine old gentleman.

ALBERT GORTON GREENE.

The Closing Year.

'T is midnight's holy hour,—and silence now
Is brooding like a gentle spirit o'er
The still and pulseless world. Hark! on the winds
The bell's deep tones are swelling,—'t is the knell
Of the departed year. No funeral train
Is sweeping past; yet, on the stream and wood,
With melancholy light, the moon-beams rest
Like a pale, spotless shroud; the air is stirred
As by a mourner's sigh; and on yon cloud
That floats so still and placidly through heaven,
The spirits of the seasons seem to stand,—
Young Spring, bright Summer, Autumn's solemn form,
And Winter with its aged locks,—and breathe,
In mournful cadences that come abroad
Like the far wind-harp's wild and touching wail,
A melancholy dirge o'er the dead year,
Gone from the Earth forever.

                   'T is a time
For memory and for tears. Within the deep,

Still chambers of the heart, a spectre dim,
Whose tones are like the wizard voice of Time
Heard from the tomb of ages, points its cold
And solemn finger to the beautiful
And holy visions that have passed away,
And left no shadow of their loveliness
On the dead waste of life.　That spectre lifts
The coffin-lid of Hope, and Joy, and Love,
And, bending mournfully above the pale,
Sweet forms, that slumber there, scatters dead flowers
O'er what has passed to nothingness.

　　　　　　　The year
Has gone, and, with it, many a glorious throng
Of happy dreams.　Its mark is on each brow,
Its shadow in each heart.　In its swift course,
It waved its sceptre o'er the beautiful,—
And they are not.　It laid its pallid hand
Upon the strong man,—and the haughty form
Is fallen, and the flashing eye is dim.
It trod the hall of revelry, where thronged
The bright and joyous,—and the tearful wail
Of stricken ones　is heard where erst the song
And reckless shout resounded.

　　　　　　　　It passed o'er
The battle-plain, where sword, and spear, and shield,
Flashed in the light of midday,—and the strength
Of serried hosts is shivered, and the grass,
Green from the soil of carnage, waves above
The crushed and mouldering skeleton.　It came,
And faded like a wreath of mist at eve;
Yet, ere it melted in the viewless air,
It heralded its millions to their home
In the dim land of dreams.

　　　　　　　Remorseless Time!
Fierce spirit of the glass and scythe!—what power

Can stay him in his silent course, or melt
His iron heart to pity? On, still on,
He presses, and forever. The proud bird,
The condor of the Andes, that can soar
Through heaven's unfathomable depths, or brave
The fury of the northern hurricane,
And bathe his plumage in the thunder's home,
Furls his broad wings at nightfall, and sinks down
To rest upon his mountain crag,—but Time
Knows not the weight of sleep or weariness,
And night's deep darkness has no chain to bind
His rushing pinions.

               Revolutions sweep
O'er earth, like troubled visions o'er the breast
Of dreaming sorrow,—cities rise and sink
Like bubbles on the water,—fiery isles
Spring blazing from the ocean, and go back
To their mysterious caverns,—mountains rear
To heaven their bald and blackened cliffs, and bow
Their tall heads to the plain,—new empires rise,
Gathering the strength of hoary centuries,
And rush down like the Alpine avalanche,
Startling the nations,—and the very stars,
Yon bright and burning blazonry of God,
Glitter a while in their eternal depths,
And, like the Pleiad, loveliest of their train,
Shoot from their glorious spheres, and pass away
To darkle in the trackless void. Yet, Time,
Time, the tomb-builder, holds his fierce career,
Dark, stern, all-pitiless, and pauses not
Amid the mighty wrecks that strew his path,
To sit and muse, like other conquerors,
Upon the fearful ruin he has wrought.

                         GEORGE DENISON PRENTICE.

A Health.

I FILL this cup to one made up
  Of loveliness alone,
A woman, of her gentle sex
  The seeming paragon;
To whom the better elements
  And kindly stars have given
A form so fair, that, like the air,
  'T is less of earth than heaven.

Her every tone is music's own,
  Like those of morning birds,
And something more than melody
  Dwells ever in her words;
The coinage of her heart are they,
  And from her lips each flows
As one may see the burdened bee
  Forth issue from the rose.

Affections are as thoughts to her,
  The measures of her hours;
Her feelings have the fragrancy,
  The freshness of young flowers;
And lovely passions, changing oft,
  So fill her, she appears
The image of themselves by turns,—
  The idol of past years!

Of her bright face one glance will trace
  A picture on the brain,
And of her voice in echoing hearts
  A sound must long remain;
But memory, such as mine of her,
  So very much endears,
When death is nigh my latest sigh
  Will not be life's, but hers.

I fill this cup to one made up
    Of loveliness alone,
A woman, of her gentle sex
    The seeming paragon,—
Her health! and would on earth there stood
    Some more of such a frame,
That life might be all poetry,
    And weariness a name.
                    EDWARD COATE PINKNEY.

The Three Sons.

I HAVE a son, a little son, a boy just five years old,
With eyes of thoughtful earnestness, and mind of gentle
    mould.
They tell me that unusual grace in all his ways appears,
That my child is grave and wise of heart beyond his child-
    ish years.
I cannot say how this may be; I know his face is fair—
And yet his chiefest comeliness is his sweet and serious
    air:
I know his heart is fond and kind; I know he loveth me:
But loveth yet his mother more with grateful fervency.
But that which others most admire, is the thought which
    fills his mind,
The food for grave inquiring speech he everywhere doth
    find.
Strange questions doth he ask of me, when we together
    walk;
He scarcely thinks as children think, or talks as children
    talk.
Nor cares he much for childish sports, dotes not on bat or
    ball,
But looks on manhood's ways and works, and aptly mimics
    all.
His little heart is busy still, and oftentimes perplexed

With thoughts about this world of ours, and thoughts about
    the next.
He kneels at his dear mother's knee; she teacheth him to
    pray;
And strange, and sweet, and solemn then are the words
    which he will say.
O, should my gentle child be spared to manhood's years
    like me,
A holier and a wiser man I trust that he will be;
And when I look into his eyes, and stroke his thoughtful
    brow,
I dare not think what I should feel, were I to lose him now.

I have a son, a second son, a simple child of three;
I'll not declare how bright and fair his little features be,
How silver sweet those tones of his when he prattles on
    my knee;
I do not think his light-blue eye is, like his brother's, keen,
Nor his brow so full of childish thought as his hath ever
    been;
But his little heart's a fountain pure of kind and tender feel-
    ing;
And his every look's a gleam of light, rich depths of love
    revealing.
When he walks with me, the country folk, who pass us in
    the street,
Will shout for joy and bless my boy, he looks so mild and
    sweet.
A playfellow is he to all; and yet, with cheerful tone,
Will sing his little song of love, when left to sport alone.
His presence is like sunshine sent to gladden home and
    hearth,
To comfort us in all our griefs, and sweeten all our mirth.
Should he grow up to riper years, God grant his heart may
    prove
As sweet a home for heavenly grace as now for earthly
    love;

And if, beside his grave, the tears our aching eyes must
    dim,
God comfort us for all the love which we shall lose in him!

I have a son, a third sweet son; his age I cannot tell,
For they reckon not by years and months where he is gone
    to dwell.
To us, for fourteen anxious months, his infant smiles were
    given;
And then he bade farewell to earth, and went to live in
    heaven.
I cannot tell what form is his, what looks he weareth now,
Nor guess how bright a glory crowns his shining seraph
    brow.
The thoughts that fill his sinless soul, the bliss which he
    doth feel,
Are numbered with the secret things which God will not
    reveal.
But I know (for God hath told me this) that he is now at ·
    rest,
Where other blessed infants be, on their Saviour's loving
    breast.
I know his spirit feels no more this weary load of flesh,
But his sleep is blessed with endless dreams of joy forever
    fresh.
I know the angels fold him close beneath their glittering
    wings,
And soothe him with a song that breathes of heaven's di-
    vinest things.
I know that we shall meet our babe (his mother dear and I)
Where God for aye shall wipe away all tears from every
    eye.
Whate'er befalls his brethren twain, his bliss can never
    cease;
Their lot may here be grief and fear, but his is certain
    peace.
It may be that the tempter's wiles their souls from bliss
    may sever;

But, if our own poor faith fail not, he must be ours forever.
When we think of what our darling is, and what we still
    must be—
When we muse on that world's perfect bliss, and this
    world's misery—
When we groan beneath this load of sin, and feel this grief
    and pain—
O! we 'd rather lose our other two, than have him here
    again.

JOHN MOULTRIE.

The Annuity.

I GAED to spend a week in Fife—
    An unco week it proved to be—
For there I met a waesome wife
    Lamentin' her viduity.
Her grief brak out sae fierce and fell,
I thought her heart wad burst the shell;
And,—I was sae left to mysel,—
    I sell't her an annuity.

The bargain lookit fair eneugh—
    She just was turned o' saxty-three—
I couldna guessed she'd prove sae teugh,
    By human ingenuity.
But years have come, and years have gane,
And there she 's yet as stieve as stane—
The limmer 's growin' young again,
    Since she got her annuity.

She 's crined' awa' to bane and skin,
    But that, it seems, is nought to me;
She 's like to live—although she 's in
    The last stage o' tenuity.
She munches wi' her wizen'd gums,
An' stumps about on legs o' thrums;

But comes, as sure as Christmas comes,
　　To ca' for her annuity.

I read the tables drawn wi' care
　　For an insurance company;
Her chance o' life was stated there,
　　Wi' perfect perspicuity.
But tables here or tables there,
She 's lived ten years beyond her share,
An' 's like to live a dozen mair,
　　To ca' for her annuity.

Last Yule she had a fearfu' host,
　　I thought a kink might set me free—
I led her out, 'mang snaw and frost,
　　Wi' constant assiduity.
But deil ma' care—the blast gaed by,
And miss'd the auld anatomy—
It just cost me a tooth, for bye
　　Discharging her annuity.

If there 's a sough o' cholera,
　　Or typhus,—wha sae gleg as she?
She buys up baths, an' drugs, an' a',
　　In siccan superfluity!
She doesna need—she 's fever proof—
The pest walked o'er her very roof—
She tauld me sae—an' then her loof
　　Held out for her annuity.

Ae day she fell, her arm she brak—
　　A compound fracture as could be—
Nae leech the cure wad undertake,
　　Whate'er was the gratuity.
It 's cured!　She handles 't like a flail--
It does as weel in bits as hale—
But I 'm a broken man mysel'
　　Wi' her and her annuity.

Her broozled flesh and broken banes
　　Are weel as flesh and banes can be;
She beats the toads that live in stanes,
　　An' fatten in vacuity!
They die when they 're exposed to air,
They canna thole the atmosphere—
But her! expose her onywhere,
　　She lives for her annuity.

If mortal means could nick her thread,
　　Sma' crime it wad appear to me—
Ca't murder—or ca't homicide—
　　I 'd justify 't—an' do it tae.
But how to fell a withered wife
That 's carved out o' the tree of life—
The timmer limmer dares the knife
　　To settle her annuity.

I 'd try a shot—but whar's the mark?
　　Her vital parts are hid frae me;
Her backbone wanders through her sark
　　In an unkenn'd corkscrewity.
She 's palsified, an' shakes her head
Sae fast about, ye scarce can see 't,
It 's past the power o' steel or lead
　　To settle her annuity.

She might be drowned; but go she 'll not
　　Within a mile o' loch or sea;
Or hanged—if cord could grip a throat
　　O' siccan exiguity.
It 's fitter far to hang the rope—
It draws out like a telescope;
'T wad tak' a dreadfu' length o' drop
　　To settle her annuity.

Will poison do it? It has been tried,
　　But be 't in hash or fricassee,

That 's just the dish she can't abide,
   Whatever kind o' gout it hae.
It 's needless to assail her doubts,
She gangs by instinct, like the brutes,
An' only eats an' drinks what suits
   Hersel' and her annuity.

The Bible says the age o' man
   Threescore and ten, perchance, may be;
She 's ninety-four.   Let them who can,
   Explain the incongruity.
She should hae lived afore the flood—
She 's come o' patriarchal blood,
She 's some auld Pagan mummified
   Alive for her annuity.

She 's been embalmed inside and oot—
   She 's sauted to the last degree—
There 's pickle in her very snoot
   Sae caper-like an' cruety.
Lot's wife was fresh compared to her—
They 've kyanized the useless knir,
She canna decompose—nae mair
   Than her accursed annuity.

The water-drop wears out the rock,
   As this eternal jaud wears me;
I could withstand the single shock,
   But not the continuity.
It 's pay me here, an' pay me there,
An' pay me, pay me, evermair—
I 'll gang demented wi' despair—
   I 'm charged for her annuity.

GEORGE OUTRAM.

13

The Forging of the Anchor.

COME, see the Dolphin's anchor forged; 't is at a white heat
    now:
The bellows ceased, the flames decreased; though on the
    forge's brow
The little flames still fitfully play through the sable mound;
And fitfully you still may see the grim smiths ranking
    round,
All clad in leathern panoply, their broad hands only bare;
Some rest upon their sledges here, some work the windlass
    there.

The windlass strains the tackle-chains, the black mound
    heaves below,
And red and deep a hundred veins burst out at every throe;
It rises, roars, rends all outright,—O Vulcan, what a glow!
'T is blinding white, 't is blasting bright, the high sun shines
    not so!
The high sun sees not, on the earth, such fiery fearful
    show,—
The roof-ribs swarth, the candent hearth, the ruddy, lurid
    row
Of smiths that stand, an ardent band, like men before the
    foe;
As, quivering through his fleece of flame, the sailing mon-
    ster slow
Sinks on the anvil,—all about the faces fiery grow,—
"Hurrah!" they shout, "leap out, leap out:" bang, bang,
    the sledges go;
Hurrah! the jetted lightnings are hissing high and low;
A hailing fount of fire is struck at every squashing blow;
The leathern mail rebounds the hail; the rattling cinders
    strew
The ground around; at every bound the sweltering fount-
    ains flow;
And thick and loud the swinking crowd, at every stroke,
    pant "Ho!"

Leap out, leap out, my masters; leap out and lay on load!
Let 's forge a goodly anchor, a bower, thick and broad;
For a heart of oak is hanging on every blow, I bode,
And I see the good ship riding, all in a perilous road;
The low reef roaring on her lee, the roll of ocean poured
From stem to stern, sea after sea, the mainmast by the
    board;
The bulwarks down, the rudder gone, the boats stove at the
    chains,
But courage still, brave mariners, the bower still remains,
And not an inch to flinch he deigns save when ye pitch sky-
    high,
Then moves his head, as though he said, " Fear nothing,
    here am I! "
Swing in your strokes in order, let foot and hand keep time,
Your blows make music sweeter far than any steeple's
    chime!
But while you sling your sledges, sing; and let the burden
    be,
The Anchor is the Anvil King, and royal craftsmen we;
Strike in, strike in, the sparks begin to dull their rustling
    red!
Our hammers ring with sharper din, our work will soon be
    sped;
Our anchor soon must change his bed of fiery rich array
For a hammock at the roaring bows, or an oozy couch of
    clay;
Our anchor soon must change the lay of merry craftsmen
    here,
For the Yeo-heave-o, and the Heave-away, and the sighing
    seaman's cheer;
When, weighing slow, at eve they go far, far from love and
    home,
And sobbing sweethearts, in a row, wail o'er the ocean foam.

In livid and obdurate gloom, he darkens down at last.
A shapely one he is, and strong as e'er from cat was cast.

O trusted and trustworthy guard, if thou hadst life like me,
What pleasures would thy toils reward beneath the deep
       green sea!
O deep sea-diver, who might then behold such sights as
       thou?   .
The hoary monsters' palaces! methinks what joy 't were
       now
To go plumb plunging down amid the assembly of the
       whales,
And feel the churned sea round me boil beneath their
       scourging tails!
Then deep in tangle-woods to fight the fierce sea unicorn,
And send him foiled and bellowing back, for all his ivory
       horn ;
To leave the subtle sworder-fish of bony blade forlorn ;
And for the ghastly-grinning shark, to laugh his jaws to
       scorn ;
To leap down on the kraken's back, where 'mid Norwegian
       isles
He lies, a lubber anchorage for sudden shallowed miles,
Till snorting, like an under-sea volcano, off he rolls;
Meanwhile to swing, a-buffeting the far astonished shoals
Of his black-browsing ocean-calves, or haply in a cove
Shell-strown, and consecrate of old to some Undine's love,
To find the long-haired mermaidens; or, hard by icy lands,
To wrestle with the sea-serpent, upon cerulean sands.

O broad-armed fisher of the deep, whose sports can equal
       thine?
The Dolphin weighs a thousand tons, that tugs thy cable
       line ;
And night by night 't is thy delight, thy glory day by day,
Through sable sea and breaker white, the giant game to play.
But, shamer of our little sports, forgive the name I gave!
A fisher's joy is to destroy—thine office is to save.
O lodger in the sea-kings' halls, couldst thou but understand

Whose be the white bones by thy side, or who that drip-
    ping band,
Slow swaying in the heaving wave, that round about thee
    bend,
With sounds like breakers in a dream, blessing their ancient
    friend—
Oh, couldst thou know what heroes glide with larger steps
    round thee,
Thine iron side would swell with pride; thou 'dst leap with-
    in the sea!
Give honor to their memories who left the pleasant strand,
To shed their blood so freely for the love of Fatherland;
Who left their chance of quiet age and grassy church-yard
    grave,
So freely, for a restless bed amid the tossing wave.
Oh, though our anchor may not be all I have fondly sung,
Honor him for their memory whose bones he goes among!

SAMUEL FERGUSON.

The Bells of Shandon.

WITH deep affection
And recollection
I often think of
    Those Shandon bells,
Whose sounds so wild would,
In the days of childhood,
Fling round my cradle
    Their magic spells.

On this I ponder
Where'er I wander,
And thus grow fonder,
    Sweet Cork, of thee,—
With thy bells of Shandon,
That sound so grand on

The plesant waters
  Of the river Lee.

I 've heard bells chiming
Full many a clime in,
Tolling sublime in
  Cathedral shrine,
While at a glibe rate
Brass tongues would vibrate;
But all their music
  Spoke naught like thine.

For memory, dwelling
On each proud swelling
Of thy belfry, knelling
  Its bold notes free,
Made the bells of Shandon
Sound far more grand on
The pleasant waters
    Of the river Lee.

I 've heard bells tolling
Old Adrian's Mole in,
Their thunder rolling
  From the Vatican,—
And cymbals glorious
Swinging uproarious
In the gorgeous turrets
  Of Notre Dame;

But thy sounds were sweeter
Than the dome of Peter
Flings o'er the Tiber,
  Pealing solemnly.
Oh! the bells of Shandon
Sound far more grand on
The pleasant waters
    Of the river Lee.

There 's a bell in Moscow;
While on tower and kiosk O
In St. Sophia
   The Turkman gets,
And loud in air
Calls men to prayer,
From the tapering summit
   Of tall minarets.

Such empty phantom
I freely grant them;
But there 's an anthem
   More dear to me,—
'T is the bells of Shandon,
That sound so grand on
The pleasant waters
   Of the river Lee.

FRANCIS MAHONY.

The Death of Napoleon.

WILD was the night, yet a wilder night
  Hung round the soldier's pillow;
In his bosom there waged a fiercer fight
  Than the fight on the wrathful billow.

A few fond mourners were kneeling by,
  The few that his stern heart cherished;
They knew, by his glazed and unearthly eye,
  That life had nearly perished.

They knew by his awful and kingly look,
  By the order hastily spoken,
That he dreamed of days when the nations shook,
  And the nations' hosts were broken.

He dreamed that the Frenchman's sword still slew,
    And triumphed the Frenchman's eagle,
And the struggling Austrian fled anew,
    Like the hare before the beagle.

The bearded Russian he scourged again,
    The Prussian's camp was routed,
And again on the hills of haughty Spain
    His mighty armies shouted.

Over Egypt's sands, over Alpine snows,
    At the pyramids, at the mountain,
Where the wave of the lordly Danube flows,
    And by the Italian fountain,

On the snowy cliffs where mountain streams
    Dash by the Switzer's dwelling,
He led again, in his dying dreams,
    His hosts, the broad earth quelling.

Again Marengo's field was won,
    And Jena's bloody battle;
Again the world was overrun,
    Made pale at his cannon's rattle.

He died at the close of that darksome day,
    A day that shall live in story;
In the rocky land they placed his clay,
    "And left him alone with his glory."

                        ISSAC McCLELLAN.

The Grave of Bonaparte.

On a lone barren isle, where the wild roaring billows
    Assail the stern rock, and the loud tempests rave,
The hero lies still, while the dew-drooping willows,
    Like fond weeping mourners, lean over the grave.

The lightnings may flash, and the loud thunders rattle:
  He heeds not, he hears not, he 's free from all pain;—
He sleeps his last sleep—he has fought his last battle!
  No sound can awake him to glory again!

O shade of the mighty, where now are the legions
  That rush'd but to conquer when thou led'st them on?
Alas! they have perish'd in far hilly regions,
  And all save the fame of their triumph is gone!
The trumpet may sound, and the loud cannon rattle!
  They heed not, they hear not, they 're free from all pain:
They sleep their last sleep, they have fought their last battle!
  No sound can awake them to glory again!

Yet, spirit immortal, the tomb cannot bind thee,
  For, like thine own eagle that soar'd to the sun,
Thou springest from bondage and leavest behind thee
  A name which before thee no mortal had won.
Though nations may combat, and war's thunders rattle,
  No more on the steed wilt thou sweep o'er the plain:
Thou sleep'st thy last sleep, thou hast fought thy last battle!
  No sound can awake thee to glory again!

ANONYMOUS.

Widow Malone.

DID you hear of the Widow Malone,
    Ohone!
Who lived in the town of Athlone,
    Alone!
    O, she melted the hearts
    Of the swains in them parts,—
So lovely the Widow Malone,
    Ohone!
So lovely the Widow Malone.

Of lovers she had a full score,
    Or more,

13*

And fortunes they all had galore,
    In store;
  From the minister down
  To the clerk of the Crown,
All were courting the Widow Malone,
    Ohone!
All were courting the Widow Malone.

But so modest was Mistress Malone,
    'T was known
That no one could see her alone,
    Ohone!
  Let them ogle and sigh,
  They could ne'er catch her eye,
So bashful the Widow Malone,
    Ohone!
So bashful the Widow Malone.

Till one Misther O'Brien, from Clare,
    (How quare!
It 's little for blushing they care
    Down there)
  Put his arm round her waist,—
  Gave ten kisses at laste,—
"O," says he, "you 're my Molly Malone,
    My own!"
"O," says he, "you 're my Molly Malone."

And the widow they all thought so shy,
    My eye!
Ne'er thought of a simper or sigh,—
    For why?
  But, "Lucius," says she,
  "Since you've now made so free,
You may marry your Mary Malone,
    Ohone!
You may marry your Mary Malone."

There 's a moral contained in my song,
    Not wrong;
And one comfort, it 's not very long,
    But strong :
    If for widows you die,
    Learn to kiss, not to sigh;
For they 're all like sweet Mistress Malone,
    Ohone!
O, they 're all like sweet Mistress Malone.

CHARLES LEVER.

Lament of the Irish Emigrant.

I 'M sittin' on the stile, Mary,
    Where we sat side by side,
On a bright May mornin' long ago,
    When first you were my bride;
The corn was springin' fresh and green,
    And the lark sang loud and high;
And the red was on your lip, Mary,
    And the love-light in your eye.

The place is little changed, Mary;
    The day is bright as then;
The lark's loud song is in my ear,
    And the corn is green again;
But I miss the soft clasp of your hand,
    And your breath, warm on my cheek;
And I still keep list'nin' for the words
    You never more will speak.

'T is but a step down yonder lane,
    And the little church stands near,
The church where we were wed, Mary;
    I see the spire from here.
But the grave-yard lies between, Mary,
    And my step might break your rest,

For I 've laid you, darling, down to sleep,
　　With your baby on your breast.

I 'm very lonely now, Mary—
　　For the poor make no new friends;
But, O, they love the better still
　　The few our Father sends!
And you were all I had, Mary,
　　My blessin' and my pride:
There 's nothing left to care for now,
　　Since my poor Mary died.

Yours was the good, brave heart, Mary,
　　That still kept hoping on,
When the trust in God had left my soul,
　　And my arm's young strength was gone;
There was comfort ever on your lip,
　　And the kind look on your brow,
I bless you, Mary, for that same,
　　Though you cannot hear me now.

I thank you for the patient smile
　　When your heart was fit to break,
When the hunger-pain was gnawin' there,
　　And you hid it for my sake;
I bless you for the pleasant word,
　　When your heart was sad and sore,
Oh! I 'm thankful you are gone, Mary,
　　Where grief can't reach you more!

I 'm biddin' you a long farewell,
　　My Mary, kind and true!
But I 'll not forget you, darling,
　　In the land I 'm goin' to;
They say there 's bread and work for all,
　　And the sun shines always there,
But I 'll not forget old Ireland,
　　Were it fifty times as fair!

And often in those grand old woods
  I 'll sit, and shut my eyes,
And my heart will travel back again
  To the place where Mary lies;
And I 'll think I see the little stile
  Where we sat side by side,
And the springin' corn, and the bright May morn,
  When first you were my bride.
LADY DUFFERIN.

The Happy Land.

THERE is a happy land,
  Far, far away,
Where saints in glory stand,
  Bright, bright as day.
Oh, how they sweetly sing,
Worthy is our Saviour King;
Loud let his praises ring—
  Praise, praise for aye.

Come to this happy land—
  Come, come away;
Why will ye doubting stand—
  Why still delay?
Oh, we shall happy be,
When, from sin and sorrow free,
Lord, we shall live with thee—
  Blest, blest for aye.

Bright in that happy land
  Beams every eye:
Kept by a Father's hand,
  Love cannot die.
On then to glory run;
Be a crown and kingdom won;
And bright above the sun,
  Reign, reign for aye.
ANDREW YOUNG.

Gluggity Glug.

A JOLLY fat friar loved liquor good store,
    And he had drunk stoutly at supper;
He mounted his horse in the night at the door,
    And sat with his face to the crupper.
"Some rogue," quoth the friar, "quite dead to remorse,
    Some thief, whom a halter will throttle,
Some scoundrel has cut off the head of my horse,
    While I was engaged at the bottle,
        Which went gluggity, gluggity—glug—glug—glug."

The tail of the steed pointed south on the dale,
    'T was the friar's road home, straight and level;
But, when spurred, a horse follows his nose, not his tail,
    So he scampered due north like a devil.
"This new mode of docking," the friar then said,
    "I perceive does n't make a horse trot ill;
"And 't is cheap, for he never can eat off his head
    While I am engaged at the bottle,
        Which goes gluggity, gluggity—glug—glug—glug."

The steed made a stop—in a pond he had got,
    He was rather for drinking than grazing;
Quoth the friar, "'T is strange headless horses should trot,
    But to drink with their tails is amazing!"
Turning round to see whence this phenomenon rose,
    In the pond fell this son of a pottle;
Quoth he, "The head 's found, for I 'm under his nose,—
    I wish I were over a bottle,
        Which goes gluggity, gluggity—glug—glug—glug."
                      ANONYMOUS.

Here she Goes—and There she Goes.

Two Yankee wags, one summer day,
Stopped at a tavern on their way;

Supped, frolicked, late retired to rest,
And woke to breakfast on the best.

The breakfast over, Tom and Will
Sent for the landlord and the bill;
Will looked it over; " Very right—
But hold! what wonder meets my sight?
Tom! the surprise is quite a shock! "
" What wonder? where? "   " The clock! the clock! "

Tom and the landlord in amaze
Stared at the clock with stupid gaze,
And for a moment neither spoke;
At last the landlord silence broke:

" You mean the clock that 's ticking there?
  I see no wonder, I declare;
  Though may be, if the truth were told,
  'T is rather ugly—somewhat old;
  Yet time it keeps to half a minute,
  But, if you please, what wonder 's in it? "

" Tom, do n't you recollect," said Will,
" The clock in Jersey near the mill,
  The very image of this present,
  With which I won the wager pleasant? "
  Will ended with a knowing wink—
  Tom scratched his head, and tried to think.
" Sir, begging pardon for inquiring,"
  The landlord said, with grin admiring,
" What wager was it? "

                " You remember,
It happened, Tom, in last December.
In sport I bet a Jersey Blue
That it was more than he could do,
To make his finger go and come

In keeping with the pendulum,
Repeating, till one hour should close,
Still '*Here she goes—and there she goes*'—
He lost the bet in half a minute."

"Well, if I would, the deuce is in it!"
Exclaimed the landlord; "try me yet,
And fifty dollars be the bet."
"Agreed, but we will play some trick
To make you of the bargain sick!"
"I 'm up to that!"

　　　　　"Do n't make us wait;
Begin, the clock is striking eight."
He seats himself, and left and right
His finger wags with all his might,
And hoarse his voice, and hoarser grows,
With "*Here she goes—and there she goes!*"

"Hold," said the Yankee, "plank the ready!"
The landlord wagged his fingers steady
While his left hand, as well as able,
Conveyed a purse upon the table.
"Tom, with the money let 's be off!"
This made the landlord only scoff.

He heard them running down the stair,
But was not tempted from his chair.
Thought he, "The fools! I 'll bite them yet!
So poor a trick sha' n't win the bet."
And loud and loud the chorus rose
Of "*Here she goes—and there she goes!*"
While right and left his finger swung,
In keeping to his clock and tongue.

His mother happened in, to see
Her daughter. "Where is Mrs. B—
When will she come, as you suppose?
Son!"

" *Here she goes—and there she goes !* "
" Here! where ? "—the lady in surprise
  His finger followed with her eyes;
" Son, why that steady gaze and sad ?
  Those words—that motion—are you mad ?
  But here 's your wife—perhaps she knows,
  And—"
    " *Here she goes—and there she goes !* "

His wife surveyed him with alarm,
And rushed to him and seized his arm;
He shook her off, and to and fro
His finger persevered to go,
While curled his very nose with ire,
That *she* against him should conspire,
And with more furious tone arose
The " *Here she goes—and there she goes !* "

" Lawks! " screamed the wife, " I 'm in a whirl!
  Run down and bring the little girl;
  She is his darling, and who knows
  But—"
    " *Here she goes—and there she goes !* "

" Lawks! he is mad!   What made him thus ?
  Good Lord! what will become of us ?
  Run for a doctor—run—run—run —
  For Doctor Brown, and Doctor Dun,
  And Doctor Black, and Doctor White,
  And Doctor Grey, with all your might."

The doctors came, and looked and wondered,
And shook their heads, and paused and pondered,
Till one proposed he should be bled,
" No—leeched, you mean," the other said—
" Clap on a blister," roared another,
" No—cup him "—" No—trepan him, brother! "

A sixth would recommend a purge,
The next would an emetic urge,
The eighth, just come from a dissection,
His verdict gave for an injection;
The last produced a box of pills,
A certain cure for earthly ills;
"I had a patient yesternight,"
Quoth he, "and wretched was her plight,
And as the only means to save her,
Three dozen patent pills I gave her,
And by to-morrow, I suppose
That—"
    "*Here she goes—and there she goes!*"

"You all are fools," the lady said,
"The way is, just to shave his head,
  Run, bid the barber come anon—"
"Thanks, mother," thought her clever son,
" *You* help the knaves that would have bit me,
  But all creation sha' n't outwit me!"
Thus to himself, while to and fro
His finger perseveres to go,
And from his lips no accent flows
But "*Here she goes—and there she goes!*"
The barber came—"Lord help him! what
A queer customer I 've got;
But we must do our best to save him—
So hold him, gemmen, while I shave him!"
But here the doctors interpose—
"A woman never—"
       "*There she goes!*"

"A woman is no judge of physic,
  Not even when her baby is sick.
  He must be bled"—"No—no—a blister"—
"A purge you mean"—"I say a clyster"—
"No—cup him"—"leech him"—"pills! pills! pills!"
And all the house the uproar fills.

What means that smile?   What means that shiver?
The landlord's limbs with rapture quiver,
And triumph brightens up his face—
His finger yet shall win the race!
The clock is on the stroke of nine—
And up he starts—"'T is mine! 't is mine!"
"What do you mean?"

"I mean the fifty!
I never spent an hour so thrifty;
But you, who tried to make me lose,
Go, burst with envy, if you choose!
But how is this!   Where are they?"

"Who?"
"The gentlemen—I mean the two
Came yesterday—are they below?"
"They galloped off an hour ago."
"Oh, purge me! blister! shave and bleed!
For, hang the knaves, I 'm mad indeed!"

JAMES NACK.

She Died in Beauty.

SHE died in beauty,—like a rose
  Blown from its parent stem;
She died in beauty,—like a pearl
  Dropped from some diadem.

She died in beauty,—like a lay
  Along a moonlit lake;
She died in beauty,—like the song
  Of birds amid the brake.

She died in beauty,—like the snow
  On flowers dissolved away;
She died in beauty,—like a star
  Lost on the brow of day.

She lives in glory,—like night's gems
　　Set round the silver moon ;
She lives in glory,—like the sun
　　Amid the blue of June.

CHARLES DOYNE SILLERY.

The New Tale of a Tub.

THE Orient day was fresh and and fair,
A breeze sang soft in the ambient air,
Men almost wondered to find it there,
　　Blowing so near Bengal,
Where waters bubble as boiled in a pot,
And the gold of the sun spreads melting hot,
And there 's hardly a breath of wind to be got
　　At any price at all.
Unless, indeed, when the great Simoom
Gets up from its bed with the voice of doom,
　　And deserts no rains e'er drench
Rise up and roar with a dreadful gust,
Pillars of sand and clouds of dust
Rushing on drifted, and rapid to burst,
And filling all India's throat with thirst
　　That its Ganges couldn't quench.

No great Simoom rose up to-day,
　　But only a gentle breeze,
And that of such silent and voiceless play
　　　That a lady's bustle
　　　Had made more rustle
　　Than *it* did among the trees.
'T was not like the breath of a British vale,
Where each Green acre is blessed with a Gale
　　Whenever the natives please ;
But it was of that soft inviting sort
That it tempted to revel in picnic sport
　　A couple of Bengalese.

Two Bengalese
Resolved to seize
The balmy chance of that cool-winged weather,
To revel in Bengal ease together.
One was tall, the other was stout,
They were natives both of the glorious East,
And both so fond of a rural feast
That off they roamed to a country plain,
Where the breeze roved free about,
That during its visits brief, at least,
If it never were able to blow again,
It might blow upon their blow-out.

The country plain gave a view as small
As ever man clapped his eyes on,
Where the sense of sight did easily pall,
For it kept on seeing nothing at all,
As far as the far horizon.
Nothing at all!—Oh! what do I say?—
Something certainly stood in the way
(Though it had neither cloth nor tray,
With its " tiffin " I would n't quarrel)—
It was a sort of hermaphrodite thing,
(It might have been filled with sugar or ling
But is very unfit for a muse to sing),
Betwixt a tub and a barrel.

It stood in the midst of that Indian plain,
Burning with sunshine, pining for rain,
A parenthesis balanced 'twixt pleasure and pain,
And as stiff as if it were starching,—
When up to it, over the brown and green
Of that Indian soil, were suddenly seen
Two gentlemen anxiously marching.
Those two gentlemen were, if you please,
The aforesaid couple of Bengalese;
And the tub or barrel that stood beyond—
14*

For short we will call it Tub—
   Contained with pride,
   In its jolly inside,
The prize of which they were dotingly fond,
   The aforesaid gentlemen's grub.

"Leave us alone—come man or come beast,"
Said the eldest, "We 'll soon have a shy at the feast."

They are now at their picnic with might and with main.
But what do we see in the front of the plain?
   A jungle, a thicket of bush, weed, and grass,
   And in it reposing—eh?—no, not an ass—
   Not an ass, not an ass,—that could not come to pass;
No donkey, no donkey, no donkey at all,
But, superb in his slumber, a Royal Bengal.
   Though Royal, he was n't a king—
   No such thing!
He did n't rule lands from the Thames to the Niger,
   But he did hold a reign
   O'er that jungle and plain,
And besides was a very magnificent Tiger.

   There he lay, in his skin so gay,
His passions at rest, and his appetites curbed;
   A Minister Prime,
   In his proudest time,
Asleep, was never more undisturbed;
   For who would come to shake him?
O, it 's certain sure, in his dream demure,
   That none would dare to wake him.
Only the Royal snore may creep
Over the dreams of a Tiger's sleep.

The Bengalese, in cool apparel,
Meanwhile have reached their picnic barrel;
In other words, they have tossed the grub

Out of their great provision Tub,
  And, standing it up for shelter,
Sit guzzling underneath its shade,
With a glorious dinner ready-made,
  Which they're eating helter-skelter.
Ham and chicken, and bread and cheese,
  They make a pass to spread on the grass.
They sit at ease, with their plates on their knees,
And now their hungry jaws they appease,
  And now they turn to the glass;
      For Hodgson's ale
      Is genuine pale,
      And the bright champagne
      Flows not in vain,
      The most convivial souls to please
      Of these very thirsty Bengalese.

Ha! one of the two has relinquished his fork,
And wakes up the Tiger by drawing a cork.

      Blurting and spurting!
      List! O list!
      Perhaps the Tiger thinks he is hissed.
Effervescing and whizzed and phizzed!
Perhaps his Majesty thinks he is quizzed,
      Or haply deems,
      As he 's roused from his dreams,
That his visions have come to a thirsty stop,
And resolves to moisten his throat with a drop.

At all events, with body and soul,
He gives in his jungle a stretch and a roll,
Then regally rises to go for a stroll,
      With a temperate mind,
      For a beast of his kind,
      And a tail uncommonly long behind.

He knows of no water,
　By field or by flood;　·
He does not seek slaughter,
　He does not scent blood.
　　　No! the utmost scope
　　　Of his limited hope
　　　　Is, that these
　　　　Bengalese,
When they find he arrives,
May not rise from their picnic and run for their lives,
　But simply bow on that beautiful plain,
　And offer Sir Tiger a glass of champagne.
　"From my jungle it true is
　　They woke me, I think,
　So the least they can do is
　　To give me some drink."

Gently Tiger crouches along,
Humming a kind of animal song,
　A sweet subdued familiar lay
　As ever was warbled by beast of prey;
And all so softly, tunefully done,
　That it made no more sound
　Than his shade on the ground;
So the Bengalese heard it, never a one!

Gently Tiger steals along,
　"Mild as a moonbeam," meek as a lamb,—
What so suddenly changes his song
　　From a tune to a growl?
　　"Och! by my sowl,
　Nothing on earth but the smell of the ham!"
　　He quickens his pace,
　　　The illigant baste,
　　And he's running a race
　　　With himself for a taste.
And he's taken to roaring, and given up humming,
Just to let the two Bengalese know he is coming.

What terrors sieze
The Bengalese
As the roar of the Tiger reaches the ear,
Their hair is standing on end with fear.
Short-and-stout, with *his* hair all gray,
Has a rattling note in his jolly old throat;
If choking his laugh with a truss of hay,
He could n't more surely have stifled the gay.
While Tall-and-thin with *his* hair all carroty,
Looks thrice as red with fright as his head,
And his face bounds plump, at a single jump,
Into horror, and out of hilarity.
All they can hear, in their terrible fear,
Behind and before, is the Tiger's roar;
Again and again, o'er the plain,
Clearer and clearer, nearer and nearer,
Into the Tub now its way it has found,
Where its echoes keep rolling round and round,
Till out of the bung-hole they bursting come,
Like a regiment of thunders escaped from a drum.

If an earthquake had shattered a thousand kegs,
The terrified Bengalese could n't, i' fegs,
Have leapt more rapidly on to their legs.
He 's at 'em, he 's on 'em, the jungle guest!
When a man's life by peril is prest,
His wits will sometimes be at their best.
So the presence of Tiger, I find,
Inspires our heroes with presence of mind.
There 's no time to be lost—
Down the glasses are tossed;
The Bengalese have abandoned their grub,
And they 're dodging their gentleman round the Tub.
Active and earnest they nowhere lodge,
And he can't get at them, because of their dodge.
Short-and-stout and Tall-and-thin
Never before such a scrape were in,

15

Nor ever yet used—can you well have a doubt of it?—
So uncommonly artful a dodge to get out of it.
   Tiger keeps prowling,
    Howling, and growling;
  He feels himself that their dodge is clever;
But the quick fresh blood of the Bengalese
Nicer and nicer he snuffs on the breeze.
The more they practice their dodge recitals,
The more he longs to dine on their vitals.
His passion is up, his hunger is keen,
His jaws are ready, his teeth are clean,
  And sharpened their limbs to sever.
 The fire is flashing in light from his eyes;
 In his own peculiar manner he cries,
   The while they shine,
   "If I mean to dine,
   I had better begin,"
   And then, with a grin,
And a voice the loudest that ever was heard,
He roars, "Never trust to a tiger's word,
  If this dodge shall last much longer!
  No, no, no, no,—it shall be no go!
There 's a way of disturbing this Tub's repose;
   So down on your knees,
   You Bengalese,
  And prepare to be eaten up, if you please.
   Here goes!
Here goes! here goes!" and he gave a spring.
The gentlemen, looking for no such thing,
Might have fallen a prey to the Tiger's fling;
  But a certain interference,
Which bursts from their most intelligent Tub,
May enable them to return to their grub,
  On the selfsame plain a year hence.
The Tub, though empty of roll and ration,
Is full of a certain preservation,
 Of which—though it does not follow

In every case of argumentation-
    It is full because it is hollow.
For, not having a top, and no inside things,
It turns top-heavy when Tiger springs,
And, making a kind of balancing pause,
Keeps holding the animal up by his claws,
        In a manner that seems to fret it;
While Short-and-stout, in a state of doubt,
Keeps on his belly a sharp lookout;
And Tall-and-thin, with an impudent grin,
            Exults in his way,
            As much as to say,
    "I only wish you may get it!
But much as I may respect your ability,
I don't see at present the great probability."

The Tiger has leapt up, heart and soul.
It 's clear he meant to go the whole
Hog, in his hungry efforts to seize
The two defianceful Bengalese.
            But the Tub! the Tub!
            Ay, there 's the rub!
            At present he 's balanced atop of the Tub,
            His fore legs inside,
            And the rest of his hide,
Not weighing so much as his head and his legs,
            And having no hand in
            A pure understandin'
Of the just equilibrium of casks and of kegs,
            Not bred up in attics,
            Nor taught mathematics,
To work out the problems of Euclid with pegs,—
He has plunged with the impetus wild of a lover,
And the Tub has loomed large, balanced, paused, and
        turned over.

The Tiger at first had a hobby-horse ride,
But now he is decently quartered inside;

And the question is next, long as fortune may frown on
    him,
How the two Bengalese are to keep the Tub down on
    him.
      'Bout this there's no blunder,
      The Tiger is under
        The Tub!
      My verse need not run
        To the length of a sonnet,
      To tell how the Bengalese
        Both jumped upon it,
      While the beautiful barrel
        Keeps acting as bonnet
      To the Tiger inside,
      Who no more in his pride
Can roam over jungle and plain,
But sheltered alike from the sun and the rain,
    Around its interior his sides deigns to rub
    With a fearful hub-bub,
And longs for his freedom again.

      The two Bengalese,
      Not at all at their ease,
      Hear him roar,
      And deplore
      Their prospects as sore,
    Forgetting both picnic and flask;
      Each, wondering, dumb,
      What of both will become,
    Helps the other to press on the cask;
      Resigned to their fate,
      But increasing their weight
    By action of muscle and sinew,
      In order that forcibly you, Mr. Tub,
        Whom their niggers this morning
    Rolled here with their grub,
    May still keep the Tiger within you.

On the top of the Tub,
In the warmest of shirts,
The thin man stands,
While the fat by his skirts
Holds, anxiously puffing and blowing;
And the thin peers over the top of the cask,
"Is there any hope for us?"
As much as to ask,
With a countenance cunning and knowing;
And just as he mournfully 'gins to bewail,
In a grief-song that ought to be sung whole,
He twigs the long end of the old Tiger's tail
As it twists itself out of the bung-hole.
Then, sharp on the watch,
He gives it a catch,
And shouts to the Tiger,
"You 've now got your match;
You may rush and may riot, may wriggle and roar,
But I 'm blest if I 'll let your tail go any more!"
It 's as safe as a young roasted pig in a larder,
And no two Bengalese could hold on by it harder.
With the Tiger's tail clenched fast in his fist,
And his own coat-tail grasped fast to assist,
Stands Tall-and-thin with Short-and-stout,
Both on the top of the Tub to scout,
Tiger within and they without,
And both in a pretty pickle.
The Tiger begins by giving a bound;
The Tub 's half turned, but the men are found
To have very carefully jumped to the ground—
At trifles they must not stickle.
It 's no use quaking and turning pale,
Pluck and patience must now prevail,
They must keep a hold on the Tiger's tail,
And neither one be fickle.
There they must pull, if they pull for weeks,
Straining their stomachs and bursting their cheeks,

While Tiger alternately roars and squeaks,
    Trying to break away from 'em;
They must keep the Tub turned over his back,
And never let his long tail get slack,
    For fear he should win the day from 'em.
Yes, yes, they must hold him tight,
From night till morning, from morn till night,—
Must n't stop to eat, must n't stop to weep,
Must n't stop to drink, must n't stop to sleep,—
No cry, no laugh, no rest, no grub,
Till they starve the Tiger under the Tub,
        Till the animal dies,
        To his own surprise,
With two Bengalese in a deadly quarrel,
And his tail thrust through the hole of a barrel.

Oh dear! oh dear! it 's very clear
They can't live so; but they dare n't let go—
Fate for a pitying world to wail,
Starving behind a Tiger's tail.
If Invention be Necessity's son,
Now let him tell them what 's to be done.
What 's to be done! ha! I see a grin
Of joy on the face of Tall-and-thin,
Some new device he has hit in a trice,
The which he is telling all about
To the gratified gentleman, Short-and-stout.
What 's to be done! what precious fun!
Have n't they found out what 's to be done!
See! see! what glorious glee!
Note! mark! what a capital lark!
Tiger and Tub, and bung-hole and all,
Baffled by what is about to befall.
Excellent! marvelous! beautiful! O!
Is n't it now an original go!
What, stop! I 'm ready to drop.
Hold! stay! I 'm fainting away.

Laughter I 'm certain will kill me to-day;
And Short-and-stout is bursting his skin,
And almost in fits is Tall-and-thin,
And Tiger is free, yet they do not quail,
  Though temper has all gone wrong with him.
No! they 've tied a knot in the Tiger's tail,
  And he carried the Tub along with him;
He 's a freehold for life, with a tail out of joint,
And has made his last climax a true knotty point.

FREDERICK W. N. BAYLEY.

The Old Sexton.

NIGH to a grave that was newly made,
Leaned a sexton old on his earth-worn spade;
His work was done, and he paused to wait
The funeral-train at the open gate.
A relic of by-gone days was he,
And his locks were gray as the foamy sea;
And these words came from his lips so thin:
" I gather them in—I gather them in—
  Gather—gather—I gather them in.

" I gather them in; for man and boy,
  Year after year of grief and joy,
  I 've builded the houses that lie around
  In every nook of this burial ground.
  Mother and daughter, father and son,
  Come to my solitude one by one;
  But come they stranger, or come they kin,
  I gather them in—I gather them in.

" Many are with me, yet I 'm alone;
  I 'm King of the Dead, and I make my throne
  On a monument slab of marble cold—
  My sceptre of rule is the spade I hold.

Come they from cottage, or come they from hall,
Mankind are my subjects, all, all, all!
May they loiter in pleasure, or toilfully spin,
I gather them in—I gather them in.

" I gather them in, and their final rest
Is here, down here, in the earth's dark breast ! "
And the sexton ceased as the funeral-train
Wound mutely over that solemn plain;
And I said to myself: When time is told,
A mightier voice than that sexton's old,
Will be heard o'er the last trump's dreadful din;
" I gather them in—I gather them in—
Gather—gather—gather them in."

PARK BENJAMIN.

The Private of the Buffs.

LAST night among his fellow-roughs,
    He jested, quaffed, and swore;
A drunken private of the Buffs,
    Who never looked before.
To-day, beneath the foeman's frown,
    He stands in Elgin's place,
Ambassador from Britain's crown,
    And type of all her race.

Poor, reckless, rude, low-born, untaught,
    Bewildered, and alone,
A heart with English instinct fraught
    He yet can call his own.
Ay, tear his body limb from limb,
    Bring cord or axe or flame,
He only knows that not through him
· Shall England come to shame.

Far Kentish hop-fields round him seemed,
    Like dreams, to come and go;

Bright leagues of cherry-blossom gleamed,
   One sheet of living snow;
The smoke above his father's door
   In gray soft eddyings hung;
Must he then watch it rise no more,
   Doomed by himself so young?

Yes, honor calls!—with strength like steel
   He put the vision by;
Let dusky Indians whine and kneel,
   An English lad must die.
And thus, with eyes that would not shrink,
   With knee to man unbent,
Unfaltering on its dreadful brink,
   To his red grave he went.

Vain mightiest fleets of iron framed,
   Vain those all-shattering guns,
Unless proud England keep untamed
   The strong heart of her sons;
So let his name through Europe ring,—
   A man of mean estate,
Who died, as firm as Sparta's king,
   Because his soul was great.
             SIR FRANCIS HASTINGS DOYLE.

Light.

FROM the quickened womb of the primal gloom
   The sun rolled black and bare,
Till I wove him a vest for his Ethiop breast
   Of the threads of my golden hair;
And when the broad tent of the firmament
   Arose on its airy spars,
I penciled the hue of its matchless blue,
   And spangled it round with stars.
    15*

I painted the flowers of the Eden bowers,
    And their leaves of living green,
And mine were the dyes in the sinless eyes
    Of Eden's virgin queen;
And when the fiend's art on the trustful heart
    Had fastened its mortal spell,
In the silvery sphere of the first-born tear
    To the trembling earth I fell.

When the waves that burst o'er the world accurs'd
    Their work of wrath had sped,
And the Ark's lone few, the tried and true,
    Came forth among the dead;
With the wond'rous gleams of my bridal beams,
    I bade their terrors cease,
As I wrote, on the roll of the storm's dark scroll,
    God's covenant of peace!

Like a pall at rest on a senseless breast,
    Night's funeral shadow slept;—
Where shepherd swains on the Bethlehem plains
    Their lonely vigils kept—
When I flashed on their sight the heralds bright
    Of Heaven's redeeming plan,
As they chanted the morn of a Saviour born—
    Joy, joy to the outcast man!

Equal favor I show to the lofty and low,
    On the just and unjust I descend;
E'en the blind, whose vain spheres roll in darkness and tears,
    Feel my smile, the blest smile of a friend.
Nay, the flower of the waste by my love is embraced,
    As the rose in the garden of Kings;
At the chrysalis bier of the worm I appear,
    And lo! the gay butterfly wings.

The desolate Morn, like a mourner forlorn,
    Conceals all the pride of her charms,

Till I bid the bright hours chase night from her bowers,
  And lead the young day to her arms;
And when the gay Rover seeks Eve for his lover,
  And sinks to her balmy repose,
I wrap their soft rest by the zephyr-fanned west,
  In curtains of amber and rose.

From my sentinel steep, by the night-brooded deep,
  I gaze with unslumbering eye,
When the cynosure star of the mariner
  Is blotted from out of the sky;
And guided by me through the merciless sea,
  Though sped by the hurricane's wings,
His compassless bark, lone, weltering dark,
  To the haven-home safely he brings.

I waken the flowers in their dew-spangled bowers,
  The birds in their chambers of green,
And mountain and plain glow with beauty again,
  As they bask in my matinal sheen.
Oh, if such the glad worth of my presence to earth,
  Though fitful and fleeting the while,
What glories must rest on the home of the blest,
  Ever bright with the Deity's smile!

WILLIAM PITT PALMER.

A Death=Bed.

Her suffering ended with the day;
  Yet lived she at its close,
And breathed the long, long night away
  In statue-like repose.

But when the sun, in all his state,
  Illumed the eastern skies,
She passed through glory's morning-gate,
  And walked in Paradise.

JAMES ALDRICH.

A Christmas Hymn.

It was the calm and silent night!
  Seven hundred years and fifty-three
Had Rome been growing up to might,
  And now was queen of land and sea.
No sound was heard of clashing wars,—
  Peace brooded o'er the hushed domain:
Apollo, Pallas, Jove, and Mars
  Held undisturbed their ancient reign,
      In the solemn midnight,
        Centuries ago.

'T was in the calm and silent night!
  The senator of haughty Rome,
Impatient, urged his chariot's flight,
  From lordly revel rolling home;
Triumphal arches, gleaming, swell
  His breast with thoughts of boundless sway;
What recked the Roman what befell
  A paltry province far away,
      In the solemn midnight,
        Centuries ago?

Within that province far away
  Went plodding home a weary boor;
A streak of light before him lay,
  Fallen through a half-shut stable-door,
Across his path.   He passed, for naught
  Told what was going on within;
How keen the stars, his only thought—
  The air, how calm, and cold, and thin,
      In the solemn midnight,
        Centuries ago!

Oh, strange indifference! low and high
  Drowsed over common joys and cares;

The earth was still, but knew not why;
  The world was listening, unawares.
How calm a moment may precede
  One that shall thrill the world forever!
To that still moment, none would heed,
  Man's doom was linked no more to sever,
    In the solemn midnight,
      Centuries ago!

It is the calm and solemn night!
  A thousand bells ring out, and throw
Their joyous peals abroad, and smite
  The darkness, charmed and holy now!
The night that erst no name had worn,
  To it a happy name is given;
For in that stable lay, new-born,
  The peaceful Prince of earth and heaven,
    In the solemn midnight,
      Centuries ago!

ALFRED DOMMET.

The Ivy Green.

O, A DAINTY plant is the ivy green,
  That creepeth o'er ruins old!
Of right choice food are his meals, I ween,
  In his cell so lone and cold.
The walls must be crumbled, the stones decayed,
  To pleasure his dainty whim;
And the mouldering dust that years have made
  Is a merry meal for him.
    Creeping where no life is seen,
    A rare old plant is the ivy green.

Fast he stealeth on, though he wears no wings,
  And a stanch old heart has he!
16

How closely he twineth, how tight he clings
  To his friend, the huge oak-tree!
And slyly he traileth along the ground,
  And his leaves he gently waves,
And he joyously twines and hugs around
  The rich mould of dead men's graves.
    Creeping where no life is seen,
    A rare old plant is the ivy green.

Whole ages have fled, and their works decayed,
  And nations have scattered been;
But the stout old ivy shall never fade
  From its hale and hearty green.
The brave old plant in its lonely days
  Shall fatten upon the past;
For the stateliest building man can raise
  Is the ivy's food at last.
    Creeping where no life is seen,
    A rare old plant is the ivy green.
                CHARLES DICKENS.

The Polish Boy.

WHENCE come those shrieks so wild and shrill,
  That cut, like blades of steel, the air,
Causing the creeping blood to chill
  With the sharp cadence of despair?

Again they come, as if a heart
  Were cleft in twain by one quick blow,
And every string had voice apart
  To utter its peculiar woe.

Whence come they? From yon temple, where
An altar, raised for private prayer,
Now forms the warrior's marble bed
Who Warsaw's gallant armies led.

The dim funereal tapers throw
A holy lustre o'er his brow,
And burnish with their rays of light
The mass of curls that gather bright
Above the haughty brow and eye
Of a young boy that 's kneeling by.

What hand is that, whose icy press
  Clings to the dead with death's own grasp,
But meets no answering caress?
  No thrilling fingers seek its clasp.
It is the hand of her whose cry
  Rang wildly, late, upon the air,
When the dead warrior met her eye
  Outstretched upon the altar there.

With pallid lip and stony brow
She murmurs forth her anguish now.
But hark! the tramp of heavy feet
Is heard along the bloody street;
Nearer and nearer yet they come,
With clanking arms and noiseless drum.
Now whispered curses, low and deep,
Around the holy temple creep;
The gate is burst; a ruffian band
Rush in, and savagely demand,
With brutal voice and oath profane,
The startled boy for exile's chain.

The mother sprang with gesture wild,
And to her bosom clasped her child;
Then, with pale cheek and flashing eye,
Shouted with fearful energy,
" Back, ruffians, back! nor dare to tread
Too near the body of my dead;
Nor touch the living boy; I stand
Between him and your lawless band.

Take *me*, and bind these arms, these hands,
With Russia's heaviest iron bands,
And drag me to Siberia's wild
To perish, if 't will save my child!"

"Peace, woman, peace!" the leader cried,
Tearing the pale boy from her side,
And in his ruffian grasp he bore
His victim to the temple door.
"One moment!" shrieked the mother; "one!
Will land or gold redeem my son?
Take heritage, take name, take all,
But leave him free from Russia's thrall!
Take these!" and her white arms and hands
She stripped of rings and diamond bands,
And tore from braids of long black hair
The gems that gleamed like starlight there;
Her cross of blazing rubies, last,
Down at the Russian's feet she cast.
He stooped to seize the glittering store;—
Up springing from the marble floor,
The mother, with a cry of joy,
Snatched to her leaping heart the boy.
But no!   The Russian's iron grasp
Again undid the mother's clasp.
Forward she fell, with one long cry
Of more than mortal agony.

But the brave child is roused at length,
    And, breaking from the Russian's hold,
He stands, a giant in the strength
    Of his young spirit, fierce and bold.
Proudly he towers; his flashing eye,
    So blue, and yet so bright,
Seems kindled from the eternal sky,
    So brilliant is its light.
His curling lips and crimson cheeks
Foretell the thought before he speaks;

With a full voice of proud command
He turned upon the wondering band:
" Ye hold me not! no! no, nor can;
This hour has made the boy a man.
I knelt before my slaughtered sire,
Nor felt one throb of vengeful ire.
I wept upon his marble brow,
Yes, wept! I was a child; but now
My noble mother, on her knee,
Hath done the work of years for me ! "
He drew aside his broidered vest,
And there, like slumbering serpent's crest,
The jeweled haft of poniard bright
Glittered a moment on the sight.
" Ha! start ye back? Fool! coward! knave!
Think ye my noble father's glaive
Would drink the life-blood of a slave?
The pearls that on the handle flame,
Would blush to rubies in their shame;
The blade would quiver in thy breast
Ashamed of such ignoble rest.
No! thus I rend the tyrant's chain,
And fling him back a boy's disdain! "

A moment, and the funeral light
Flashed on the jeweled weapon bright;
Another, and his young heart's blood
Leaped to the floor, a crimson flood.
Quick to his mother's side he sprang,
And on the air his clear voice rang:
" Up, mother, up! I 'm free! I 'm free!
The choice was death or slavery.
Up, mother, up! Look on thy son!
His freedom is forever won;
And now he waits one holy kiss
To bear his father home in bliss,
One last embrace, one blessing,—one!
To prove thou know'st, approv'st thy son.

What! silent yet?   Canst thou not feel
My warm blood o'er thy heart congeal?
Speak, mother, speak! lift up thy head!
What! silent still?   Then art thou dead!
——Great God, I thank thee!   Mother, I
Rejoice with thee,—and thus—to die."
One long, deep breath, and his pale head
Lay on his mother's bosom,—dead.

Ann S. Stephens.

Balaklava.

O THE charge at Balaklava!
    O that rash and fatal charge!
Never was a fiercer, braver,
    Than that charge at Balaklava,
        On the battle's bloody marge!
All the day the Russian columns,
        Fortress huge, and blazing banks,
Poured their dread destructive volumes
        On the French and English ranks,—
        On the gallant allied ranks!
Earth and sky seemed rent asunder
By the loud incessant thunder!
When a strange but stern command—
Needless, heedless, rash command—
Came to Lucan's little band,—
Scarce six hundred men and horses
Of those vast contending forces:—
" England 's lost unless you save her!
Charge the pass at Balaklava! "
        O that rash and fatal charge,
        On the battle's bloody marge!

Far away the Russian Eagles
    Soar o'er smoking hill and dell,
And their hordes, like howling beagles,
    Dense and countless, round them yell!

Thundering cannon, deadly mortar,
Sweep the field in every quarter!
Never, since the days of Jesus,
Trembled so the Chersonesus!
    Here behold the Gallic Lilies—
    Stout St. Louis' golden Lilies—
    Float as erst at old Ramillies!
    And beside them, lo! the Lion!
    With her trophied Cross, is flying!
Glorious standards!—shall they waver
On the field of Balaklava?
No, by Heavens! at that command—
Sudden, rash, but stern command—
Charges Lucan's little band!
    Brave Six Hundred! lo! they charge,
    On the battle's bloody marge!

Down yon deep and skirted valley,
    Where the crowded cannon play,—
Where the Czar's fierce cohorts rally,
Cossack, Calmuck, savage Kalli,—
    Down that gorge they swept away!
Down the new Thermopylæ,
Flashing swords and helmets see!
Underneath the iron shower,
    To the brazen cannon's jaws,
Heedless of their deadly power,
    Press they without fear or pause,—
    To the very cannon's jaws!
Gallant Nolan, brave as Roland
    At the field of Roncesvalles,
    Dashes down the fatal valley,
Dashes on the bolt of death,
Shouting with his latest breath,
"Charge, then, gallants! do not waver,
Charge the pass at Balaklava!"
    O that rash and fatal charge,
    On the battle's bloody marge!

Now the bolts of volleyed thunder
Rend the little band asunder,
Steed and rider wildly screaming,
    Screaming wildly, sink away ;
Late so proudly, proudly gleaming,
    Now but lifeless clods of clay,—
    Now but bleeding clods of clay !
Never since the days of Jesus,
Saw such sight the Chersonesus !
Yet your remnant, brave Six Hundred,
Presses onward, onward, onward,
    Till they storm the bloody pass,—
    Till, like brave Leonidas,
    They storm the deadly pass !
Sabring Cossack, Calmuck, Kalli,
In that wild shot-rended valley,—
Drenched with fire and blood, like lava,
Awful pass at Balaklava !
    O that rash and fatal charge,
    On that battle's bloody marge !

For now Russia's rallied forces,
Swarming hordes of Cossack horses,
Trampling o'er the reeking corses,
    Drive the thinned assailants back,
    Drive the feeble remnant back,
    O'er their late heroic track !
Vain, alas ! now rent and sundered,
Vain your struggles, brave Two Hundred !
Thrice your number lie asleep,
In that valley dark and deep.
Weak and wounded you retire
From that hurricane of fire,—
That tempestuous storm of fire,—
But no soldiers firmer, braver,
    Ever trod the field of fame,
Then the Knights of Balaklava,—
    Honor to each hero's name !

Yet their country long shall mourn
For her ranks so rashly shorn,—
So gallantly, but madly shorn
    In that fierce and fatal charge,
    On the battle's bloody marge.

               ALEXANDER B. MEEK.

The Pauper's Drive.

THERE 's a grim one-horse hearse in a jolly round trot—
To the church-yard a pauper is going, I wot;
The road it is rough, and the hearse has no springs;
And hark to the dirge which the mad driver sings:
   Rattle his bones over the stones!
   He 's only a pauper, whom nobody owns!

Oh, where are the mourners?   Alas! there are none—
He has left not a gap in the world, now he 's gone—
Not a tear in the eye of child, woman, or man;
To the grave with his carcass as fast as you can:
   Rattle his bones over the stones!
   He 's only a pauper, whom nobody owns!

What a jolting, and creaking, and splashing, and din!
The whip, how it cracks! and the wheels, how they spin!
How the dirt, right and left, o'er the hedges is hurled!
The pauper at length makes a noise in the world!
   Rattle his bones over the stones!
   He 's only a pauper, whom nobody owns!

Poor pauper defunct! he has made some approach
To gentility, now that he 's stretched in a coach!
He 's taking a drive in his carriage at last;
But it will not be long, if he goes on so fast.
   Rattle his bones over the stones!
   He 's only a pauper, whom nobody owns!

You bumpkins, who stare at your brother conveyed,
Behold what respect to a cloddy is paid!
  16*

And be joyful to think, when by death you 're laid low,
You 've a chance to the grave like a gemman to go !
   Rattle his bones over the stones!
   He 's only a pauper, whom nobody owns!

But a truce to this strain; for my soul it is sad,
To think that a heart in humanity clad
Should make, like the brutes, such a desolate end,
And depart from the light without leaving a friend.
   Bear soft his bones over the stones!
   Though a pauper, he 's one whom his Maker yet owns!
THOMAS NOEL.

Florence Vane.

I LOVED thee long and dearly,
   Florence Vane;
My life's bright dream and early
   Hath come again ;
I renew in my fond vision
   My heart's dear pain,
My hopes and thy derision,
   Florence Vane!

The ruin, lone and hoary,
   The ruin old,
Where thou didst hark my story,
   At even told,
That spot, the hues elysian
   Of sky and plain
I treasure in my vision,
   Florence Vane!

Thou wast lovelier than the roses
   In their prime;
Thy voice excelled the closes
   Of sweetest rhyme;

Thy heart was as a river
 Without a main,
Would I had loved thee never,
 Florence Vane.

But fairest, coldest wonder!
 Thy glorious clay
Lieth the green sod under;
 Alas the day!
And it boots not to remember
 Thy disdain,
To quicken love's pale ember,
 Florence Vane!

The lilies of the valley
 By young graves weep,
The daisies love to dally
 Where maidens sleep,
May their bloom, in beauty vying,
 Never wane
Where thine earthly part is lying,
 Florence Vane.

     PHILIP PENDLETON COOKE.

The Dule 's i' this Bonnet o' Mine.

THE dule 's i' this bonnet o' mine:
 My ribbins 'll never be reet;
Here, Mally, aw 'm like to be fine,
 For Jamie 'll be comin' to-neet;
He met me i' th' lone t' other day
 (Aw wur gooin' for wayter to th' well),
An' he begged that aw 'd wed him i' May,
 Bi th' mass, if he'll let me, aw will!

When he took my two honds into his,
 Good Lord, heaw they trembled between!

An' aw durst n't look up in his face,
　　Becose on him seein' my e'en.
My cheek went as red as a rose;
　　There 's never a mortal con tell
Heaw happy aw felt,—for, thae knows,
　　One could n't ha' axed him theirsel'.

But th' tale wur at th' end o' my tung:
　　To let it eawt would n't be reet,
For aw thought to seem forrud wur wrong;
　　So aw towd him aw 'd tell him to-neet.
But, Mally, thae knows very weel,
　　Though it is n't a thing one should own,
Iv aw 'd th' pikein' o' th' world to mysel',
　　Aw 'd oather ha' Jamie or noan.

Neaw, Mally, aw 're towd thae my mind;
　　What would to do iv 't wur thee?
"Aw 'd tak him just while he 's inclined,
　　An' a farrantly bargain he 'll be;
For Jamie 's as greadly a lad
　　As ever stept eawt into th' sun.
Go, jump at thy chance, an' get wed;
　　An' mak th' best o' th' job when it 's done!"

Eh, dear! but it 's time to be gwon:
　　Aw should n't like Jamie to wait;
Aw connut for shame be too soon,
　　An' aw would n't for th' wuld be too late.
Aw 'm o' ov a tremble to th' heel:
　　Dost think 'at my bonnet 'll do?
"Be off, lass,—thae looks very weel;
　　He wants noan o' th' bonnet, thae foo!"

　　　　　　　　　　　　　　EDWIN WAUGH.

Abraham Lincoln.

FIRST PUBLISHED IN PUNCH.

You lay a wreath on murdered Lincoln's bier,
  You, who with mocking pencil wont to trace,
Broad for the self-complacent British sneer,
  His length of shambling limb, his furrowed face,

His gaunt, gnarled hands, his unkempt, bristling hair,
  His garb uncouth, his bearing ill at ease,
His lack of all we prize as debonair,
  Of power or will to shine, of art to please;

You, whose smart pen backed up the pencil's laugh,
  Judging each step as though the way were plain;
Reckless, so it could point its paragraph,
  Of chief's perplexity or people's pain,—

Beside this corpse, that bears for winding-sheet
  The Stars and Stripes he lived to rear anew,
Between the mourners at his head and feet,
  Say, scurrile jester, is there room for *you*?

Yes: he had lived to shame me from my sneer,
  To lame my pencil and confute my pen;
To make me own this hind of princes peer,
  This rail-splitter, a true-born king of men.

My shallow judgment I had learned to rue,
  Noting how to occasion's height he rose;
How his quaint wit made home-truth seem more true;
  How, iron-like, his temper grew by blows;

How humble, yet how hopeful he could be;
  How in good fortune and in ill the same;
Nor bitter in success, nor boastful he,
  Thirsty for gold, nor feverish for fame.

17

He went about his work, such work as few
  Ever had laid on head and heart and hand,
As one who knows, where there 's a task to do,
  Man's honest will must Heaven's good grace command;

Who trusts the strength will with the burden grow,
  That God makes instruments to work his will,
If but that will we can arrive to know,
  Nor tamper with the weights of good and ill.

So he went forth to battle, on the side
  That he felt clear was Liberty's and Right's,
As in his peasant boyhood he had plied
  His warfare with rude Nature's thwarting mights—

The uncleared forest, the unbroken soil,
  The iron bark that turns the lumberer's axe,
The rapid that o'erbears the boatman's toil,
  The prairie hiding the mazed wanderer's tracks,

The ambushed Indian, and the prowling bear,—
  Such were the deeds that helped his youth to train:
Rough culture, but such trees large fruit may bear,
  If but their stocks be of right girth and grain.

So he grew up, a destined work to do,
  And lived to do it; four long-suffering years'
Ill fate, ill feeling, ill report lived through,
  And then he heard the hisses change to cheers,

The taunts to tribute, the abuse to praise,
  And took both with the same unwavering mood,—
Till, as he came on light, from darkling days,
  And seemed to touch the goal from where he stood,

A felon hand, between the goal and him,
  Reached from behind his back, a trigger prest,
And those perplexed and patient eyes were dim,
  Those gaunt, long-laboring limbs were laid to rest.

The words of mercy were upon his lips,
  Forgiveness in his heart and on his pen,
When this vile murderer brought swift eclipse
  To thoughts of peace on earth, good will to men.

The Old World and the New, from sea to sea,
  Utter one voice of sympathy and shame.
Sore heart, so stopped when it at last beat high!
  Sad life, cut short just as its triumph came!

A deed accursed! Strokes have been struck before
  By the assassin's hand, whereof men doubt
If more of horror or disgrace they bore;
  But thy foul crime, like Cain's, stands darkly out,

Vile hand, that brandest murder on a strife,
  Whate'er its grounds, stoutly and nobly striven,
And with the martyr's crown crownest a life
  With much to praise, little to be forgiven.
Tom Taylor.

The Memory of the Dead.

WHO fears to speak of Ninety-Eight?
  Who blushes at the name?
When cowards mock the patriot's fate,
  Who hangs his head for shame?
He 's all a knave, or half a slave,
  Who slights his country thus;
But a true man, like you, man,
  Will fill your glass with us.

We drink the memory of the brave,
  The faithful and the few—
Some lie far off beyond the wave—
  Some sleep in Ireland, too;
All, all are gone—but still lives on
  The fame of those who died—

All true men, like you, men,
　　Remember them with pride.

Some on the shores of distant lands
　　Their weary hearts have laid,
And by the stranger's heedless hands
　　Their lonely graves were made;
But, though their clay be far away
　　Beyond the Atlantic foam—
In true men, like you, men,
　　Their spirit 's still at home.

The dust of some is Irish earth;
　　Among their own they rest;
And the same land that gave them birth
　　Has caught them to her breast;
And we will pray that from their clay
　　Full many a race may start
Of true men, like you, men,
　　To act as brave a part.

They rose in dark and evil days
　　To right their native land;
They kindled here a living blaze
　　That nothing shall withstand.
Alas! that might can vanquish right—
　　They fell and passed away;
But true men, like you, men,
　　Are plenty here to-day.

Then here 's their memory—may it be
　　For us a guiding light,
To cheer our strife for liberty,
　　And teach us to unite.
Through good and ill, be Ireland's still,
　　Though sad as theirs your fate;
And true men, be you, men,
　　Like those of Ninety-Eight!
　　　　　　　　　　JOHN KELLS INGRAM.

The Bivouac of the Dead.

THE muffled drum's sad roll has beat
  The soldier's last tattoo;
No more on life's parade shall meet
  That brave and fallen few.
On fame's eternal camping ground
  Their silent tents are spread,
And glory guards, with solemn round,
  The bivouac of the dead.

No rumor of the foe's advance
  Now swells upon the wind;
No troubled thought at midnight haunts
  Of loved ones left behind;
No vision of the morrow's strife
  The warrior's dream alarms;
No braying horn nor screaming fife
  At dawn shall call to arms.

Their shivered swords are red with rust,
  Their plumèd heads are bowed;
Their haughty banner, trailed in dust,
  Is now their martial shroud.
And plenteous funeral tears have washed
  The red stains from each brow,
And the proud forms, by battle gashed,
  Are free from anguish now.

The neighing troop, the flashing blade,
  The bugle's stirring blast,
The charge, the dreadful cannonade,
  The din and shout are past;
Nor war's wild note nor glory's peal
  Shall thrill with fierce delight
Those breasts that never more may feel
  The rapture of the fight.

Like the fierce northern hurricane
 That sweeps his great plateau,
Flushed with the triumph yet to gain,
 Came down the serried foe.
Who heard the thunder of the fray
 Break o'er the field beneath,
Knew well the watchword of that day
 Was "Victory or death."

Long has the doubtful conflict raged
 O'er all that stricken plain,
For never fiercer fight had waged
 The vengeful blood of Spain;
And still the storm of battle blew,
 Still swelled the gory tide;
Not long, our stout old chieftain knew,
 Such odds his strength could bide.

'T was in that hour his stern command
 Called to a martyr's grave
The flower of his belovèd land,
 The nation's flag to save.
By rivers of their fathers' gore
 His first-born laurels grew,
And well he deemed the sons would pour
 Their lives for glory too.

Full many a norther's breath had swept
 O'er Angostura's plain—
And long the pitying sky has wept
 Above the mouldering slain.
The raven's scream, or eagle's flight,
 Or shepherd's pensive lay,
Alone awakes each sullen height
 That frowned o'er that dread fray.

Sons of the Dark and Bloody Ground,
 Ye must not slumber there,

Where stranger steps and tongues resound
  Along the heedless air;
Your own proud land's heroic soil
  Shall be your fitter grave;
She claims from war his richest spoil—
  The ashes of her brave.

So, 'neath their parent turf they rest,
  Far from the gory field,
Borne to a Spartan mother's breast,
  On many a bloody shield;
The sunshine of their native sky
  Smiles sadly on them here,
And kindred eyes and hearts watch by
  The heroes' sepulchre.

Rest on, embalmed and sainted dead,
  Dear as the blood ye gave;
No impious footstep here shall tread
  The herbage of your grave;
Nor shall your glory be forgot
  While Fame her record keeps,
Or Honor points the hallowed spot
  Where Valor proudly sleeps.

Yon marble minstrel's voiceless stone,
  In deathless song shall tell,
When many a vanished age hath flown,
  The story how ye fell;
Nor wreck, nor change, nor winter's blight,
  Nor Time's remorseless doom,
Shall dim one ray of glory's light
  That gilds your deathless tomb.

THEODORE O'HARA.

Nearer, my God, to Thee.

  NEARER, my God, to thee,
    Nearer to thee!

E'en though it be a cross
  That raiseth me;
Still all my song shall be,
Nearer, my God, to thee,
  Nearer to thee!

Though, like the wanderer,
  The sun gone down,
Darkness be over me,
  My rest a stone;
Yet in my dreams I 'd be
Nearer, my God, to thee,
  Nearer to thee!

There let the way appear
  Steps unto heaven;
All that thou sendest me
  In mercy given;
Angels to beckon me
Nearer, my God, to thee,
  Nearer to thee!

Then with my waking thoughts
  Bright with thy praise,
Out of my stony griefs
  Bethel I 'll raise;
So by my woes to be
Nearer, my God, to thee,
  Nearer to thee!

Or if on joyful wing
  Cleaving the sky,
Sun, moon, and stars forgot,
  Upward I fly;
Still all my song shall be,—
Nearer, my God, to thee,
  Nearer to thee.

                SARAH FLOWER ADAMS.

Lines on a Skeleton.

BEHOLD this ruin! 'T was a skull
Once of ethereal spirit full.
This narrow cell was Life's retreat,
This space was Thought's mysterious seat.
What beauteous visions filled this spot,
What dreams of pleasure long forgot!
Nor hope, nor joy, nor love, nor fear,
Have left one trace of record here.

Beneath this mouldering canopy
Once shone the bright and busy eye,
But start not at the dismal void,—
If social love that eye employed,
If with no lawless fire it gleamed,
But through the dews of kindness beamed,
That eye shall be forever bright
When stars and sun are sunk in night.

Within this hollow cavern hung
The ready, swift, and tuneful tongue;
If Falsehood's honey it disdained,
And when it could not praise was chained;
If bold in Virtue's cause it spoke,
Yet gentle concord never broke,—
This silent tongue shall plead for thee
When Time unveils Eternity!

Say, did these fingers delve the mine?
Or with the envied rubies shine?
To hew the rock, or wear a gem,
Can little now avail to them.
But if the page of Truth they sought,
Or comfort to the mourner brought,
These hands a richer meed shall claim
Than all that wait on Wealth and Fame.

17*

Avails it whether bare or shod
These feet the paths of duty trod?
If from the bowers of Ease they fled,
To seek Affliction's humble shed;
If Grandeur's guilty bribe they spurned,
And home to Virtue's cot returned,—
These feet with angel-wings shall vie,
And tread the palace of the sky.

ANONYMOUS.

The Place where Man should Die.

How little recks it where men lie,
  When once the moment 's past
In which the dim and glazing eye
  Has looked on earth its last,—
Whether beneath the sculptured urn
  The coffined form shall rest,
Or in its nakedness return
  Back to its mother's breast!

Death is a common friend or foe,
  As different men may hold,
And at his summons each must go,
  The timid and the bold;
But when the spirit, free and warm,
  Deserts it, as it must,
What matter where the lifeless form
  Dissolves again to dust?

The soldier falls 'mid corses piled
  Upon the battle-plain,
Where reinless war-steeds gallop wild
  Above the mangled slain;
But though his corse be grim to see,
  Hoof-trampled on the sod,
What recks it, when the spirit free
  Has soared aloft to God?

The coward's dying eyes may close
  Upon his downy bed,
And softest hands his limbs compose,
  Or garments o'er them spread.
But ye who shun the bloody fray,
  When fall the mangled brave,
Go—strip his coffin-lid away,
  And see him in his grave!

'T were sweet, indeed, to close our eyes,
  With those we cherish near,
And, wafted upwards by their sighs,
  Soar to some calmer sphere.
But whether on the scaffold high,
  Or in the battle's van,
The fittest place where man can die
  Is where he dies for man!

MICHAEL JOSEPH BARRY.

A Hundred Years to Come.

WHERE, where will be the birds that sing,
  A hundred years to come?
The flowers that now in beauty spring,
  A hundred years to come?
The rosy lips, the lofty brow,
The heart that beats so gayly now,
Oh, where will be love's beaming eye,
Joy's pleasant smile, and sorrow's sigh,
  A hundred years to come?

Who 'll press for gold this crowded street,
  A hundred years to come?
Who 'll tread yon church with willing feet,
  A.hundred years to come?
Pale trembling age, and fiery youth,
And childhood with its brow of truth;

The rich and poor, on land and sea,—
Where will the mighty millions be
    A hundred years to come?

We all within our graves shall sleep,
    A hundred years to come;
No living soul for us will weep,
    A hundred years to come.
But other men our lands shall till,
And others, then, our streets will fill,
While other birds will sing as gay,
As bright the sunshine as to-day,
    A hundred years to come.

                    WILLIAM GOLDSMITH BROWN.

The Song of Steam.

HARNESS me down with your iron bands,
    Be sure of your curb and rein,
For I scorn the strength of your puny hands
    As the tempest scorns a chain.
How I laughed as I lay concealed from sight,
    For many a countless hour,
At the childish boast of human might,
    And the pride of human power.

When I saw an army upon the land,
    A navy upon the seas,
Creeping along, a snail-like band,
    Or waiting the wayward breeze,—
When I marked the peasant faintly reel
    With the toil which he daily bore,
As he feebly turned the tardy wheel,
    Or tugged at the weary oar,—

When I measured the panting courser's speed,
    The flight of the carrier dove,

As they bore the law a king decreed,
　Or the lines of impatient love,
I could but think how the world would feel,
　As these were outstripped afar,
When I should be bound to the rushing keel,
　Or chained to the flying car.

Ha, ha, ha!　They found me at last,
　They invited me forth at length,
And I rushed to my throne with a thunder blast,
　And laughed in my iron strength!
Oh! then ye saw a wondrous change
　On the earth and the ocean wide,
Where now my fiery armies range,
　Nor wait for wind or tide.

The ocean pales where'er I sweep,
　To hear my strength rejoice,
And monsters of the briny deep
　Cower trembling at my voice.
I carry the wealth and the lord of earth,
　The thoughts of his godlike mind;
The wind lags after my going forth,
　The lightning is left behind.

In the darksome depths of the fathomless mine,
　My tireless arm doth play;
Where the rocks never saw the sun decline,
　Or the dawn of a glorious day;
I bring earth's glittering jewels up
　From the hidden caves below,
And I make the fountain's granite cup
　With a crystal gush o'erflow.

I blow the bellows, I forge the steel,
　In all the shops of trade;
I hammer the ore and turn the wheel
　Where my arms of strength are made.

18

I manage the furnace, the mill, the mint,—
  I carry, I spin, I weave;
And all my doings I put into print
  On every Saturday eve.

I 've no muscle to weary, no brains to decay,
  No bones to be "laid on the shelf,"
And soon I intend you may " go and play,"
  While I manage the world myself.
But harness me down with your iron bands,
  Be sure of your curb and rein,
For I scorn the strength of your puny hands
  As the tempest scorns a chain.

GEORGE W. CUTTER.

Why thus Longing?

WHY thus longing, thus forever sighing,
  For the far-off, unattained and dim,
While the beautiful, all round thee lying,
  Offers up its low, perpetual hymn?

Wouldst thou listen to its gentle teaching,
  All thy restless yearnings it would still;
Leaf and flower and laden bee are preaching
  Thine own sphere, though humble, first to fill.

Poor indeed thou must be, if around thee
  Thou no ray of light and joy canst throw—
If no silken cord of love hath bound thee
  To some little world through weal and woe;

If no dear eyes thy fond love can brighten—
  No fond voices answer to thine own;
If no brother's sorrow thou canst lighten,
  By daily sympathy and gentle tone.

Not by deeds that win the crowd's applauses,
   Not by works that give thee world-renown,
Not by martyrdom or vaunted crosses,
   Canst thou win and wear the immortal crown.

Daily struggling, though unloved and lonely,
   Every day a rich reward will give;
Thou wilt find, by hearty striving only,
   And truly loving, thou canst truly live.

Dost thou revel in the rosy morning,
   When all nature hails the lord of light,
And his smile, the mountain-tops adorning,
   Robes yon fragrant fields in radiance bright?

Other hands may grasp the field and forest,
   Proud proprietors in pomp may shine;
But with fervent love if thou adorest,
   Thou art wealthier—all the world is thine.

Yet if through earth's wide domains thou rovest,
   Sighing that they are not thine alone,
Not those fair fields, but thyself thou lovest,
   And their beauty and thy wealth are gone.

Nature wears the color of the spirit;
   Sweetly to her worshiper she sings;
All the glow, the grace she doth inherit,
   Round her trusting child she fondly flings.
                 HARRIET WINSLOW SEWALL.

Nothing to Wear.

MISS FLORA M'FLIMSEY, of Madison Square,
Has made three separate journeys to Paris,
And her father assures me, each time she was there,
That she and her friend Mrs. Harris

(Not the lady whose name is so famous in history,
But plain Mrs. H., without romance or mystery)
Spent six consecutive weeks, without stopping,
In one continuous round of shopping,—
Shopping alone, and shopping together,
At all honrs of the day, and in all sorts of weather,
For all manner of things that a woman çan put
On the crown of her head, or the soul of her foot,
Or wrap round her shoulders, or fit round her waist,
Or that can be sewed on, or pinned on, or laced,
Or tied with a string, or stitched with a bow,
In front or behind, above or below;
For bonnets, mantillas, capes, collars, and shawls;
Dresses for breakfast, and dinners, and balls;
Dresses to sit in, and stand in, and walk in;
Dresses to dance in, and flirt in, and talk in;
Dresses in which to do nothing at all;
Dresses for Winter, Spring, Summer, and Fall;—
All of them different in color and shape,
Silk, muslin, and lace, velvet, satin, and crape,
Brocade and broadcloth, and other material,
Quite as expensive and much more ethereal;
In short, for all things that could ever be thought of,
Or milliner, *modiste*, or tradesman be bought of,
    From ten-thousand-franc robes to twenty-sous frills;
In all quarters of Paris, and to every store,
While M'Flimsey in vain stormed, scolded, and swore,
    They footed the streets, and he footed the bills!

The last trip, their goods shipped by the steamer *Argo*,
Formed, M'Flimsey declares, the bulk of her cargo,
Not to mention a quantity kept from the rest,
Sufficient to fill the largest sized chest,
Which did not appear on the ship's manifest,
But for which the ladies themselves manifested
Such particular interest, that they invested
Their own proper persons in layers and rows

Of muslins, embroideries, worked under-clothes,
Gloves, handkerchiefs, scarfs, and such trifles as those;
Then, wrapped in great shawls, like Circassian beauties,
Gave *good by* to the ship, and *go by* to the duties.
Her relations at home all marveled, no doubt,
Miss Flora had grown so enormously stout
    For an actual belle and a possible bride;
But the miracle ceased when she turned inside out,
    And the truth came to light, and the dry-goods beside;
Which, in spite of Collector and Custom-House sentry,
Had entered the port without any entry.
And yet, though scarce three months have passed since
      the day
This merchandise went, on twelve carts, up Broadway,
This same Miss M'Flimsey, of Madison Square,
The last time we met was in utter despair,
Because she had nothing whatever to wear!

NOTHING TO WEAR! Now, as this is a true ditty,
    I do not assert—this, you know, is between us—
That she 's in a state of absolute nudity,
    Like Powers' Greek Slave, or the Medici Venus;
But I do mean to say, I have heard her declare,
    When at the same moment she had on a dress
    Which cost five hundred dollars, and not a cent less,
    And jewelry worth ten times more, I should guess,
That she had not a thing in the wide world to wear!

I should mention just here, that out of Miss Flora's
Two hundred and fifty or sixty adorers,
I had just been selected as he who should throw all
The rest in the shade, by the gracious bestowal
On myself, after twenty or thirty rejections,
Of those fossil remains which she called her "affections,"
And that rather decayed, but well-known work of art,
Which Miss Flora persisted in styling her "heart."
So we were engaged. Our troth had been plighted,

Not by moonbeam or starbeam, by fountain or grove,
But in a front parlor, most brilliantly lighted,
Beneath the gas-fixtures, we whispered our love.
Without any romance, or raptures, or sighs,
Without any tears in Miss Flora's blue eyes,
Or blushes, or transports, or such silly actions,
It was one of the quietest business transactions,
With a very small sprinkling of sentiment, if any,
And a very large diamond imported by Tiffany.
On her virginal lips while I printed a kiss,
She exclaimed, as a sort of parenthesis,
And by way of putting me quite at my ease,
" You know I 'm to polka as much as I please,
And flirt when I like—now, stop, do n't you speak—
And you must not come here more than twice in the
        week,
Or talk to me either at party or ball,
But always be ready to come when I call;
So do n't prose to me about duty and stuff,
If we do n't break this off, there will be time enough
For that sort of thing; but the bargain must be
That, as long as I choose, I am perfectly free,—
For this is a kind of engagement, you see,
Which is binding on you, but not binding on me."

Well, having thus wooed Miss M'Flimsey and gained her,
With the silks, crinolines, and hoops that contained her,
I had, as I thought, a contingent remainder
At least in the property, and the best right
To appear as its escort by day and by night;
And it being the week of the Stuckup's grand ball,—
    Their cards had been out a fortnight or so,
    And set all the Avenue on the tiptoe,—
I considered it only my duty to call,
    And see if Miss Flora intended to go.
I found her—as ladies are apt to be found,
When the time intervening between the first sound

Of the bell and the visitor's entry is shorter
Than usual—I found; I won't say—I caught her,
Intent on the pier-glass, undoubtedly meaning
To see if perhaps it did n't need cleaning.
She turned as I entered,—" Why, Harry, you sinner,
I thought that you went to the Flashers' to dinner!"
" So I did," I replied, " but the dinner is swallowed,
    And digested, I trust, for 't is now nine and more,
So being relieved from that duty, I followed
    Inclination, which led me, you see, to your door;
And now will your ladyship so condescend
As just to inform me if you intend
Your beauty, and graces, and presence to lend
(All of which, when I own, I hope no one will borrow)
To the Stuckups, whose party, you know, is to-morrow?"
The fair Flora looked up, with a pitiful air,
And answered quite promptly, " Why, Harry, *mon cher*,
I should like above all things to go with you there,
But really and truly—I 've nothing to wear."
" Nothing to wear! go just as you are;
    Wear the dress you have on, and you 'll be by far,
I engage, the most bright and particular star
    On the Stuckup horizon—" I stopped, for her eye,
Notwithstanding this delicate onset of flattery,
Opened on me at once a most terrible battery
    Of scorn and amazement. She made no reply,
But gave a slight turn to the end of her nose,
    (That pure Grecian feature,) as much to say,
" How absurd that any sane man should suppose
That a lady would go to a ball in the clothes,
    No matter how fine, that she wears every day!"

So I ventured again: " Wear your crimson brocade;"
(Second turn up of nose)—" That 's too dark by a shade."
' Your blue silk "—" That 's too heavy." " Your pink "—
    " That's too light."
" Wear tulle over satin "—" I can't endure white."

"Your rose-colored, then, the best of the batch."
"I have n't a thread of point-lace to match."
"Your brown *moire antique*"—"Yes, and look like a Qua-
    ker;"
"The pearl-colored"—"I would, but that plaguy dress-
    maker
  Has had it a week."—"Then that exquisite lilac,
  In which you would melt the heart of a Shylock;"
(Here the nose took again the same elevation)—
"I would n't wear that for the whole of creation."
   "Why not? It's my fancy, there's nothing could strike it
    As more *comme il faut*"—"Yes, but, dear me, that lean
     Sophronia Stuckup has got one just like it,
   And I won't appear dressed like a chit of sixteen."
"Then that splendid purple, that sweet Mazarine;
  That superb *point d'aiguille*, that imperial green,
  That zephyr-like tarletan, that rich *grenadine*"—
"Not one of all which is fit to be seen,"
  Said the lady, becoming excited and flushed.
"Then wear," I exclaimed in a tone which quite crushed
   Opposition, "that gorgeous *toilette* which you sported
  In Paris last spring, at the grand presentation,
  When you quite turned the head of the head of the nation,
   And by all the grand court were so very much courted."
   The end of the nose was portentously tipped up,
And both the bright eyes shot forth indignation,
As she burst upon me with the fierce exclamation,
"I have worn it three times, at the least calculation,
   And that and most of my dresses are ripped up!"
Here I *ripped out* something, perhaps rather rash,
   Quite innocent, though; but, to use an expression
More striking than classic, it "settled my hash,"
   And proved very soon the last of our session.
"Fiddlesticks, is it, sir? I wonder the ceiling
  Does n't fall down and crush you,—you men have no feel-
    ing;

You selfish, unnatural, illiberal creatures,
Who set yourselves up as patterns and preachers,
Your silly pretense,—why, what a mere guess it is!
Pray, what do you know of a woman's necessities?
I have told you and shown you I 've nothing to wear,
And it 's perfectly plain you not only do n't care,
But you do not believe me," (here the nose went still
    higher.)
"I suppose, if you dared, you would call me a liar.
Our engagement is ended, sir,—yes, on the spot;
You 're a brute, and a monster, and—I do n't know what."
I mildly suggested the words Hottentot,
Pickpocket, and cannibal, Tartar, and thief,
As gentle expletives which might give relief;
But this only proved as a spark to the powder,
And the storm I had raised came faster and louder;
It blew and it rained, thundered, lightened, and hailed
Interjections, verbs, pronouns, till language quite failed
To express the abusive, and then its arrears
Were brought up all at once by a torrent of tears,
And my last faint, despairing attempt at an obs-
Ervation was lost in a tempest of sobs.
Well, I felt for the lady, and felt for my hat, too,
Improvised on the crown of the latter a tattoo,
In lieu of expressing the feelings which lay
Quite too deep for words, as Wordsworth would say;
Then, without going through the form of a bow,
Found myself in the entry, I hardly knew how,
On door-step and side-walk, past lamp-post and square,
At home and up-stairs, in my own easy-chair;
    Poked my feet into slippers, my fire into blaze,
And said to myself, as I lit my cigar,
"Supposing a man had the wealth of the Czar
    Of the Russias to boot, for the rest of his days,
On the whole do you think he would have much to spare,
If he married a woman with nothing to wear?"
Since that night, taking pains that it should not be bruited
    18*

Abroad in society, I 've instituted
A course of inquiry, extensive and thorough,
On this vital subject, and find, to my horror,
That the fair Flora's case is by no means surprising;
    But that there exists the greatest distress
In our female community, solely arising
    From this unsupplied destitution of dress,
Whose unfortunate victims are filling the air
With the pitiful wail of "Nothing to wear."

Researches in some of the "Upper Ten" districts
Reveal the most painful and startling statistics,
Of which let me mention only a few:
In one single house, on the Fifth Avenue,
Three young ladies were found, all below twenty-two,
Who have been three whole weeks without anything new
In the way of flounced silks, and thus left in the lurch,
Are unable to go to ball, concert, or church.
In another large mansion, near the same place,
Was found a deplorable, heart-rending case
Of entire destitution of Brussels point-lace.
In a neighboring block there was found, in three calls,
Total want, long continued, of camel's-hair shawls;
And a suffering family, whose case exhibits
The most pressing need of real ermine tippets;
One deserving young lady almost unable
To survive for the want of a new Russian sable;
Still another, whose tortures have been most terrific
Ever since the sad loss of the steamer *Pacific*,
In which were ingulfed, not friend or relation,
(For whose fate she perhaps might have found consolation,
Or borne it, at least, with serene resignation,)
But the choicest assortment of French sleeves and collars
Ever sent out from Paris, worth thousands of dollars,
And all as to style most *recherché* and rare,
The want of which leaves her with nothing to wear,
And renders her life so drear and dyspeptic

That she 's quite a recluse, and almost a skeptic,
For she touchingly says, that this sort of grief
Cannot find in Religion the slightest relief,
And Philosophy has not a maxim to spare
For the victims of such overwhelming despair.
But the saddest, by far, of all these sad features,
Is the cruelty practiced upon the poor creatures
By husbands and fathers, real Bluebeards and Timons,
Who resist the most touching appeals made for diamonds
By their wives and their daughters, and leave them for days
Unsupplied with new jewelry, fans, or bouquets,
Even laugh at their miseries whenever they have a chance,
And deride their demands as useless extravagance;
One case of a bride was brought to my view,
Too sad for belief, but, alas! 't was too true,
Whose husband refused, as savage as Charon,
To permit her to take more than ten trunks to Sharon.
The consequence was, that when she got there,
At the end of three weeks she had nothing to wear,
And when she proposed to finish the season
At Newport, the monster refused, out and out,
For his infamous conduct alleging no reason,
Except that the waters were good for his gout;
Such treatment as this was too shocking, of course,
And proceedings are now going on for divorce.

But why harrow the feelings by lifting the curtain
From these scenes of woe?   Enough, it is certain,
Has here been disclosed to stir up the pity
Of every benevolent heart in the city,
And spur up Humanity into a canter
To rush and relieve these sad cases instanter.
Won't somebody, moved by this touching description,
Come forward to-morrow and head a subscription?
Won't some kind philanthropist, seeing that aid is
So needed at once by these indigent ladies,
Take charge of the matter?   Or won't Peter Cooper

The corner-stone lay of some new splendid super-
Structure, like that which to-day links his name
In the Union unending of Honor and Fame,
And found a new charity just for the care
Of these unhappy women with nothing to wear,
Which, in view of the cash which would daily be claimed,
The *Laying-out* Hospital well might be named?
Won't Stewart, or some of our dry-goods importers,
Take a contract for clothing our wives and our daughters?
Or, to furnish the cash to supply these distresses,
And life's pathway strew with shawls, collars, and dresses,
Ere the want of them makes it much rougher and thornier,
Won't some one discover a new California?

O ladies, dear ladies, the next sunny day
Please trundle your hoops just out of Broadway,
From its whirl and its bustle, its fashion and pride,
And the temples of Trade which tower on each side,
To the alleys and lanes, where Misfortune and Guilt
Their children have gathered, their city have built;
Where Hunger and Vice, like twin beasts of prey,
　　Have hunted their victims to gloom and despair;
Raise the rich, dainty dress, and the fine broidered skirt,
Pick your delicate way through the dampness and dirt,
　　Grope through the dark dens, climb the rickety stair
To the garret, where wretches, the young and the old,
Half starved and half naked, lie crouched from the cold;
See those skeleton limbs, those frost-bitten feet,
All bleeding and bruised by the stones of the street;
Hear the sharp cry of childhood, the deep groans that swell
　　From the poor dying creature who writhes on the floor;
Hear the curses that sound like the echoes of Hell,
　　As you sicken and shudder and fly from the door;
Then home to your wardrobes, and say, if you dare,--
Spoiled children of fashion,--you 've nothing to wear!

And O, if perchance there should be a sphere
Where all is made right which so puzzles us here,

Where the glare and the glitter and tinsel of Time
Fade and die in the light of that region sublime,
Where the soul, disenchanted of flesh and of sense,
Unscreened by its trappings and shows and pretense,
Must be clothed for the life and the service above,
With purity, truth, faith, meekness, and love,
O daughters of Earth! foolish virgins, beware!
Lest in that upper realm you have nothing to wear!

WILLIAM ALLEN BUTLER.

Antony and Cleopatra.

I AM dying, Egypt, dying,
  Ebbs the crimson life-tide fast,
And the dark Plutonian shadows
  Gather on the evening blast;
Let thine arms, O Queen, infold me;
  Hush thy sobs and bow thine ear;
Listen to the great heart-secrets,
  Thou, and thou alone, must hear.

Though my scarred and veteran legions
  Bear their eagles high no more,
And my wrecked and scattered galleys
  Strew dark Actium's fatal shore;
Though no glittering guards surround me,
  Prompt to do their master's will,
I must perish like a Roman,
  Die the great Triumvir still.

Let not Cæsar's servile minions
  Mock the lion thus laid low;
'T was no foeman's arm that felled him—
  'T was his own that struck the blow,—
His who, pillowed on thy bosom,
  Turned aside from glory's ray—
His who, drunk with thy caresses,
  Madly threw a world away.

19

Should the base plebeian rabble
　Dare assail my name at Rome,
Where my noble spouse, Octavia,
　Weeps within her widowed home,
Seek her; say the gods bear witness—
　Altars, augurs, circling wings—
That her blood, with mine commingled,
　Yet shall mount the throne of kings.

As for thee, star-eyed Egyptian!
　Glorious sorceress of the Nile,
Light the path to Stygian horrors
　With the splendors of thy smile.
Give the Cæsar crowns and arches,
　Let his brow the laurel twine;
I can scorn the Senate's triumphs,
　Triumphing in love like thine.

I am dying, Egypt, dying;
　Hark! the insulting foeman's cry.
They are coming! quick, my falchion!
　Let me front them ere I die.
Ah! no more amid the battle
　Shall my heart exulting swell—
Isis and Osiris guard thee!
　Cleopatra, Rome, farewell!

　　　　　　　　WILLIAM HAINES LYTLE.

The Nautilus and the Ammonite.

THE nautilus and the ammonite
　Were launched in friendly strife,
Each sent to float in its tiny boat
　On the wide, wide sea of life.

For each could swim on the ocean's brim,
　And, when wearied, its sail could furl,

And sink to sleep in the great sea-deep,
  In its palace all of pearl.

And theirs was a bliss more fair than this
  Which we taste in our colder clime;
For they were rife in a tropic life—
  A brighter and better clime.

They swam 'mid isles whose summer smiles
  Were dimmed by no alloy;
Whose groves were palm, whose air was balm,
  And life one only joy.

They sailed all day through creek and bay,
  And traversed the ocean deep;
And at night they sank on a coral bank,
  In its fairy bowers to sleep.

And the monsters vast of ages past
  They beheld in their ocean caves;
They saw them ride in their power and pride,
  And sink in their deep-sea graves.

And hand in hand, from strand to strand,
  They sailed in mirth and glee;
These fairy shells, with their crystal cells,
  Twin sisters of the sea.

And they came at last to a sea long past,
  But as they reached its shore,
The Almighty's breath spoke out in death,
  And the ammonite was no more.

So the nautilus now in its shelly prow,
  As over the deep it strays,
Still seems to seek, in bay and creek,
  Its companion of other days.

And alike do we, on life's stormy sea,
  As we roam from shore to shore,
Thus tempest-tossed, seek the loved, the lost,
  And find them on earth no more.

Yet the hope how sweet, again to meet,
  As we look to a distant strand,
Where heart meets heart, and no more they part
  Who meet in that better land.

ANONYMOUS.

Carmen Bellicosum.

IN their ragged regimentals
Stood the old Continentals,
    Yielding not,
When the grenadiers were lunging,
And like hail fell the plunging
    Cannon-shot;
    When the files
    Of the isles,   [rampant
From the smoky night encampment, bore the banner of the
       Unicorn,   [drummer,
And grummer, grummer, grummer rolled the roll of the
       Through the morn!

Then with eyes to the front all,
And with guns horizontal,
    Stood our sires;
And the balls whistled deadly,
And in streams flashing redly
    Blazed the fires;
    As the roar
    On the shore,
Swept the strong battle-breakers o'er the green-sodded acres
       Of the plain;
And louder, louder, louder cracked the black gunpowder,
       Cracking amain!

Now like smiths at their forges
Worked the red St. George's
  Cannoneers;
And the "villainous saltpetre"
Rung a fierce, discordant metre
  Round their ears;
  As the swift
  Storm-drift,
With hot sweeping anger, came the horse-guard's clangor
  On our flanks.
Then higher, higher, higher burned the old-fashioned fire
  Through the ranks!

  Then the old-fashioned colonel
  Galloped through the white infernal
   Powder-cloud;
  And his broadsword was swinging,
  And his brazen throat was ringing
   Trumpet loud.
   Then the blue
   Bullets flew,
And the trooper-jackets redden at the touch of the leaden
   Rifle-breath;
And rounder, rounder, rounder roared the iron six-pounder,
   Hurling death!

     Guy Humphrey McMaster.

Doris.

I sat with Doris, the shepherd maiden;
 Her crook was laden with wreathèd flowers.
I sat and wooed her through sunlight wheeling,
 And shadows stealing for hours and hours.

And she my Doris, whose lap incloses
 Wild summer roses of faint perfume,
The while I sued her, kept hushed and hearkened
 Till shades had darkened from gloss to gloom.

She touched my shoulder with fearful finger;
    She said, "We linger, we must not stay;
My flock 's in danger, my sheep will wander;
    Behold them yonder, how far they stray!"

I answered bolder, "Nay, let me hear you,
    And still be near you, and still adore!
No wolf nor stranger will touch one yearling—
    Ah! stay my darling a moment more!"

She whispered sighing, "There will be sorrow
    Beyond to-morrow, if I lose to-day;
My fold unguarded, my flock unfolded—
    I shall be scolded and sent away!"

Said I replying, "If they do miss you,
    They ought to kiss you when you get home;
And well rewarded by friend and neighbor
    Should be the labor from which you come."

"They might remember," she answered meekly,
    "That lambs are weakly and sheep are wild;
But if they love me it 's none so fervent—
    I am a servant and not a child."

Then each hot ember glowed quick within me,
    And love did win me to swift reply:
"Ah! do but prove me, and none shall bind you,
    Nor fray nor find you until I die!"

She blushed and started, and stood awaiting,
    As if debating in dreams divine;
But I did brave them—I told her plainly,
    She doubted vainly, she must be mine.

So we twin-hearted, from all the valley
    Did rouse and rally her nibbling ewes;
And homeward drove them, we two together,
    Through blooming heather and gleaming dews.

That simple duty such grace did lend her,
   My Doris tender, my Doris true,
That I her warder did always bless her,
   And often press her to take her due.

And now in beauty she fills my dwelling
   With love excelling, and undefiled;
And love doth guard her, both fast and fervent,
   No more a servant, nor yet a child.

Arthur Munby.

The Exile to his Wife.

Come to me, darling, I 'm lonely without thee;
Day-time and night-time I 'm dreaming about thee;
Night-time and day-time in dreams I behold thee,
Unwelcome the waking that ceases to fold thee.
Come to me, darling, my sorrows to lighten;
Come in thy beauty, to bless and to brighten;
Come in thy womanhood, meekly and lowly;
Come in thy lovliness, queenly and holy.

Swallows shall flit round the desolate ruin,
Telling of Spring and its joyous renewing;
As thoughts of thy love and its manifest treasure
Are circling my heart with a promise of pleasure.
O Spring of my heart! O May of my bosom!
Shine out on my soul till it bourgeon and blossom.
The waste of my life has a rose-root within it,
And thy fondness alone to the sunshine can win it.

Figure which moves like a song through the even,
Features lit up with a reflex of heaven,
Eyes like the skies of poor Erin, our mother,
Where sunshine and shadow are chasing each other;
Smiles coming seldom, but childlike and simple;
And opening their eyes from the heart of a dimple;
O, thanks to the Saviour that even the seeming
Is left to the exile, to brighten his dreaming.

You have been glad when you knew I was gladdened;
Dear, are you sad now to hear I am saddened?
Our hearts ever answer in tune and in time, love,
As octave to octave, and rhyme unto rhyme, love;
I cannot smile but your cheeks will be glowing;
You cannot weep but my tears will be flowing;
You will not linger when I shall have died, love;
I could not live without you at my side, love.

Come to me, dear, ere I die of my sorrow;
Rise on my gloom like the sun of to-morrow;
Come swift and strong as the words which I speak, love,
With a song on your lip and a smile on your cheek, love;
Come, for my heart in your absence is dreary;
Haste, for my spirit is sickened and weary;
Come to the arms which alone shall caress thee;
Come to the heart that is throbbing to press thee.

JOSEPH BRENAN.

Rock me to Sleep.

BACKWARD, turn backward, O Time, in your flight,
Make me a child again just for to-night!
Mother, come back from the echoless shore,
Take me again to your heart as of yore;
Kiss from my forhead the furrows of care,
Smooth the few silver threads out of my hair;
Over my slumbers your loving watch keep;—
Rock me to sleep, mother—rock me to sleep!

Backward, flow backward, O tide of the years!
I am so weary of toil and of tears,—
Toil without recompense, tears all in vain,—
Take them, and give me my childhood again!
I have grown weary of dust and decay,—
Weary of flinging my soul-wealth away;
Weary of sowing for others to reap;—
Rock me to sleep, mother,—rock me to sleep!

Tired of the hollow, the base, the untrue,
Mother, O mother, my heart calls for you!
Many a summer the grass has grown green,
Blossomed and faded, our faces between;
Yet, with strong yearning and passionate pain,
Long I to-night for your presence again;
Come from the silence so long and so deep;—
Rock me to sleep, mother,—rock me to sleep!

Over my heart, in the days that are flown,
No love like mother-love ever has shone;
No other worship abides and endures,
Faithful, unselfish, and patient like yours;
None like a mother can charm away pain
From the sick soul and the world-weary brain:
Slumber's soft calms o'er my heavy lids creep;—
Rock me to sleep, mother,—rock me to sleep!

Come, let your brown hair, just lighted with gold,
Fall on your shoulders again as of old;
Let it drop over my forehead to-night,
Shading my faint eyes away from the light;
For with its sunny-edged shadows once more
Haply will throng the sweet visions of yore;
Lovingly, softly, its bright billows sweep;—
Rock me to sleep, mother,—rock me to sleep!

Mother, dear mother, the years have been long
Since I last listened your lullaby song;
Sing, then, and unto my soul it shall seem
Womanhood's years have been only a dream;
Clasped to your heart in a loving embrace,
With your light lashes just sweeping my face,
Never hereafter to wake or to weep;—
Rock me to sleep, mother,—rock me to sleep!

ELIZABETH AKERS ALLEN.

19*

Only a Baby Small.

Only a baby small,
  Dropt from the skies;
Only a laughing face,
  Two sunny eyes;
Only two cherry lips,
  One chubby nose;
Only two little hands,
  Ten little toes.

Only a golden head,
  Curly and soft;
Only a tongue that wags
  Loudly and oft;
Only a little brain,
  Empty of thought;
Only a little heart,
  Troubled with nought.

Only a tender flower
  Sent us to rear;
Only a life to love
  While we are here;
Only a baby small,
  Never at rest;
Small, but how dear to us,
  God knoweth best.

Matthias Barr.

The Jolly Old Pedagogue.

'T was a jolly old pedagogue, long ago,
  Tall and slender, and sallow, and dry;
His form was bent, and his gait was slow,
His long, thin hair was as white as snow;
  But a wonderful twinkle shone in his eye,

And he sang every night as he went to bed,
"Let us be happy down here below;
The living should live, though the dead be dead,"
Said the jolly old pedagogue, long ago.

He taught his scholars the rule of three,
Writing, and reading, and history too,
Taking the little ones on his knee,
For a kind old heart in his breast had he,
And the wants of the smallest child he knew:
"Learn while you 're young," he often said,
"There is much to enjoy down here below;
Life for the living, and rest for the dead,"
Said the jolly old pedagogue, long ago.

With stupidest boys, he was kind and cool,
Speaking only in gentlest tones;
The rod was scarcely known in his school;
Whipping to him was a barbarous rule,
And too hard work for his poor old bones;
"Besides, it was painful,"—he sometimes said,
"We should make life pleasant here below,
The living need charity more than the dead,"
Said the jolly old pedagogue, long ago.

He lived in the house by the hawthorn lane,
With roses and woodbine over the door;
His rooms were quiet and neat and plain,
But a spirit of comfort there held reign,
And made him forget he was old and poor.
"I need so little," he often said,
"And my friends and relatives here below
Won't litigate over me when I am dead,"
Said the jolly old pedagogue, long ago.

But the most pleasant times that he had, of all,
Were the sociable hours he used to pass,

With his chair tipped back to a neighbor's wall,
Making an unceremonious call,
  Over a pipe and a friendly glass;—
"This was the sweetest pleasure," he said,
  "Of the many I share in here below;
Who has no cronies, had better be dead,"
  Said the jolly old pedagogue, long ago.

The jolly old pedagogue's wrinkled face
  Melted all over in sunshiny smiles;—
He stirred his glass with an old-school grace,
Chuckled, and sipped, and prattled apace,
  Till the house grew merry from cellar to tiles;—
"I'm a pretty old man," he gently said,
  "I've lingered a long while here below,
But my heart is fresh, if my youth be fled!"
  Said the jolly old pedagogue, long ago.

He smoked his pipe in the balmy air,
  Every night when the sun went down,
While the soft wind played in his silvery hair,
Leaving its tenderest kisses there
  On the jolly old pedagogue's jolly old crown;
And feeling the kisses, he smiled and said,
  "'T is a glorious world down here below;
Why wait for happiness till we are dead?"
  Said the jolly old pedagogue, long ago.

He sat at his door one midsummer night,
  After the sun had sunk in the west,
And the lingering beams of golden light
Made his kindly old face look warm and bright,
  While the odorous night-wind whispered "Rest!"
Gently, gently he bowed his head,—
  There were angels waiting for him, I know;
He was sure of happiness, living or dead,
  This jolly old pedagogue, long ago.

GEORGE ARNOLD.

Ode on the Centenary of Burns.

WE hail this morn
A century's noblest birth;
　A Poet peasant-born,
Who more of Fame's immortal dower
　Unto his country brings
　Than all her kings!

　As lamps high set
Upon some earthly eminence;
And to the gazer brighter thence
Than the sphere lights they flout—
　Dwindle in distance and die out,
　While no star waneth yet;
So through the past's far-reaching night
　Only the star-souls keep their light.

　A gentle boy,
With moods of sadness and of mirth,
　Quick tears and sudden joy,
Grew up beside the peasant's hearth.
　His father's toil he shares;
　But half his mother's cares
　From his dark, searching eyes,
Too swift to sympathize,
　Hid in her heart she bears.

　At early morn
His father calls him to the field;
Through the stiff soil that clogs his feet,
　Chill rain, and harvest heat,
He plods all day; returns at eve outworn,
　To the rude fare a peasant's lot doth yield—
To what else was he born?

　The God-made king
　Of every living thing;
20

(For his great heart in love could hold them all);
The dumb eyes meeting his by hearth and stall—
    Gifted to understand!—
    Knew it and sought his hand;
And the most timorous cretaure had not fled
    Could she his heart have read,
Which fain all feeble things had blessed and sheltered.

    To Nature's feast,
  Who knew her noblest guest
  And entertained him best,
Kingly he came. Her chambers of the east
  She draped with crimson and with gold,
    And poured her pure joy wines
      For him the poet-souled;
      For him her anthem rolled
  From the storm-wind among the winter pines,
      Down to the slenderest note
Of a love-warble from the linnet's throat.

    But when begins
The array for battle, and the trumpet blows,
A king must leave the feast and lead the fight;
  And with its mortal foes,
Grim gathering hosts of sorrows and of sins,
  Each human soul must close;
  And Fame her trumpet blew
Before him, wrapped him in her purple state,
And made him mark for all the shafts of Fate
  That henceforth round him flew.

    Though he may yield,
Hard-pressed, and wounded fall
  Forsaken on the field;
  His regal vestments soiled;
  His crown of half its jewels spoiled;
    He is a king for all.

Had he but stood aloof!
Had he arrayed himself in armor proof
  Against temptation's darts!
So yearn the good—so those the world calls wise,
  With vain, presumptuous hearts,
    Triumphant moralize.

  Of martyr-woe
A sacred shadow on his memory rests—
  Tears have not ceased to flow—
Indignant grief yet stirs impetuous breasts,
  To think—above that noble soul brought low,
That wise and soaring spirit fooled, enslaved—
  Thus, thus he had been saved!

  It might not be!
  That heart of harmony
  Had been too rudely rent;
Its silver chords, which any hand could wound,
  By no hand could be tuned,
Save by the Maker of the instrument,
  Its every string who knew,
And from profaning touch his heavenly gift withdrew.

  Regretful love
  His country fain would prove,
By grateful honors lavished on his grave;
  Would fain redeem her blame
That he so little at her hands can claim,
  Who unrewarded gave
To her his life-bought gift of song and fame.

  The land he trod
Hath now become a place of pilgrimage;
  Where dearer are the daisies of the sod
  That could his song engage.
  The hoary hawthorn, wreathed
Above the bank on which his limbs he flung

While some sweet plaint he breathed;
　The streams he wandered near;
The maidens whom he loved; the songs he sung—
　All, all are dear!

　　The arch blue eyes—
　Arch but for love's disguise—
Of Scotland's daughters, soften at his strain;
Her hardy sons, sent forth across the main
To drive the plowshare through earth's virgin soils,
　Lighten with it their toils:
And sister-lands have learned to love the tongue
　In which such songs are sung.

　　For doth not song
　To the whole world belong?
Is it not given wherever tears can fall,
Wherever hearts can melt, or blushes glow,
Or mirth and sadness mingle as they flow,
　A heritage to all?

ISA CRAIG KNOX.

Over the River.

OVER the river they beckon to me—
　Loved ones who 've passed to the further side;
The gleam of their snowy robes I see,
　But their voices are lost in the dashing tide.
There 's one with ringlets of sunny gold,
　And eyes the reflection of heaven's own blue;
He crossed in the twilight gray and cold,
　And the pale mist hid him from mortal view;
We saw not the angels who met him there,
　The gates of the city we could not see—
Over the river, over the river,
　My brother stands waiting to welcome me!

Over the river the boatman pale
  Carried another, the household pet;
Her brown curls waved in the gentle gale—
  Darling Minnie! I see her yet.
She crossed on her bosom her dimpled hands,
  And fearlessly entered the phantom bark,
We felt it glide from the silver sands,
  And all our sunshine grew strangely dark;
We know she is safe on the further side,
  Where all the ransomed and angels be—
Over the river, the mystic river,
  My childhood's idol is waiting for me.

For none return from those quiet shores,
  Who cross with the boatman cold and pale;
We hear the dip of the golden oars,
  And catch a gleam of the snowy sail;
And lo! they have passed from our yearning heart,
  They cross the stream and are gone for aye,
We may not sunder the vail apart
  That hides from our vision the gates of day;
We only know that their barks no more
  May sail with us o'er life's stormy sea—
Yet, somewhere, I know, on the unseen shore,
  They watch, and beckon, and wait for me.

And I sit and think, when the sunset's gold
  Is flushing river and hill and shore,
I shall one day stand by the water cold
  And list for the sound of the boatman's oar;
I shall watch for a gleam of the flapping sail,
  I shall hear the boat as it gains the strand;
I shall pass from sight with the boatman pale,
  To the better shore of the spirit land.
I shall know the loved who have gone before,
  And joyfully sweet will the meeting be,
When over the river, the peaceful river,
  The Angel of Death shall carry me.

NANCY PRIEST WAKEFIELD.

The Old Sergeant.

"Come a little nearer, Doctor,—thank you!—let me take
    the cup:
Draw your chair up,—draw it closer,—just another little
    , sup!
May be you may think I 'm better; but I 'm pretty well
    used up,—
Doctor, you 've done all you could do, but I 'm just a
    going up!

"Feel my pulse, sir, if you want to, but it ain't much use to
    try "—
"Never say that," said the Surgeon, as he smothered down
    a sigh;
"It will never do, old comrade, for a soldier to say die! "
"What you *say* will make no difference, Doctor, when you
    come to die.

"Doctor, what has been the matter?" "You were very
    faint, they say;
You must try to get to sleep now." "Doctor, have I been
    away?"
"Not that anybody knows of!" "Doctor—Doctor, please
    to stay!
There is something I must tell you, and you won't have
    long to stay!

"I have got my marching orders, and I 'm ready now to go;
Doctor, did you say I fainted?—but it could n't ha' been
    so,—
For as sure as I 'm a Sergeant, and was wounded at Shi-
    loh,
I 've this very night been back there, on the old field of Shi-
    loh!

"This is all that I remember: The last time the Lighter
 came,
 And the lights had all been lowered, and the noises much
  the same,
 He had not been gone five minutes before something called
  my name:
'ORDERLY SERGEANT—ROBERT BURTON !'—just that way it
 called my name.

"And I wondered who could call me so distinctly and so
 slow,
 Knew it could n't be the Lighter,—he could not have
  spoken so;
 And I tried to answer, 'Here, sir !' but I could n't make
  it go;
 For I could n't move a muscle, and I could n't make it go !

"Then I thought: It 's all a nightmare, all a humbug and a
 bore;
 Just another foolish *grape-vine**—and it won't come any
  more;
 But it came, sir, notwithstanding, just the same way as before:
'ORDERLY SERGEANT—ROBERT BURTON !' even plainer than
 before.

"That is all that I remember, till a sudden burst of light,
 And I stood beside the River, where we stood that Sunday
  night,
 Waiting to be ferried over to the dark bluffs opposite,
 When the river was perdition and all hell was opposite !

"And the same old palpitation came again in all its power,
 And I heard a Bugle sounding, as from some celestial
  Tower;

---

*Canard.

And the same mysterious voice said: 'IT IS THE ELEVENTH
    HOUR!
ORDERLY SERGEANT—ROBERT BURTON—IT IS THE ELEVENTH
    HOUR!'

"Doctor Austin!—what *day* is this?" "It is Wednesday
    night, you know."
"Yes,—to-morrow will be New Year's, and a right good
    time below!
What *time* is it, Doctor Austin?" "Nearly Twelve." "Then
    do n't you go!
Can it be that all this happened—all this—not an hour ago!

"There was where the gun-boats opened on the dark, re-
    bellious host;
And where Webster semicircled his last guns upon the
    coast;
There were still the two log-houses, just the same, or else
    their ghost,—
And the same old transport came and took me over—or its
    ghost!

"And the old field lay before me all deserted far and wide;
There was where they fell on Prentiss,—there McClernand
    met the tide;
There was where stern Sherman rallied, and where Hurl-
    but's heroes died,—
Lower down, where Wallace charged them, and kept
    charging till he died.

"There was where Lew Wallace showed them he was of
    the canny kin,
There was where old Nelson thundered, and where Rous-
    seau waded in;
There McCook sent 'em to breakfast, and we all began to
    win—
There was where the grape-shot took me, just as we be-
    gan to win.

"Now, a shroud of snow and silence over everything was
  spread;
  And but for this old blue mantle and the old hat on my
    head,
  I should not have even doubted, to this moment, I was
    dead,—
  For my footsteps were as silent as the snow upon the dead!

"Death and silence!—Death and silence! all around me as
    I sped!
  And behold, a mighty TOWER, as if builded to the dead,—
  To the Heaven of the heavens, lifted up its mighty head,
  Till the Stars and Stripes of Heaven all seemed waving
    from its head!

"Round and mighty-based it towered—up into the infinite—
  And I knew no mortal mason could have built a shaft so
    bright;
  For it shone like solid sunshine; and a winding stair of
    light,
  Wound around it and around it till it wound clear out of
    sight!

"And, behold, as I approached it—with a rapt and dazzled
    stare,—
  Thinking that I saw old comrades just ascending the great
    Stair,—
  Suddenly the solemn challenge broke of—'Halt, and who
    goes there!'
  'I 'm a friend,' I said, 'if you are.'—'Then advance, sir, to
    the Stair!'

"I advanced!—That sentry, Doctor, was Elijah Ballan-
    tyne!—
  First of all to fall on Monday, after we had formed the
    line:
    20*

'Welcome, my old Sergeant, welcome! Welcome by that
    countersign!'
And he pointed to the scar there, under this old cloak of
    mine!

"As he grasped my hand, I shuddered, thinking only of the
    grave;
But he smiled and pointed upward with a bright and
    bloodless glaive:
'That's the way, sir, to Head-quarters.'—'What Head-
    quarters?'—'Of the Brave.'
'But the great Tower?'—'That,' he answered, 'Is the way,
    sir, of the Brave!'

"Then a sudden shame came o'er me at his uniform of light;
At my own so old and tattered, and at his so new and
    bright;
'Ah!' said he, 'you have forgotten the New Uniform to-
    night,—
Hurry back, for you must be here at just twelve o'clock
    to-night!'

"And the next thing I remember, you were sitting there,
    and I—
Doctor—did you hear a footstep? Hark!—God bless you
    all! Good-by!
Doctor, please to give my musket and my knapsack, when
    I die,
To my Son—my Son that's coming,—he won't get here
    till I die!

"Tell him his old father blessed him as he never did before,—
And to carry that old musket"—Hark! a knock is at the
    door!—
"Till the Union"—See! it opens!—"Father! Father! speak
    once more!"
"*Bless you!*"—gasped the old gray Sergeant, and he lay
    and said no more.

                              FORCEYTHE WILLSON.

Too Late.

"Ah! si la jeunesse savait,—si la vieillesse pouvait!"

THERE sat an old man on a rock,
　And unceasing bewailed him of Fate,—
That concern where we all must take stock,
　Though our vote has no hearing or weight;
　　And the old man sang him an old, old song,—
　　Never sang voice so clear and strong
　　That it could drown the old man's for long,
　　　For he sang the song "Too late! too late!"

'When we want, we have for our pains
　The promise that if we but wait
Till the want has burned out of our brains,
　Every means shall be present to state;
　　While we send for the napkin the soup gets cold,
　　While the bonnet is trimming the face grows old,
　　When we 've matched our buttons the pattern is sold,
　　　And everything comes too late,—too late!

" When strawberries seemed like red heavens,—
　Terrapin stew a wild dream,—
When my brain was at sixes and sevens,
　If my mother had 'folks' and ice cream,
　　Then I gazed with a lickerish hunger
　　At the restaurant man and fruit-monger,—
　　But oh! how I wished I were younger
　　　When the goodies all came in a stream! in a stream!

" I 've a splendid blood horse, and—a liver
　That it jars into torture to trot;
My row-boat 's the gem of the river,—
　Gout makes every knuckle a knot!
　　I can buy boundless credits on Paris and Rome,
　　But no palate for *ménus*,—no eyes for a dome,—
　　Those belonged to the youth who must tarry at home,
　　　When no home but an attic he 'd got,— he 'd got!

"How I longed, in that lonest of garrets,
    Where the tiles baked my brains all July,
For ground to grow two pecks of carrots,
    Two pigs of my own in a sty,
        A rosebush,—a little thatched cottage,—
        Two spoons—love—a basin of pottage!—
        Now in freestone I sit,—and my dotage,—
            With a woman's chair empty close by, close by!

"Ah! now, though I sit on a rock,
    I have shared one seat with the great;
I have sat—knowing naught of the clock—
    On love's high throne of state;
        But the lips that kissed, and the arms that caressed,
        To a mouth grown stern with delay were pressed,
        And circled a breast that their clasp had blessed,
            Had they only not come too late,—too late!"

                                FITZ HUGH LUDLOW.

What the End shall be.

WHEN another life is added
    To the heaving, turbid mass;
When another breath of being
    Stains creation's tarnished glass;
When the first cry, weak and piteous,
    Heralds long-enduring pain,
And a soul from non-existence
    Springs, that ne'er can die again;
When the mother's passionate welcome,
    Sorrow-like, bursts forth in tears,
And a sire's self-gratulation
    Prophesies of future years,—
            It is well we cannot see
            What the end shall be.

When across the infant features
    Trembles the faint dawn of mind,

And the heart looks from the windows
  Of the eyes that were so blind;
When the inarticulate murmurs
  Syllable each swaddled thought,
To the fond ear of affection
  With a boundless promise fraught;
Kindling great hopes for to-morrow
  From that dull, uncertain ray,
As by glimmering of the twilight
  Is foreshown the perfect day,—
        It is well we cannot see
        What the end shall be.

When the boy, upon the threshold
  Of his all-comprising home,
Puts aside the arm maternal
  That enlocks him ere he roam;
When the canvas of his vessel
  Flutters to the favoring gale,
Years of solitary exile
  Hid behind the sunny sail:
When his pulses beat with ardor,
  And his sinews stretch for toil,
And a hundred bold emprises
  Lure him to that eastern soil,—
        It is well we cannot see
        What the end shall be.

When the youth beside the maiden
  Looks into her credulous eyes,
And the heart upon the surface
  Shines too happy to be wise;
He by speeches less than gestures
  Hinteth what her hopes expound,
Laying out the waste hereafter
  Like enchanted garden-ground;
He may falter—so do many;
  She may suffer—so must all:

21

Both may yet, world-disappointed,
  This lost hour of love recall,—
      It is well we cannot see
      What the end shall be.

When the altar of religion
  Greets the expectant bridal pair,
And the vow that lasts till dying
  Vibrates on the sacred air;
When man's lavish protestations
  Doubts of after-change defy,
Comforting the frailer spirit
  Bound his servitor for aye;
When beneath love's silver moonbeams
  Many rocks in shadow sleep,
Undiscovered, till possession
  Shows the danger of the deep,—
      It is well we cannot see
      What the end shall be.

Whatsoever is beginning,
  That is wrought by human skill;
Every daring emanation
  Of the mind's ambitious will;
Every first impulse of passion,
  Gush of love or twinge of hate;
Every launch upon the waters
  Wide-horizoned by our fate;
Every venture in the chances
  Of life's sad, oft desperate game,
Whatsoever be our motive,
  Whatsoever be our aim,—
      It is well we cannot see
      What the end shall be.

                Anonymous.

The Two Worlds.

Two worlds there are.   To one our eyes we strain,
Whose magic joys we shall not see again;
 Bright haze of morning veils its glimmering shore.
  Ah, truly breathed we there
  Intoxicating air—
 Glad were our hearts in that sweet realm of
  Nevermore.

The lover there drank her delicious breath
Whose love has yielded since to change or death;
 The mother kissed her child, whose days are o'er.
  Alas! too soon have fled
  The irreclaimable dead:
 We see them—visions strange—amid the
  Nevermore.

The merrysome maiden used to sing—
The brown, brown hair that once was wont to cling
 To temples long clay-cold: to the very core
  They strike our weary hearts,
  As some vexed memory starts
 From that long faded land—the realm of
  Nevermore.

It is perpetual summer there.   But here
Sadly may we remember rivers clear,
 And harebells quivering on the meadow-floor.
  For brighter bells and bluer,
  For tenderer hearts and truer
 People that happy land—the realm of
  Nevermore.

Upon the frontier of this shadowy land
We pilgrims of eternal sorrow stand:
 What realm lies forward, with its happier store

Of forests green and deep,
Of valleys hushed in sleep,
And lakes most peaceful? 'T is the land of
Evermore.

Very far off its marble cities seem—
Very far off—beyond our sensual dream—
Its woods, unruffled by the wild wind's roar;
Yet does the turbulent surge
Howl on its very verge.
One moment—and we breathe within the
Evermore.

They whom we loved and lost so long ago
Dwell in those cities, far from mortal wo—
Haunt those fresh woodlands, whence sweet carolings
soar.
Eternal peace have they;
God wipes their tears away:
They drink that river of life which flows from
Evermore.

Thither we hasten through these regions dim,
But, lo, the wide wings of the Seraphim
Shine in the sunset! On that joyous shore
Our lightened hearts shall know
The life of long ago:
The sorrow-burdened past shall fade for
Evermore.

MORTIMER COLLINS.

Rain on the Roof.

WHEN the humid shadows hover
Over all the starry spheres,
And the melancholy darkness
Gently weeps in rainy tears,

What a bliss to press the pillow
　　Of a cottage-chamber bed
And to listen to the patter
　　Of the soft rain overhead!

Every tinkle on the shingles
　　Has an echo in the heart;
And a thousand dreamy fancies
　　Into busy being start,
And a thousand recollections
　　Weave their air-threads into woof,
As I listen to the patter
　　Of the rain upon the roof.

Now in memory comes my mother,
　　As she used long years agone,
To regard the darling dreamers
　　Ere she left them till the dawn:
O! I see her leaning o'er me,
　　As I list to this refrain
Which is played upon the shingles
　　By the patter of the rain.

Then my little seraph sister,
　　With her wings and waving hair,
And her star-eyed cherub brother—
　　A serene angelic pair!—
Glide around my wakeful pillow,
　　With their praise or mild reproof,
As I listen to the murmur
　　Of the soft rain on the roof.

And another comes, to thrill me
　　With her eyes' delicious blue;
And I mind not, musing on her,
　　That her heart was all untrue:
I remember but to love her
　　With a passion kin to pain,

And my heart's quick pulses vibrate
    To the patter of the rain.

Art hath naught of tone or cadence
    That can work with such a spell
In the soul's mysterious fountains.
    Whence the tears of rapture well,
As that melody of nature,
    That subdued, subduing strain
Which is played upon the shingles
    By the patter of the rain.

COATES KINNEY.

Willie Winkie.

Wee Willie Winkie rins through the town,
Up-stairs and doon-stairs, in his nicht-gown,
Tirlin' at the window, cryin' at the lock,
"Are the weans in their bed?—for it 's now ten o'clock."

Hey, Willie Winkie! are ye comin' ben?
The cat 's singin' gay thrums to the sleepin' hen,
The doug's speldered on the floor, and disna gie a cheep;
But here 's a waukrife laddie, that winna fa' asleep.

Ony thing but sleep, ye rogue! glow'rin' like the moon,
Rattlin' in an airn jug wi' an airn spoon,
Rumblin' tumblin' roun' about, crowin' like a cock,
Skirlin' like a kenna-what—wauknin' sleepin' folk.

Hey, Willie Winkie! the wean 's in a creel!
Waumblin' aff a body's knee like a vera eel,
Ruggin' at the cat's lug, and ravellin' a' her thrums,—
Hey, Willie Winkie!—See, there he comes!

Wearie is the mither that has a storie wean,
A wee stumpie stoussie, that canna rin his lane,
That has a battle aye wi' sleep, before he 'll close an ee;
But a kiss frae aff his rosy lips gies strength anew to me.

WILLIAM MILLER.

The Old Canoe.

Where the rocks are gray and the shore is steep,
And the waters below look dark and deep,
Where the rugged pine, in its lonely pride,
Leans gloomily over the murky tide,
Where the reeds and rushes are long and rank,
And the weeds grow thick on the winding bank,
Where the shadow is heavy the whole day through,—
There lies at its moorings the old canoe.

The useless paddles are idly dropped,
Like a sea-bird's wings that the storm had lopped,
And crossed on the railing one o'er one,
Like the folded hands when the work is done;
While busily back and forth between
The spider stretches his silvery screen,
And the solemn owl, with his dull " too-hoo,"
Settles down on the side of the old canoe.

The stern, half sunk in the slimy wave,
Rots slowly away in its living grave,
And the green moss creeps o'er its dull decay,
Hiding its mouldering dust away,
Like the hand that plants o'er the tomb a flower,
Or the ivy that mantles the falling tower;
While many a blossom of loveliest hue
Springs up o'er the stern of the old canoe.

The currentless waters are dead and still,
But the light wind plays with the boat at will,
And lazily in and out again
It floats the length of the rusty chain,
Like the weary march of the hands of time,
That meet and part at the noontide chime;
And the shore is kissed at each turning anew,
By the drippling bow of the old canoe.

Oh, many a time, with a careless hand,
I have pushed it away from the pebbly strand,
And paddled it down where the stream runs quick,
Where the whirls are wild and the eddies are thick,
And laughed as I leaned o'er the rocking side,
And looked below in the broken tide,
To see that the faces and boats were two,
That were mirrored back from the old canoe.

But now, as I lean o'er the crumbling side,
And look below in the sluggish tide,
The face that I see there is graver grown,
And the laugh that I hear has a soberer tone,
And the hands that lent to the light skiff wings
Have grown familiar with sterner things.
But I love to think of the hours that sped
As I rocked where the whirls their white spray shed,
Ere the blossoms waved, or the green grass grew
O'er the mouldering stern of the old canoe.

ANONYMOUS.

Only Waiting.

*A very old man in an alms-house was asked what he was doing now.
He replied, "Only waiting."*

Only waiting till the shadows
  Are a little longer grown;
Only waiting till the glimmer
  Of the day's last beam is flown;
Till the night of earth is faded
  From the heart once full of day;
Till the stars of heaven are breaking
  Through the twilight soft and gray.

Only waiting till the reapers
  Have the last sheaf gathered home;

For the summer-time is faded,
    And the autumn winds have come.
Quickly, reapers, gather quickly
    The last ripe hours of my heart,
For the bloom of life is withered,
    And I hasten to depart.

Only waiting till the angels
    Open wide the mystic gate,
At whose feet I long have lingered,
    Weary, poor, and desolate.
Even now I hear the footsteps,
    And their voices far away;
If they call me, I am waiting,
    Only waiting to obey.

Only waiting till the shadows
    Are a little longer grown;
Only waiting till the glimmer
    Of the day's last beam is flown;
Then from out the gathered darkness,
    Holy, deathless stars shall rise,
By whose light my soul shall gladly
    Tread its pathway to the skies.

ANONYMOUS.

The Burial of Moses.

"And he buried him in a valley in the land of Moab, over against Beth-peor; but no man knoweth of his sepulchre unto this day." DEUT. xxxiv : 6.

By Nebo's lonely mountain,
    On this side Jordan's wave,
In a vale in the land of Moab,
    There lies a lonely grave;
But no man dug that sepulchre,
    And no man saw it e'er,

21*

For the angels of God upturned the sod,
    And laid the dead man there.

That was the grandest funeral
    That ever passed on earth;
But no man heard the tramping,
    Or saw the train go forth;
Noiselessly as the daylight
    Comes when the night is done,
And the crimson streak on ocean's cheek
    Grows into the great sun,—

Noiselessly as the spring-time
    Her crown of verdure weaves,
And all the trees on all the hills
    Open their thousand leaves,—
So, without sound of music,
    Or voice of them that wept,
Silently down from the mountain crown
    The great procession swept.

Perchance the bald old eagle,
    On gray Beth-peor's height,
Out of his rocky eyrie,
    Looked on the wondrous sight.
Perchance the lion, stalking,
    Still shuns the hallowed spot;
For beast and bird have seen and heard
    That which man knoweth not.

Lo! when the warrior dieth,
    His comrades in the war,
With arms reversed, and muffled drum,
    Follow the funeral car.
They show the banners taken,
    They tell his battles won,
And after him lead his masterless steed,
    While peals the minute gun.

Amid the noblest of the land
  Men lay the sage to rest,
And give the bard an honored place,
  With costly marble dressed,
In the great minster transept,
  Where lights like glories fall,
And the choir sings, and the organ rings
  Along the emblazoned wall.

This was the bravest warrior
  That ever buckled sword;
This the most gifted poet
  That ever breathed a word;
And never earth's philosopher
  Traced, with his golden pen,
On the deathless page, truths half so sage
  As *he* wrote down for men.

And had he not high honor?
  The hill-side for his pall,
To lie in state while angels wait,
  With stars for tapers tall;
And the dark rock pines, like tossing plumes,
  Over his bier to wave;
And God's own hand, in that lonely land,
  To lay him in the grave,—

In that deep grave, without a name,
  Whence his uncoffined clay
Shall break again,—O wondrous thought!—
  Before the judgment day;
And stand, with glory wrapped around,
  On the hills he never trod,
And speak of the strife that won our life,
  With the incarnate Son of God.

O lonely tomb in Moab's land!
  O dark Beth-peor's hill!

Speak to these curious hearts of ours,
　　And teach them to be still.
God hath his mysteries of grace,—
　　Ways that we cannot tell;
He hides them deep, like the secret sleep
　　Of him he loved so well.

　　　　　　　　　CECIL FRANCES ALEXANDER.

Milton's Prayer of Patience.

　　I AM old and blind!
Men point at me as smitten by God's frown;
Afflicted and deserted of my kind,
　　Yet am I not cast down.

　　I am weak, yet strong:
I murmur not that I no longer see;
Poor, old, and helpless, I the more belong,
　　Father Supreme, to Thee.

　　O merciful One!
When men are farthest, then art Thou most near;
When friends pass by, my weaknesses to shun,
　　Thy chariot I hear.

　　Thy glorious face
Is leaning towards me, and its holy light
Shines in upon my lonely dwelling-place,—
　　And there is no more night.

　　On my bended knee,
I recognize Thy purpose, clearly shown;
My vision thou hast dimmed, that I may see
　　Thyself—Thyself alone.

　　I have naught to fear;
This darkness is the shadow of Thy wing;
Beneath it I am almost sacred,—here
　　Can come no evil thing.

Oh, I seem to stand
Trembling, where foot of mortal ne'er hath been,
Wrapped in the radiance of Thy sinless hand
　　Which eye hath never seen.

Visions come and go,—
Shapes of resplendent beauty round me throng ;
From angel lips I seem to hear the flow
　　Of soft and holy song.

It is nothing now,—
When Heaven is ripening on my sightless eyes,
When airs from Paradise refresh my brow,
　　That earth in darkness lies.

In a purer clime,
My being fills with rapture,—waves of thought
Roll in upon my spirit,—strains sublime
　　Break over me unsought.

Give me now my lyre !
I feel the stirrings of a gift divine ;
Within my bosom glows unearthly fire,
　　Lit by no skill of mine.

ELIZABETH LLOYD HOWELL.

Curfew Must not Ring To=night.

ENGLAND s sun was slowly setting o'er the hills so far away,
Filling all the land with beauty at the close of one sad
　　day ;
And the last rays kiss'd the forehead of a man and maiden
　　fair,
He with step so slow and weakened, she with sunny,
　　floating hair ;
He with sad bowed head, and thoughtful, she with lips so
　　cold and white,
Struggling to keep back the murmur, " Curfew must not
　　ring to-night."

"Sexton," Bessie's white lips faltered, pointing to the prison
    old,
  With its walls so dark and gloomy,—walls so dark, and
    damp, and cold,—
"I 've a lover in that prison, doomed this very night to die,
  At the ringing of the Curfew, and no earthly help is nigh.
  Cromwell will not come till sunset," and her face grew
    strangely white,
  As she spoke in husky whispers, "Curfew must not ring
    to-night."

"Bessie," calmly spoke the sexton—every word pierced her
    young heart
  Like a thousand gleaming arrows—like a deadly poisoned
    dart;
"Long, long years I 've rung the Curfew from that gloomy
    shadowed tower;
  Every evening, just at sunset, it has told the twilight hour;
  I have done my duty ever, tried to do it just and right,
  Now I 'm old, I will not miss it; girl, the Curfew rings to-
    night!"

Wild her eyes and pale her features, stern and white her
    thoughtful brow,
  And within her heart's deep centre, Bessie made a solemn
    vow;
  She had listened while the judges read, without a tear or
    sigh,
"At the ringing of the Curfew—Basil Underwood *must die.*"
  And her breath came fast and faster, and her eyes grew
    large and bright—
  One low murmur, scarcely spoken—"Curfew *must not* ring
    to-night!"

She with light step bounded forward, sprang within the old
    church door,
  Left the old man coming slowly, paths he 'd trod so oft be-
    fore;

Not one moment paused the maiden, but with cheek and
    brow aglow,
Staggered up the gloomy tower, where the bell swung to
    and fro:
Then she climbed the slimy ladder, dark, without one ray
    of light,
Upward still, her pale lips saying: "Curfew shall not ring
    , to-night."

She has reached the topmost ladder, o'er her hangs the
    great dark bell,
And the awful gloom beneath her, like the pathway down
    to hell;
See, the ponderous tongue is swinging, 't is the hour of
    Curfew now—
And the sight has chilled her bosom, stopped her breath
    and paled her brow.
Shall she let it ring?   No, never!   her eyes flash with sud-
    den light,
As she springs and grasps it firmly—"Curfew shall not
    ring to-night!"

Out she swung, far out, the city seemed a tiny speck be-
    low;
There, 'twixt heaven and earth suspended, as the bell
    swung to and fro;
And the half-deaf Saxon ringing (years he had not heard
    the bell,)
And he thought the twilight Curfew rang young Basil's
    funeral knell;
Still the maiden clinging firmly, cheek and brow so pale
    and white,
Stilled her frightened heart's wild beating—" *Curfew shall
    not ring to-night.*"

It was o'er—the bell ceased swaying, and the maiden
    stepped once more
Firmly on the damp old ladder, where for hundred years
    before

Human foot had not been planted; and what she this
    night had done,
Should be told in long years after—as the rays of setting
    sun
Light the sky with mellow beauty, aged sires with heads
    of white,
Tell their children why the Curfew did not ring that one
    sad night.

O'er the distant hills came Cromwell; Bessie saw him,
    and her brow,
Lately white with sickening terror, glows with sudden
    beauty now;
At his feet she told her story, showed her hands all bruised
    and torn;
And her sweet young face so haggard, with a look so sad
    and worn,
Touched his heart with sudden pity—lit his eyes with
    misty light;
"Go, your lover lives!" cried Cromwell; "Curfew shall not
    ring to-night."

ANONYMOUS.

Revelry in India.

WE meet 'neath the sounding rafter,
    And the walls around are bare;
As they echo the peals of laughter
    It seems that the dead are there;
But stand to your glasses steady,
    We drink to our comrades' eyes;
Quaff a cup to the dead already—
    And hurrah for the next that dies!

Not here are the goblets flowing,
    Not here is the vintage sweet;
'T is cold, as our hearts are growing,
    And dark as the doom we meet.

But stand to your glasses steady,
   And soon shall our pulses rise;
A cup to the dead already—
   Hurrah for the next that dies!

Not a sigh for the lot that darkles,
   Not a tear for the friends that sink;
We 'll fall, 'midst the wine-cup's sparkles,
   As mute as the wine we drink.
So stand to your glasses steady,
   'T is in this that our respite lies;
One cup to the dead already—
   Hurrah for the next that dies!

Time was when we frowned at others,
   We thought we were wiser then;
Ha! ha! let those think of their mothers,
   Who hope to see them again.
No! stand to your glasses steady,
   The thoughtless are here the wise;
A cup to the dead already—
   Hurrah for the next that dies!

There 's many a hand that 's shaking,
   There 's many a cheek that 's sunk;
But soon, though our hearts are breaking,
   They 'll burn with the wine we 've drunk.
So stand to your glasses steady,
   'T is here the revival lies;
A cup to the dead already—
   Hurrah for the next that dies!

There 's a mist on the glass congealing,
   'T is the hurricane's fiery breath;
And thus does the warmth of feeling
   Turn ice in the grasp of death.
Ho! stand to your glasses steady;
   For a moment the vapor flies;

A cup to the dead already—
    Hurrah for the next that dies!

Who dreads to the dust returning?
    Who shrinks from the sable shore,
Where the high and haughty yearning
    Of the soul shall sing no more?
Ho! stand to your glasses steady;
    This world is a world of lies;
A cup to the dead already—
    Hurrah for the next that dies!

Cut off from the land that bore us,
    Betrayed by the land we find,
Where the brightest have gone before us,
    And the dullest remain behind—
Stand, stand to your glasses steady!
    'T is all we have left to prize;
A cup to the dead already—
    And hurrah for the next that dies!

                    BARTHOLOMEW DOWLING.

The Rising of the Moon.

" O, THEN tell me, Shawn O'Ferrall,
    Tell me why you hurry so."
" Hush, ma bouchal, hush and listen,"—
    And his cheeks were all aglow.
" I bear ordhers from the captain,
    Get you ready quick and soon,
For the pikes must be together
    At the risin' of the moon."

" O, then tell me, Shawn O'Ferrall,
    Where the gatherin' is to be."
" In the ould spot by the river,
    Right well known to you and me.

One word more—for signal token
 Whistle up the marchin' tune,
With your pike upon your shoulder,
 By the risin' of the moon."

Out from many a mud-wall cabin
 Eyes were watching through that night;
Many a manly chest was throbbing
 For the blessed warning light.
Murmurs passed along the valleys,
 Like the banshee's lonely croon,
And a thousand blades were flashing,
 At the rising of the moon.

There beside the singing river
 That dark mass of men was seen;
Far above the shining weapons
 Hung their own beloved green.
"Death to every foe and traitor!
 Forward! strike the marchin' tune,
And hurrah, my boys, for freedom!—
 'T is the risin' of the moon."

Well they fought for poor old Ireland,
 And full bitter was their fate.
O, what glorious pride and sorrow
 Fill the name of Ninety-Eight!
Yet, thank God! e'en still are beating
 Hearts in manhood's burning noon,
Who would follow in their footsteps
 At the risin' of the moon.

JOHN K. CASEY.

My Maryland.

THE despot's heel is on thy shore,
 Maryland!
His torch is at thy temple door,
 Maryland!

Avenge the patriotic gore
That flecked the streets of Baltimore,
And be the battle queen of yore,
　　Maryland, My Maryland!

Hark to a wandering son's appeal,
　　　　Maryland!
My mother state, to thee I kneel,
　　　　Maryland!
For life and death, for woe and weal,
Thy peerless chivalry reveal,
And gird thy beauteous limbs with steel,
　　Maryland, My Maryland!

Thou wilt not cower in the dust,
　　　　Maryland!
Thy beaming sword shall never rust,　·
　　　　Maryland!
Remember Carroll's sacred trust,
Remember Howard's warlike thrust,
And all thy slumberers with the just,
　　Maryland, My Maryland.

Come, 't is the red dawn of the day,
　　　　Maryland!
Come with thy panoplied array,
　　　　Maryland!
With Ringgold's spirit for the fray,
With Watson's blood at Monterey,
With fearless Lowe and dashing May,
　　Maryland, My Maryland.

Dear mother, burst the tyrant's chain,
　　　　Maryland!
Virginia should not call in vain,
　　　　Maryland!
She meets her sisters on the plain;
" Sic semper! " 't is the proud refrain,

That baffles minions back amain,
    Maryland, My Maryland!

Come, for thy shield is bright and strong,
    Maryland!
Come, for thy dalliance does thee wrong,
    Maryland!
Come to thine own heroic throng,
That stalks with liberty along,
And give a new key to thy song,
    Maryland, My Maryland!

I see the blush upon thy cheek,
    Maryland!
But thou wast ever bravely meek,
    Maryland!
But lo! there surges forth a shriek
From hill to hill, from creek to creek;
Potomac calls to Chesapeake,
    Maryland, My Maryland!

Thou wilt not yield the Vandal toll,
    Maryland!
Thou wilt not crook to his control,
    Maryland!
Better the fire upon thee roll,
Better the shot, the blade, the bowl,
Than crucifixion of the soul,
    Maryland, My Maryland!

I hear the distant thunder hum,
    Maryland!
The Old Line's bugle, fife, and drum,
    Maryland!
She is not dead, nor deaf, nor dumb—
Huzza! she spurns the Northern scum;
She breathes, she burns—she 'll come! she 'll come!
    Maryland, My Maryland!

                  JAMES R. RANDALL.

Civil War.

"Rifleman, shoot me a fancy shot
    Straight at the heart of yon prowling vidette;
Ring me a ball in the glittering spot
    That shines on his breast like an amulet!"

"Ah, captain! here goes for a fine-drawn bead,
    There 's music around when my barrel 's in tune!"
Crack! went the rifle, the messenger sped,
    And dead from his horse fell the ringing dragoon.

"Now, rifleman, steal through the bushes, and snatch
    From your victim some trinket to handsel first blood;
A button, a loop, or that luminous patch
    That gleams in the moon like a diamond stud!"

"Oh captain! I staggered, and sunk on my track,
    When I gazed on the face of that fallen vidette,
For he looked so like you, as he lay on his back,
    That my heart rose upon me, and masters me yet.

"But I snatched off the trinket,—this locket of gold;
    An inch from the centre my lead broke its way,
Scarce grazing the picture, so fair to behold,
    Of a beautiful lady in bridal array."

"Ha! rifleman, fling me the locket!—'t is she,
    My brother's young bride,—and the fallen dragoon
Was her husband—Hush! soldier, 't was Heaven's decree,
    We must bury him there, by the light of the moon!

"But, hark! the far bugles their warnings unite;
    War is a virtue, weakness a sin;
There 's a lurking and loping around us to-night;—
    Load again, rifleman, keep your hand in!"

Anonymous.

The Picket Guard.

" ALL quiet along the Potomac," they say,
  "Except now and then a stray picket
Is shot, as he walks on his beat, to and fro,
  By a rifleman hid in the thicket.
'T is nothing—a private or two, now and then,
  Will not count in the news of the battle;
Not an officer lost—only one of the men,
  Moaning out, all alone, the death-rattle."

All quiet along the Potomac to-night,
  Where the soldiers lie peacefully dreaming;
Their tents in the rays of the clear autumn moon,
  Or the light of the watch-fires, are gleaming.
A tremulous sigh, as the gentle night-wind
  Through the forest-leaves softly is creeping;
While stars up above, with their glittering eyes,
  Keep guard—for the army is sleeping.

There 's only the sound of the lone sentry's tread,
  As he tramps from the rock to the fountain,
And thinks of the two in the low trundle-bed
  Far away in the cot on the mountain.
His musket falls slack—his face, dark and grim,
  Grows gentle with memories tender,
As he mutters a prayer for the children asleep—
  For their mother—may Heaven defend her!

The moon seems to shine just as brightly as then,
  That night, when the love yet unspoken
Leaped up to his lips—when low-murmured vows
  Were pledged to be ever unbroken.
Then drawing his sleeve roughly over his eyes,
  He dashes off tears that are welling,
And gathers his gun closer up to its place
  As if to keep down the heart-swelling.

He passes the fountain, the blasted pine tree—
    The footstep is lagging and weary;
Yet onward he goes, through the broad belt of light,
    Toward the shades of the forest so dreary.
Hark! was it the night-wind that rustled the leaves?
    Was it moonlight so wondrously flashing?
It looked like a rifle—"Ah! Mary, good-bye!"
    And the life-blood is ebbing and plashing.

All quiet along the Potomac to-night,
    No sound save the rush of the river;
While soft falls the dew on the face of the dead—
    The picket's off duty forever.
                  ETHEL LYNN BEERS.

The Countersign.

ALAS! the weary hours pass slow,
    The night is very dark and still,
And in the marshes far below
    I hear the bearded whippoorwill.
I scarce can see a yard ahead;
    My ears are strained to catch each sound;
I hear the leaves about me shed,
    And the spring's bubbling through the ground.

Along the beaten path I pace,
    Where white rags mark my sentry's track;
In formless shrubs I seem to trace
    The foeman's form, with bending back;
I think I see him crouching low—
    I stop and list—I stoop and peer,
Until the neighboring hillocks grow
    To groups of soldiers far and near.

With ready piece I wait and watch,
    Until my eyes, familiar grown,

Detect each harmless earthen notch,
   And turn guerillas into stone;
And then amid the lonely gloom,
   Beneath the tall old chestnut trees,
My silent marches I resume,
   And think of other times than these.

"Halt! who goes there?" my challenge cry,
   It rings along the watchful line;
"Relief!" I hear a voice reply—,
   "Advance, and give the countersign!"
With bayonet at the charge I wait—
   The corporal gives the mystic spell;
With arms aport I charge my mate,
   Then onward pass, and all is well.

But in the tent that night awake,
   I ask, if in the fray I fall,
Can I the mystic answer make,
   When the angelic sentries call?
And pray that Heaven may so ordain,
   Where'er I go, what fate be mine,
Whether in pleasure or in pain,
   I still may have the countersign.

                      ANONYMOUS.

Sherman's March to the Sea.

Our camp-fires shone bright on the mountain
   That frowned on the river below,
As we stood by our guns in the morning,
   And eagerly watched for the foe;
When a rider came out of the darkness
   That hung over mountain and tree,
And shouted, "Boys, up and be ready!
   For Sherman will march to the sea!"

Then cheer upon cheer for bold Sherman
  Went up from each valley and glen,
And the bugles re-echoed the music
  That came from the lips of the men;
For we knew that the stars in our banner
  More bright in their splendor would be,
And that blessings from Northland would greet us,
  When Sherman marched down to the sea.

Then forward, boys! forward to battle!
  We marched on our wearisome way,
We stormed the wild hills of Resaca—
  God bless those who fell on that day!
Then Kenesaw, dark in its glory,
  Frowned down on the flag of the free;
But the East and the West bore our standard
  And Sherman marched on to the sea.

Still onward we pressed, till our banners
  Swept out from Atlanta's grim walls,
And the blood of the patriot dampened
  The soil where the traitor-flag falls;
We paused not to weep for the fallen,
  Who slept by each river and tree,
Yet we twined them a wreath of the laurel,
  As Sherman marched down to the sea.

Oh, proud was our army that morning,
  That stood where the pine darkly towers,
When Sherman said, "Boys, you are weary,
  But to-day fair Savannah is ours!"
Then sang we the song of our chieftain,
  That echoed o'er river and lea,
And the stars in our banner shone brighter
  When Sherman marched down to the sea.

                        SAMUEL H. M. BYERS.

Driving Home the Cows.

Out of the clover and blue-eyed grass
    He turned them into the river-lane;
One after another he let them pass,
    Then fastened the meadow bars again.

Under the willows, and over the hill,
    He patiently followed their sober pace;
The merry whistle for once was still,
    And something shadowed the sunny face.

Only a boy! and his father had said
    He never could let his youngest go;
Two already were lying dead
    Under the feet of the trampling foe.

But after the evening work was done,
    And the frogs were loud in the meadow-swamp,
Over his shoulder he slung his gun
    And stealthily followed the foot-path damp,

Across the clover and through the wheat
    With resolute heart and purpose grim,
Though cold was the dew on his hurrying feet,
    And the blind bat's flitting startled him.

Thrice since then had the lanes been white,
    And the orchards sweet with apple-bloom;
And now, when the cows came back at night,
    The feeble father drove them home.

For news had come to the lonely farm
    That three were lying where two had lain;
And the old man's tremulous, palsied arm
    Could never lean on a son's again.

The summer day grew cool and late,
    He went for the cows when the work was done;

But down the lane, as he opened the gate,
  He saw them coming one by one,—

Brindle, Ebony, Speckle, and Bess,
  Shaking their horns in the evening wind;
Cropping the buttercups out of the grass,—
  But who was it following close behind?

Loosely swung in the idle air
  The empty sleeve of army blue;
And worn and pale, from the crisping hair,
  Looked out a face that the father knew.

For Southern prisons will sometimes yawn,
  And yield their dead unto life again;
And the day that comes with a cloudy dawn
  In golden glory at last may wane.

The great tears sprang to their meeting eyes;
  For the heart must speak when the lips are dumb;
And under the silent evening skies
  Together they followed the cattle home.
                    KATE PUTNAM OSGOOD.

Popping Corn.

AND there they sat, a-popping corn,
  John Styles and Susan Cutter—
John Styles as fat as any ox,
  And Susan fat as butter.

And there they sat and shelled the corn,
  And raked and stirred the fire,
And talked of different kinds of corn,
  And hitched their chairs up nigher.

Then Susan she the popper shook,
  Then John he shook the popper,

Till both their faces grew as red
 As saucepans made of copper.

And then they shelled, and popped, and ate,
 All kinds of fun a-poking,
While he haw-hawed at her remarks,
 And she laughed at his joking.

And still they popped, and still they ate—
 John's mouth was like a hopper—
And stirred the fire, and sprinkled salt,
 And shook and shook the popper.

The clock struck nine—the clock struck ten,
 And still the corn kept popping ;
It struck eleven, and then struck twelve,
 And still no signs of stopping.

And John he ate, and Sue she thought—
 The corn did pop and patter—
Till John cried out, "The corn 's a-fire !
 Why, Susan, what 's the matter?"

Said she, "John Styles, it 's one o'clock ;
 You 'll die of indigestion ;
I 'm sick of all this popping corn—
 Why do n't you pop the question?"

ANONYMOUS.

The Twins.

 In form and feature, face and limb,
  I grew so like my brother,
 That folks got taking me for him,
  And each for one another.
 It puzzled all our kith and kin,
  It reached a fearful pitch ;

For one of us was born a twin,
　　And not a soul knew which.

One day to make the matter worse,
　　Before our names were fixed,
As we were being washed by nurse,
　　We got completely mixed;
And thus, you see, by fate's decree,
　　Or rather nurse's whim,
My brother John got christened me,
　　And I got christened him.

This fatal likeness ever dogged
　　My footsteps when at school,
And I was always getting flogged,
　　When John turned out a fool.
I put this question, fruitlessly,
　　To every one I knew,
"What would you do, if you were me,
　　To prove that you were you."

Our close resemblance turned the tide
　　Of my domestic life,
For somehow, my intended bride
　　Became my brother's wife.
In fact, year after year the same
　　Absurd mistakes went on,
And when I died, the neighbors came
　　And buried brother John.

HENRY S. LEIGH.

A Little Goose.

THE chill November day was done,
　　The working world home faring;
The wind came roaring through the streets
　　And set the gas-lights flaring;

And hopelessly and aimlessly
　　The scared old leaves were flying;
When, mingled with the sighing wind,
　　I heard a small voice crying.

And shivering on the corner stood
　　A child of four, or over;
No cloak or hat her small, soft arms,
　　And wind blown curls to cover.
Her dimpled face was stained with tears;
　　Her round blue eyes ran over;
She cherished in her wee, cold hand,
　　A bunch of faded clover.

And one hand round her treasure while
　　She slipped in mine the other:
Half scared, half confidential, said,
　　"Oh! please, I want my mother!"
"Tell me your street and number, pet:
　　Do n't cry, I 'll take you to it."
Sobbing she answered, "I forget:
　　The organ made me do it.

"He came and played at Milly's steps,
　　The monkey took the money;
And so I followed down the street,
　　The monkey was so funny.
I 've walked about a hundred hours,
　　From one street to another:
The monkey 's gone, I 've spoiled my flowers,
　　Oh! please, I want my mother."

"But what 's your mother's name? and what
　　The street? Now think a minute."
"My mother's name is mamma dear—
　　The street—I can't begin it."
"But what is strange about the house,
　　Or new—not like the others?"

"I guess you mean my trundle-bed,
　Mine and my little brother's.

"Oh dear! I ought to be at home
　To help him say his prayers,—
He's such a baby he forgets;
　And we are both such players;—
And there's a bar to keep us both
　From pitching on each other,
For Harry rolls when he's asleep:
　Oh dear! I want my mother."

The sky grew stormy; people passed
　All muffled, homeward faring:
"You'll have to spend the night with me,"
　I said at last, despairing.
I tied a kerchief round her neck—
　"What ribbon's this, my blossom?"
"Why don't you know?" she smiling, said,
　And drew it from her bosom.

A card with number, street, and name;
　My eyes astonished met it;
"For," said the little one, "you see
　I might sometimes forget it:
And so I wear a little thing
　That tells you all about it;
For mother says she's very sure
　I should get lost without it."
　　　　　　　ELIZA SPROAT TURNER.

Tired Mothers.

A LITTLE elbow leans upon your knee,
　Your tired knee that has so much to bear;
A child's dear eyes are looking lovingly
　From underneath a thatch of tangled hair.

Perhaps you do not heed the velvet touch
    Of warm, moist fingers, folding yours so tight;
You do not prize this blessing overmuch,—
    You almost are too tired to pray to-night.

But it is blessedness! A year ago
    I did not see it as I do to-day—
We are so dull and thankless; and too slow
    To catch the sunshine till it slips away.
And now it seems surpassing strange to me,
    That, while I wore the badge of motherhood,
I did not kiss more oft and tenderly
    The little child that brought me only good.

And if, some night when you sit down to rest,
    You miss this elbow from your tired knee,—
This restless curling head from off your breast,—
    This lisping tongue that chatters constantly;
If from your own the dimpled hands had slipped,
    And ne'er would nestle in your palm again;
If the white feet into their grave had tripped,
    I could not blame you for your heartache then.

I wonder so that mothers ever fret
    At little children clinging to their gown;
Or that the footprints, when the days are wet,
    Are ever black enough to make them frown.
If I could find a little muddy boot,
    Or cap, or jacket, on my chamber-floor,—
If I could kiss a rosy, restless foot,
    And hear it patter in my house once more,—

If I could mend a broken cart to-day,
    To-morrow make a kite to reach the sky,
There is no woman in God's world could say
    She was more blissfully content than I.
But ah! the dainty pillow next my own
    Is never rumpled by a shining head;

My singing birdling from its nest is flown,—
The little boy I used to kiss is dead!

MAY RILEY SMITH.

The Children.

WHEN the lessons and tasks are all ended,
  And the school for the day is dismissed,
The little ones gather around me
  To bid me good-night and be kissed:
Oh, the little white arms that encircle
  My neck in their tender embrace!
Oh, the smiles that are halos of heaven,
  Shedding sunshine of love on my face!

And when they are gone I sit dreaming
  Of my childhood too lovely to last;
Of joy that my heart will remember,
  While it wakes to the pulse of the past,
Ere the world and its wickedness made me
  A partner of sorrow and sin,
When the glory of God was about me,
  And the glory of gladness within.

All my heart grows as weak as a woman's,
  And the fountains of feeling will flow,
When I think of the paths, steep and stony,
  Where the feet of the dear ones must go;
Of the mountains of Sin hanging o'er them,
  Of the tempest of Fate blowing wild;
Oh! there's nothing on earth half so holy
  As the innocent heart of a child!

They are idols of hearts and of households;
  They are angels of God in disguise;
His sunlight still sleeps in their tresses,
  His glory still gleams in their eyes,
Those truants from home and from heaven,
  They have made me more manly and mild!

And I know, now, how Jesus could liken
    The kingdom of God to a child.

I ask not a life for the dear ones,
    All radiant, as others have done,
But that life may have just enough shadow
    To temper the glare of the sun;
I would pray God to guard them from evil,
    But my prayer would bound back to myself;
Ah! a seraph may pray for a sinner,
    But a sinner must pray for himself.

The twig is so easily bended,
    I have banished the rule and the rod;
I have taught them the goodness of knowledge,
    They have taught me the goodness of God;
My heart is the dungeon of darkness,
    Where I shut them for breaking a rule;
My frown is sufficient correction;
    My love is the law of the school.

I shall leave the old house in the autumn,
    To traverse its threshold no more;
Ah! how I shall sigh for the dear ones,
    That meet me each morn at the door;
I shall miss the "good nights" and the kisses,
    And the gush of their innocent glee,
The group on the green, and the flowers
    That are brought every morning for me.

I shall miss them at morn and at even,
    Their song in the school and the street;
I shall miss the low hum of their voices,
    And the tread of their delicate feet.
When the lessons of life are all ended,
    And death says "the school is dismissed,"
May the little ones gather around me,
    To bid me good-night and be kissed!

                      CHARLES M. DICKINSON.

My Mind to me a Kingdom is. *Page* 1. WILLIAM BYRD (b. 1540, d. 1623) was organist to Queen Elizabeth, and composed an immense amount of vocal music.

The Lye. *Page* 2. The authorship of this poem has been disputed, and it is commonly printed as anonymous. But Percy ascribes it to RALEIGH, and a copy of it among the Chetham manuscripts bears his signature.

Man's Mortality. *Page* 6. SIMON WASTEL (b. about 1566) published in 1629 "Microbiblion, or the Bible's Epitome in Verse," of which these famous stanzas are a fragment.

Verses. *Page* 9. The story of CHEDIOCK TICHEBORNE is told in Disraeli's "Curiosities of Literature," Vol. II.

Good Ale. *Page* 18. JOHN STILL (d. 1607), Bishop of Bath and Wells, was the author of "Gammer Gurton's Needle," one of the earliest of English comedies.

The Sailor's Wife. *Page* 76. This poem has been commonly attributed to Mickle, author of "Cumnor Hall," because an imperfect copy of it was found among his papers. He himself never claimed it, nor would he be likely to have written it, as he never lived in a seaport. Miss ADAM was a poor school-mistress, who lived near Greenock, and died in Glasgow in 1765. She published a volume of poems, and claimed this one as hers.

Helen of Kirkconnel. *Page* 93. There are numerous versions of this poem. The one here given, by JOHN MAYNE (b. 1759, d. 1836), is metrically the most perfect. It was published by Sir Walter Scott, in the Edinburgh "Annual Register" for 1815, who says : "A lady of the name of Helen Irving or Bell (for this is disputed by the two clans), daughter of the laird of Kirkconnell, in Dumfriesshire, and celebrated for her beauty, was beloved by two gentlemen in the neighborhood. The name of the favored suitor was Adam Fleming of Kirkpatrick ; that of the other has escaped tradition, although it has been alleged that he was a Bell of

24

Blacket House. The addresses of the latter were, however, favored by the friends of the lady, and the lovers were therefore obliged to meet in secret, and by night, in the church-yard of Kirkconnell, a romantic spot surrounded by the river Kirtle. During one of these private interviews, the jealous and despised lover suddenly appeared on the opposite bank of the stream, and leveled his carabine at the breast of his rival. Helen threw herself before her lover, received in her bosom the bullet, and died in his arms. A desperate and mortal combat ensued between Fleming and the murderer, in which the latter was cut to pieces. Other accounts say that Fleming pursued his enemy to Spain, and slew him in the streets of Madrid." These events occurred in the reign of Mary Queen of Scots.

The Tears I Shed. Page 99. HELEN D'ARCY CRANSTOUN (b. 1765, d. 1838) became in 1790 the second wife of Prof. Dugald Stewart. The first four lines of the last stanza were inserted by Burns.

Lucy's Flittin'. Page 105. WILLIAM LAIDLAW (b. 1780, d. 1845) was the amanuensis and confidential friend of Sir Walter Scott. "Lucy's Flittin'" was contributed to Hogg's "Forest Minstrel," and Hogg himself wrote the closing stanza.

A Riddle. Page 109. This enigma has been frequently attributed to Lord Byron, and printed in two or three editions of his works. The answer is, the letter H.

Saint Patrick. Page 113. According to Samuel Lover, these verses were written in 1814 by two gentlemen jointly, while on their way to a masquerade where they were to appear as ballad-singers, HENRY BENNETT (b. in Cork about 1785) being one of them.

The Beacon. Page 122. This little poem has been persistently attributed to Moore; but it has been conclusively shown that it is the production of P. M. JAMES, an Englishman.

I would not Live Alway. Page 128. DR. MUHLENBERG made several revisions of his famous poem. The versions in the hymn-books contain some striking lines that do not appear in his final revision, which is here presented.

The Bivouac of the Dead. Page 197. In accordance with an act of the legislature of Kentucky, the remains of the soldiers from that state who fell at Buena Vista were brought home to Frankfort, and there interred under a handsome monument. This was the occasion of O'HARA'S poem.

Lines on a Skeleton. Page 201. The manuscript of this poem was found near a skeleton in the London Royal College of Surgeons, about 1820. The author has never been found, though a reward of fifty guineas was offered for his discovery.

The Exile to his Wife. Page 223. JOSEPH BRENAN (b. 1829, d. 1857) was a native of the north of Ireland. He joined the Young Ireland party in 1848, and was one of the conductors of the "Irish Felon." He was imprisoned for nine months in Dublin, afterward edited the "Irishman," and in October, 1849, being implicated in an insurrectionary movement in Tipperary, fled to America. He was for three years connected with the New Orleans "Delta," and died in that city in May, 1857.

Ode on the Centenary of Burns. Page 229. Miss CRAIG'S ode, which bore off the prize, offered by the directors of the Crystal Palace Company, from more than six hundred competitors, is one of the few prize poems which have possessed any poetical merit.

The Old Canoe. Page 247. All efforts to discover the authorship of this popular poem have been unavailing. It has been attributed to Albert Pike, but he disclaims it.

Revelry in India. Page 256. These lines are said to have been sung by a company of British officers stationed at a frontier post in India during a pestilence. It is also said that the author of them was the next victim.

The Countersign. Page 264. Concerning the authorship of "The Countersign," we only know that it was written by a private in Company G of Stuart's Engineers, at Camp Lesley, near Washington, during the first year of the Rebellion. It seems too good to have been a first poem ; but it is to be feared that the chances of war made it the last, as it has never been claimed.

Sherman's March to the Sea. Page 265. Adjutant BYERS, Fifth Iowa Infantry, wrote this song while a prisoner at Columbia, S. C. General Sherman, to whom a copy of the lines was handed when he arrived at that place, so admired them that he sent for the author and attached him to his staff.

INDEX OF FIRST LINES.

THE END.

www.ingramcontent.com/pod-product-compliance
Lightning Source LLC
Chambersburg PA
CBHW020850020726
47497CB00005B/1337